Kansai University
Institute of Oriental and Occidental Studies
Study Report Series
54

From Medieval to Modern:
Aspects of the Western Literary Tradition

中世から現代へ
－西洋文学の伝統の様々な形

Edited by
Yoko Wada

Kansai University Press

Kansai University
Institute of Oriental and Occidental Studies

First Published in Japan in 2017
An imprint of Kyowa Printing Co., Ltd.

©2017 Yoko Wada
All rights reserved
ISBN 978-4-87354-653-7 C3098
Printed in Japan

Kansai University Press
3-3-35 Yamate-cho, Suita, Osaka, Japan

Foreword

This book is the outcome of research conducted from 2012 to 2016 by a group of six scholars at our Institute who work on Occidental studies ; their special focus was interactions between the constituent cultures of the West in the areas of literature, languages, and thought. Although our Institute was initially established to advance comparative research, with Asian Studies as its core, it now keeps a variety of other foreign cultures in view. Thanks to this institutional commitment, the research group working on western literature has been able to play an important role ; for example, by holding symposia and inviting lecturers from inside and outside Japan. I trust that its individual members will continue their good work to promote studies in western literatures and languages. And I hope that readers will learn much from the articles contributed to this book.

Keiichi Uchida
Director
Institute of Oriental and Occidental Studies
Kansai University

Preface

It was our privilege to be members of a research group tasked with studying the "Influence of different cultures on western literature, languages and thought" at the Institute of Oriental and Occidental Studies from 2012 to 2016. This book brings together the results of our individual research projects. That our specialties vary widely, both in chronology (from early medieval to post modern) and geography (from Eastern Europe to South America), not only reflects the richness of Western studies but also highlights its potential for comparison with the cultures of the East.

We thank the former director, Professor Nobuo Nakatani, and the present director, Professor Keiichi Uchida, for giving us the opportunity to publish the results of our research. We also acknowledge the great help of Ms Satoko Nasu, who assisted us at every stage during the preparation of this book. Lastly, we are grateful to Ms Chiaki Fukushima whose diligence in maintaining the facilities of our working area created an environment conducive to research.

Yoko Wada
(Chief of the Research Group)
Professor, Faculty of Foreign Studies
Kansai University

LIST OF CONTRIBUTORS

Patrick P. O'NEILL is the James Gordon Hanes Distinguished Professor of the Humanities at the Department of English and Comparative Literature, the University of North Carolina at Chapel Hill, USA. He recently published *The Old English Psalms* (Harvard University Press, 2016).

Yoko WADA is a Professor of English at the Faculty of Foreign Language Studies, Kansai University, Osaka, Japan. Her publications focus on *Ancrene Wisse* and the contents of London, British Library, MS Harley 913.

Masao KONDO is a Professor at the Faculty of Foreign Language Studies, Kansai University, Osaka, Japan. His books include *St.Petersburg : Mythology of Literary Russia and Literary Essays on the Kolomna area.*

Wataru HIRATA is Special-Contract Professor at the Faculty of Foreign Language Studies, Kansai University, Osaka, Japan. His publications focus on Ramón Gómez de la Serna, a Spanish vanguardist writer.

Shu TSUZUMI is a Professor at the Faculty of Foreign Language Studies, Kansai University, Osaka, Japan. His field of specialization is Latin-American avant-garde literature, particularly that of the Chilean poet, Vicente Huidobro. He has published Japanese translations of works by Octavio Paz, Jorge Luis Borges and others.

Morihiro KAWAKAMI is a Professor Emeritus at the Faculty of Letters, Kansai University, Osaka, Japan. He specializes in Albert Camus and Jean-Paul Sartre.

Contents

An Irish Psalter with Two Lives: the Story of the Southampton Psalter 1
Patrick P. O'NEILL

How to administer a late-fourteenth century monastic library:
the case of Dover Priory 39
Patrick P. O'NEILL

The relationship between two Anglo-Norman alliterating verses
in London, British Library, MS Harley 913 87
Yoko WADA

Ветла и образ собора в романе Достоевского «Преступление и наказание»
("White willows and the image of the church in *Crime and Punishment* by Dostoevsky") ... 99
Masao KONDO

ラモンの『サーカス』に「日本人」が登場するまで
――ジャポニスムのスペイン伝播について――
(How Japanese acrobats came to appear in Ramón Goméz de la Serna's *El Circo*.
—an influence of Japonism on Spanish Literature") 109
Wataru HIRATA

ニューヨークの詩人――ビセンテ・ウイドブロの映画／
小説『魔術師の鏡』もしくは『カリオストロ』の成立
(A Chilean Poet in New York: Vicente Huidobro's Itinerancy for
the novel-film, *Mirror of a Mage* or *Cagliostro*) 131
Shu TSUZUMI

宗教から実存へ
("From Religion to Existence") 159
Morihiro KAWAKAMI

An Irish Psalter with Two Lives :
the Story of the Southampton Psalter*

Patrick P. O'Neill

Abstract:

An investigation of the origins, purpose, and history of the "Southampton Psalter" (now housed at St John's College, Cambridge, MS C 9), a de-luxe copy of the Latin psalms which was written in Ireland around the turn of the first millennium. This study examines (1) the Psalter's early function as an exegetical tool for understanding the Latin psalms ; and (2) its subsequent fortunes in England from the twelfth century to the present.

Keywords:

Dr Owen Gwyn ; *Gallicanum* ; John Whitfield ; Oxford, Bodleian Library, MS Bodley 920 ; Pseudo-Bede *Argumenta* ; R. Benet ; St John's College, Cambridge ; St Martin's Priory, Dover ; Third Earl of Southampton (Henry Wriothesley) ; William Crashaw

In a letter dated April 1635 the Master and Fellows of St John's College, Cambridge, wrote to Elizabeth, widow of the Third Earl of Southampton,

---

* The present article is a revised version of a paper read at St. John's College, Cambridge (Mar 11th, 2014). The images of plates 1-3 are published by kind permission of the Master and Fellows of St. John's College, Cambridge. I am very grateful to Kathryn McKee, special collections Librarian, for facilitating my study of the Southampton Psalter.

thanking her for having recently delivered to the College Library the final consignment of the books promised by her late husband (who died in 1624). Understandably, their letter was effusive, couched in the florid epistolary style of the times. Among other things they expressed the hope that "in your Bookes we might learne the Alphabet of your most Honourable Disposition towards us," and promised that "in the interim, wee will reade to studie your Bookes, yf wee may deserve the perpetuity of your Favours."[1] Among the books that prompted these promises was the Southampton Psalter (now identified as MS C. 9 of St John's College Library, Cambridge).

The manuscript in its present state consists of 98 folios. It is an integral Psalter, containing the 150 Psalms in the Latin version produced by St Jerome in the late 4th century (usually called the *Gallicanum* or Vulgate) which, as suggested by its alternative names, was current in the Gallican Church during the early centuries of its existence and subsequently became the received version in most of western Europe during the medieval period. In addition the Southampton Psalter has seven Canticles from the Old Testament, three prayers (or collects), and numerous glosses entered on the margins and between the lines intended to facilitate the interpretation of this difficult text. The whole was written and decorated in Ireland around the turn of the first millennium, which makes it about a thousand years old. Looking at it today one would have to say that it carries its age rather well; some wrinkles and dry skin to be sure, but the body of the text is sound and the decoration retains much of its lustre. Incidentally, the

---

1) Printed in C. C. Stopes, *The Life of Henry, Third Earl of Southampton, Shakespeare's Patron* (Cambridge, 1922), pp. 478-79.

An Irish Psalter with Two Lives : the Story of the Southampton Psalter

present diced Russian binding is quite modern, probably from 1818.[2]

From Early Christian Ireland (the period roughly from the early seventh to the late twelfth century) some fifteen Psalters (or fragments) have survived. They fall into one of two categories : either they are display Psalters honouring the sacred text by means of monumental script and lavish decoration ; or they are study Psalters, intended for scholarly work on the Psalms. What makes the Southampton Psalter unusual is that it combines the two functions ; it has both the show (in the form of decorated carpet pages and illuminated initials) and the substance (in the form of numerous scholarly glosses). That said, it would be rash to infer that the book was originally planned to serve this dual purpose ; indeed, various pieces of evidence suggest that the scholarly apparatus was a slightly later addition and not part of the original plan.

Script :

There are three types of script employed in the Southampton Psalter :[3]

(1) Insular Half-Uncial for the main texts, comprising the Psalms, Canticles and the first prayer. This rounded, majestic script, which had a long history in Ireland going back to the seventh century, represents the most formal hand of the Irish repertoire ; it is employed, for example, in de-luxe Gospel books such as the Book of Kells and the Book of Lindisfarne.

(2) A hybrid script which combines features of the half-uncial with a new script, a large angular, pointed script (often called in Ireland "the National Hand") which was beginning to take hold during the course of the eleventh

---

2) As suggested to me by Jonathan Harrison, former Keeper of Special Collections at St John's Library.

3) See Plate 1 (fol. 6ʳ).

century and by the twelfth century had become the standard formal hand for important texts. Its influence is already evident in Southampton, notably in the rubricated heading (or title) which precedes each psalm, in the angular form of "a" (in PSALMUS)[4] and in the more frequent use of certain abbreviations.[5]

(3) Late Insular cursive minuscule for the ancillary texts, the *Argumenta* and glosses. This script is well suited to a subordinate role because of the flexibility of its form and size. The *Argumenta* are basically short paragraphs (in Latin) offering several interpretations for a particular psalm; they are normally entered on the margin close to the opening verse of the psalm, as at fol. 6^r, line 22, right margin.[6] The glosses are found mainly between the lines, usually above the immediate Latin text which they explicate or comment on, though when adequate space was wanting they were entered on the margins. These glosses were probably excerpted from a running commentary on the psalms.

So, we can literally see here a hierarchy of scripts, reflecting the relative importance of the texts themselves. In first place comes the sacred text with its semi-uncial script; then the hybrid script of the biblical title at the head of each psalm (the Irish never really accepted the titles as the actual words of Scripture) and most of the prayers; and finally the *Argumenta* and glosses in Insular minuscule, with the former elevated slightly in status over the latter by means of a slightly larger hand. Similar hierarchies

---

4) See Plate 1, line 5.
5) As in the use of the symbol " ; " for -US in "CARMINIBUS" (Plate 1, line 22). See further E. Duncan, *The Southampton Psalter: A Palaeographical and Codicological Exploration,* Anglo-Saxon, Norse and Celtic Manuscript Studies 4 (Cambridge, 2004), p. 12.
6) See Plate 1.

of script occur in other Irish manuscripts of the eleventh century, for example, the Liber Hymnorum, where they serve the same purpose of visually marking the relative status of each constituent text.

Decoration :

As one of the finest and best-preserved Irish illuminated manuscripts from the pre-Norman period, the Southampton Psalter has received considerable attention from art historians. It has four kinds of decoration.

1. The first type is the whole-page figure illumination, of which there are three (David fighting the Lion ; the Crucifixion ; and David fighting Goliath).[7] They serve to introduce Pss 1, 51 and 101, respectively, reflecting the normal division of the 150 psalms into three fifties which is typical of Irish Psalters—though by no means confined to Ireland.

2. Facing each of the three figure illuminations of no. 1 on the opposite recto, is the second type of decoration, an elaborately decorated introductory page to the first Psalm of each of the three fifties (1, 51, 101) which contains a large initial (the first letter of the psalm) made of "a ribbon-like beast on a background of interlaced paws and tails" within a decorated frame.[8] Thus, the initial "Q" of "QUID" at the beginning of Ps 51.[9] Incidentally, the scribe of the main text entered a personal note in Irish at the

---

7) The iconographic significance of these has been studied by K. M. Openshaw, "Images, Texts and Contexts : the iconography of the Tiberius Psalter, London, British Library, Cotton MSS Tiberius C. iv," unpublished doctoral dissertation, University of Toronto 1990, ch. 5 ; and "The symbolic illustration of the Psalter : an insular tradition", *Arte Medievale* n.s. 6 (1992), 41-60.
8) F. Henry, "Remarks on the Decoration of Three Irish Psalters," *Proceedings of the Royal Irish Academy* 61 C (1960-61), 23-40 at 36.
9) Fol. 39[r], Plate 2. Here, and throughout, I follow the psalm numbering of the Latin Vulgate.

top of the page directly above the point of "Q", *"Beltene inndiu .i. for cetain* ("to-day is May-Day, on a Wednesday)" adding in Latin the intercession, "miserere nobis domine miserere nobis" ('Have mercy on us, Lord, have mercy'), an odd combination since May 1 was normally a festive occasion to celebrate the arrival of Summer.

3. The third type of decoration are the smaller ornamented capitals at the beginning of each psalm, which alternate between "ribbon animal" and "knotted wire" decorations in a pattern that seems to be "conscious and deliberate".[10] Thus, on fol. 6^r the initial "D" (line 6) exemplifies the former pattern and the initial "C" (line 23) the latter.[11] They served a practical purpose, marking where a new Psalm began, since numbered psalms were not often employed in early medieval Psalters.

4. The fourth type are the small decorated initials that mark the beginning of each verse within a psalm, consisting simply of a capital letter with alternating colours (yellow, brownish purple, lighter purple and orange) added as a filler. Again, these serve in place of the numbering of verses, a system which did not fully come into use until the advent of printing.

According to the late Françoise Henry, the doyenne of Early Irish Art studies, the first two types of decoration hark back to the eighth century and were obsolescent by the second half of the eleventh century, the last manuscripts to "show examples of it" being Southampton and an earlier Irish Psalter, the Vitellius Psalter (British Library, Cotton Vitellius F. xi), which was badly damaged in the Cottonian fire of 1731.[12] In comparing

---

10) Henry, "Remarks," 36. At least two trial versions of these initials in dry-point are visible on fols. 35^v (letter "B") and 98^v (letter "L").
11) See Plate 1.
12) Henry, "Remarks," 27 and 40, respectively.

these two psalters in their decoration, Henry was rather dismissive of the Southampton Psalter, describing it as "hardly more than a slightly decadent replica of an earlier manuscript" [*sc.* the Vitellius Psalter].[13] The third type of decoration, in contrast to the first two types, is innovative for its time, representing a style that became "the inexhaustible source from which the illuminators of the late eleventh and twelfth centuries" would draw.[14] This mixture of old and new places the Southampton Psalter among a group of transitional manuscripts from the tenth and early eleventh centuries. More specifically, Henry pointed to the "nearly complete absence of spirals" in the present Psalter's animal ornaments of the first and second types of decoration, a characteristic which "is paralleled on [Irish] metalwork of around the year [a] thousand".[15]

We turn now to the main topic, the "two lives" of the Southampton Psalter proposed in the title. The underlying notion of this conceit is that over the course of its existence the manuscript went through two very different phases, together covering more than a millennium. In the first phase (roughly from the early eleventh to the late twelfth century) it was presumably in Ireland, the place of its composition, where it was used for its text and commentary ; in the second, subsequent, phase it was lodged in England where it has since served mainly as an object valued for its aesthetic appeal and antiquity.

A. The Psalter's First Life (as text and commentary)

The study of the psalms in the medieval Irish monastic schools (from the

---

13) Henry, *Irish Art in the Romanesque Period (1020-1170 A.D.)* (Ithaca, NY, 1970), p. 2
14) Henry, "Remarks," 40.
15) Henry, "Remarks," 36.

seventh to the twelfth century) occupied a position second only to that of the Gospels. What made the psalms so special compared with the many other books of the scriptural canon (both Old and New Testament) was their multiple roles in a Christian society. As one of the sapiential books, the psalms offered not just Old Testament wisdom but also (if properly interpreted) guidance for Christians in their daily living. That they were known to have been originally composed in verse lent them a certain literary appeal, so that even in Latin translation (twice removed from their Hebrew originals) they were venerated for their poetic qualities.[16] Indeed, medieval Irish writers frequently spoke of "the pure language of the *Beati*" (Psalm 118) as a stylistic model for their own vernacular prose.[17] On a more humble level the psalms also provided the text from which beginners (traditionally at the age of seven) acquired literacy, learning to read and write Latin in the setting of the monastic school. Most importantly, the psalms were a living text, one that was recited and sung every day in the liturgy of the Divine Office by clerics as well as pious laity such as King Alfred of Wessex (died 899).

For Irish ecclesiastics the special status of the Psalter was acknowledged not just in lavish decoration but also in the interpretation of its text by means of minute commentary, based on the formidable body of psalm

---

16) Early Irish scholars would have known that the psalms were originally composed as Hebrew hymns from the comment of St Jerome in the second Preface to his Latin translation of the psalms (*Gallicanum*), "Nam et titulus ipse hebraicus Sephar Thallim, quod interpretatur Volumen hymnorum" ("For even the Hebrew title itself of the psalms was *Sephar Thallim,* which translates as 'the Book of Hymns'"); R. Weber et al. (ed.), *Biblia Sacra iuxta vulgatam versionem,* 2 vols. (2nd revised edition, Stuttgart, 1975), I, p. 768, lines 15-16.

17) See *Dictionary of the Irish Language based mainly on Old and Middle Irish materials* (compact edition, Dublin, 1998), B-94 (s.v. *biait*).

exegesis that circulated in early Ireland. Admittedly, much of it had been culled from earlier commentaries composed by the Latin Church Fathers such as Augustine, Jerome and Cassiodorus, whose allegorical approach to interpreting Scripture is known as "Alexandrian exegesis" (from the place where this approach was developed and systematized). But unlike the rest of early medieval western Europe, the Irish also had access to another type of exegesis which treated the psalms not only as literature (to be analyzed according to literary criteria) but also as historical poems composed by King David, speaking sometimes of his own times and sometimes (prophetically) of later Old Testament events. This second approach to the Psalms is referred to as "Antiochene exegesis," so named from the schools of Antioch in Asia Minor where it originated. What makes the Irish tradition of psalm exegesis distinctive (and almost creative) is its eclecticism, the blending of the Alexandrian and Antiochene traditions, which allowed for individual psalms to be interpreted both historically and allegorically. Indeed, by *c.*800 the Irish had developed a system of fourfold interpretation for each psalm which blended the two approaches in the form of a (1) first historical, (2) second historical, (3) Christological, and (4) moral application. The system, which was also employed by King Alfred of Wessex for his Old English translation of the psalms (1-50) in the late 800s,[18] was widely known and practiced in Ireland. So much so that we can reasonably presume that it was familiar to the author of the putative Latin commentary that underlies the Southampton Psalter glosses, a work composed around the mid-ninth century, judging by the approximate date of the occasional Old Irish words that appear as integral syntactical components of its pre-

---

18) See P. P. O'Neill (ed. and trans.), *Old English Psalms,* Dumbarton Oaks Medieval Library 42 (Cambridge MA & London, 2016), pp. xii-xiii.

dominantly Latin text.[19]

Yet, that author chose not to employ it. Take, for example, Ps 51.[20] The *argumentum* (or interpretative paragraph) accompanying the psalm in the manuscript proposes two interpretations, that the psalm can be understood to have been sung as a response to the words of Rabsaces, who was sent by the Assyrians to threaten King Ezechias (of Juda) with annihilation if he did not surrender to them (4 Kings 18 : 17-35) ; and secondly that it could be read as the words of Christ directed against Judas, the traitor. In the terms familiar to Irish biblical exegetes the *argumentum* was providing a second historical and a Christological interpretation. For the opening verse (v. 3), "WHY DO YOU GLORY IN MALICE, YOU WHO ARE MIGHTY IN INIQUITY,"[21] the Southampton glossator identifies four different speakers : (1) Doeg (as suggested by the biblical title[22]) ; (2) Judas Iscarioth ; (3) any sinner ; and (4) Sataliel (more correctly, "Sathariel" who appears in the apocryphal Book of Enoch as one of the principal fallen angels and who in the present context seems to represent the diabolic powers).

---

19) Edited and discussed by P. P. Ó Néill, *Psalterium Suthantoniense,* Corpus Christianorum, Continuatio Mediaeualis 240 (Turnhout, 2012), pp. lxii-lxx.
20) The numbering of psalms in the *Gallicanum* or Latin Vulgate version often differs by one from the numbering that most English readers are accustomed to from the King James Bible ; thus, Ps 51 of the Vulgate is Ps 52 of KJB. For the text (and glosses) of the opening lines, see Plate 2 ; the *argumentum* is found at the top of the page.
21) "QUID GLORIARIS IN MALITIA QUI POTENS INIQUITATE" ; here and throughout quotations from the Southampton Psalter are based on the edition by Ó Néill, *Psalterium Suthantoniense,* in this instance p. 134.
22) "CUM VENIT DOEC IDUMEUS ET ADNUNTIAVIT SAUL ET DIXIT VENIT DAVID IN DOMO ACHIMELECH" (Ps 51 : 2). Note that this part of the biblical titulus is not found in the Southampton Psalter, thus offering further evidence that the gloss (and its underlying commentary) was based on a different text of the psalms.

An Irish Psalter with Two Lives : the Story of the Southampton Psalter

At first glance it would appear that what we have here is the makings of (1) a first historical interpretation (see I Sm 22 : 9-23) ; (2) a Christological interpretation ; (3) a moral interpretation ; and (4) a mystical interpretation—but no second historical interpretation. However, as we read the glosses further it becomes evident that this system is not being systematically applied. Sometimes there are references to the machinations of Doeg and Sataliel, mentioned earlier ; but the main focus of the commentary is really the just person suffering at the hands of these agents of evil (for example, Adam and Eve tempted by the Devil) but eventually emerging victorious to witness their destruction. Significantly, at v. 8, "THE JUST SHALL LAUGH AT HIM"[23] (v. 8), where the psalmist gives vent to *Schadenfreude* at the wicked man's eventual punishment, the gloss instead comments that the just man is happy (rather than triumphal) because virtue is being rewarded and vice punished.[24] In this way the composer of the gloss deftly shifts the focus away from the wicked as victims to the just man as a model of virtuous restraint in victory ; in effect, Ps 51 is being assigned a moral interpretation, with the just man held up as an example for contemporary Christians.

A more complicated example is Psalm 77. In this long psalm the psalmist take a retrospective look at Jewish history, referring to the many favours accorded by God to the chosen people of Israel especially on their exodus from Egypt into the Promised Land. With its numerous historical references to events in the Books of Exodus and Numbers this psalm would seem to invite a historical approach ; in fact, even staunch adherents

---

23) "ET SUPER EUM RIDEBUNT" ; Ó Néill, *Psalterium Suthantoniense*, p. 135, line 31.
24) "laetabuntur non super casu eius sed pro bona retributio dum non fecerunt malum" ; Ó Néill, *Psalterium Suthantoniense*, p. 135, ll.31-33.

of the Alexandrian allegorical school such as Augustine and Cassiodorus conceded as much. Yet despite this, the opening gloss in Southampton proposes two possible speakers of the psalm, Asaph, a member of the Temple choir and a contemporary of David (to whom the psalm is attributed in the titulus) and Christ himself exhorting contemporary Christians with a Christian message, thus, "Asaph speaking; alternatively, Christ speaking to Christians."[25] But it soon becomes evident that of the two Christ is the preferred persona of the psalm. In that vein we find v. 20, "BECAUSE HE STRUCK THE ROCK, AND THE WATERS GUSHED OUT," being glossed "He bestowed abundance upon us,"[26] a purely allegorical reading that makes no mention of the historical miracle in the desert performed for the benefit of the wandering Israelites. Indeed, a survey of the numerous glosses of the main scribe reveals that while they sometimes advert to Old Testament history, more often they simply ignore the historical references or read them allegorically. For example, v. 24, "HE RAINED DOWN MANNA UPON THEM TO EAT," receives absolutely no comment.[27] Likewise, in v. 13, "HE DIVIDED THE SEA" is glossed "(he divided) the world from us by baptism";[28] and the words following, "HE MADE THE WATERS TO STAND (AS IF IN A VESSEL)," are interpreted to mean,

---

25) "Assab dicit; uel Christus ad Christianos"; Ó Néill, *Psalterium Suthantoniense,* p. 198, ll.9-10.
26) "nobis dedit habundantiam," where "nobis" surely means contemporary Christians; Ó Néill, *Psalterium Suthantoniense,* p. 201, ll.86-87.
27) "ET PLUIT ILLIS MANNA AD MANDUCANDUM"; Ó Néill, *Psalterium Suthantoniense,* p. 202, l.106.
28) "INTERRUPIT . . . MARE .i. nobis saeculum babtismo"; Ó Néill, *Psalterium Suthantoniense,* p. 200, l.59.

"for us he will inflict tribulations on himself,"[29] clearly an allegorical reference to Christ taking upon himself the sufferings of mankind.

But at just this point the hand of a second glossator intrudes, adding above "IN UTREM" ("IN A VESSEL") the defining gloss in the genitive, *"Maris Robri"* (*sc.* "the vessel of the Red Sea"), with the further comment "he (*sc.* God) made the Jews stand in an assembly—the mass of the Jewish people".[30] And in the same verse he also supplied above PERDUXIT ("HE LED US") the words *"per mare"* ("through the sea"), and over the initial "I" of INTERRUPIT the gloss. *i. diuissit* ("he divided"), both clear indications of a historically oriented approach to the verse. Again, at v. 20, "BECAUSE HE STRUCK THE ROCK, AND THE WATERS GUSHED OUT," where the original glossator provided an allegorical comment referring to contemporary Christians ("he gave us an abundance of water"), the second glossator intervened with another historically based gloss stating that "it is easier for him [*sc.* God] to produce water from a rock than to prepare food —and that verse is the word of the believers from among the Israelites."[31] What we see here, I would argue, is the intervention of a glossator (writing a little later than the first glossator) who was unhappy with the primary glossator's ahistorical approach and his predilection for allegorical interpretations, especially in a context where the text of the psalm(s) called out for a historical approach. Significantly, the comments supplied by this second

---

29) "ET STATUIT AQUAS nobis, tribulationes se dabit" ; Ó Néill, *Psalterium Suthantoniense,* p. 200, l.61.
30) "QUASI IN UTREM Maris Robri. Stare in congregationem fecit ; Ebreorum aceruum" ; The text in Ó Néill, *Psalterium Suthantoniense,* pp. 200-201, ll.61-63, incorrectly reads "Roobris" for "Robri," and "Ebreos aceruam" for "Ebreorum aceruum".
31) "Facilius est ei aquam de petra producere quam escam parare ; et uox est credentium ex Israhel" ; Ó Néill, *Psalterium Suthantoniense,* pp. 201-202, ll.87-89.

glossator derive from a historically oriented commentary on the Psalms which was probably composed in Ireland in the seventh century.[32]

To return to the original glosses (entered by the first and primary scribe), which constitute the bulk of the entries in the Southampton Psalter: how should we characterize their exegetical approach? We have seen that in Ps 51 the glosses reflected a primarily moral interpretation and in Ps 77 a strong tendency towards Christian allegorization. Elsewhere, we find that they most often propose a threefold scheme of historical (usually David), mystical (usually Christ or the Early Church), and moral (the practicing Christian, called *"sanctus"* or "holy person") interpretations. For example, at Ps 34: 2, "JUDGE, LORD, THOSE WHO INJURE ME," the gloss proposes to read the psalm as spoken by (1) David, about his enemies; (2) Christ, about the Jews, his enemies; and (3) us Christians, in our struggle against demons.[33] Note how all three levels of interpretation are couched in terms of conflict: Dauid fighting his enemies (notably Saul and Absalon); Christ suffering at the hands of the Jews or Judas Iscarioth; and contemporary Christians struggling against demons or their own vices. This agonistic approach has its counterpart in the three figure illuminations of the Psalter, all of which portray the same theme (David fighting the Lion; the Crucifixion; David fighting Goliath). However, the fact that a threefold system is formally enunciated in the opening gloss to a psalm does not necessarily mean that it was applied throughout. For one thing,

---

32) See P. Ó Néill, "Some Remarks on the edition of the Southampton Psalter Irish Glosses in the *Thesaurus Palaeohibernicus,* with further addenda and corrigenda," *Ériu* 44 (1993), 99-103; and M. McNamara (ed.), *The Psalms in the Early Irish Church,* Journal for the Study of the Old Testament, Supplement Series 165 (Sheffield, 2000), pp. 219-230.

33) "IUDICA DOMINE NOCENTES ME Dauid dicit de inimicis; uel Christus iudeis; uel nos contra demones"; Ó Néill, *Psalterium Suthantoniense,* p. 81, ll.9-10.

many of the applications of the threefold system in the glosses are quite mechanical, consisting of the simple formula, "Dauid uel Christus uel sanctus", and lacking application to the immediate context. In reality, the majority of the glosses offer either a twofold or a single level of interpretation.

But what stands out in the Southampton Psalter gloss is the ubiquity and primacy of the allegorical approach, taking that term in its broadest sense of comprising any kind of figurative interpretation (*sensus*) other than the literal/historical (*historia*).[34] It is found at work in the vast majority of the glosses, and it predominates among those that propose a twofold or single level of interpretation. Correspondingly, as we have seen, historical interpretations are noticeably absent or, if mentioned, are not pursued. Indeed, some of the glosses indicate that their author entertained a less than enthusiastic attitude towards a historical reading of the Psalms. Sometimes he uses the term *secundum historiam* ("according to the historical sense") to mean nothing more than "according to the obvious meaning," as if to imply that such an approach did not constitute a proper interpretation—or warrant a comment. For example, at Ps 123: 8, "WHO CREATED HEAVEN AND EARTH" ("QUI FECIT CAELUM ET TERRAM") has the gloss, "*secundum historiam,*" which probably means no more than "in accord with the literal meaning."

Elsewhere his reservations about the historical approach are more expressive. A gloss on Ps 17: 28, "YOU WILL ABASE THE EYES OF THE PROUD" ("ET OCULOS SUPERBORUM HUMILIABIS") castigates the

---

34) What a ninth-century Irish glossator in a commentary on the psalms referred to as *rún* ("mystical sense"); see W. Stokes and J. Strachan (edd.), *Thesaurus Palaeohibernicus: a Collection of Old-Irish Glosses Scholia Prose and Verse*, 2 vols. (Cambridge, 1901; rpt. Dublin, 1987), I, p. 125 (44 b 6). See further, McNamara, *The Psalms,* pp. 95-7.

Jews because they followed only the literal sense of Scripture and failed to recognize the higher, allegorical meaning.[35] Other glosses equate such literally-minded people with insensate beasts. Thus, at Ps 106 : 38, the word "IUMENTA" ("CATTLE") is interpreted as "simple-minded people for whom the historical meaning suffices."[36] Conversely, at Ps 103 : 13 words of the psalm that invite allegorical interpretation are labelled as "lofty explanations."[37] And in the next verse the first phrase, "SUPPLYING FODDER FOR CATTLE" ("PRODUCENS FOENUM IUMENTIS"), is unfavourably interpreted as "the literal meaning which satisfies the more simple-minded" (*"historiam semplicioribus"*), in sharp contrast with the next phrase, "(SUPPLYING) HERBS FOR MANKIND" ("HERBAM SERUITUTI HOMINUM"), which is glossed "true understanding for those allegorically inclined" (*"intellectum spiritalibus"*).[38] However, it would be wrong to conclude from such comments that the author of the Southampton gloss rejected the historical approach out of hand; rather, he regarded it as a mere stepping stone to true scriptural exegesis. In that respect he was following St Jerome and the tradition of Alexandrian exegesis which was dominant in the early medieval Western Church.

This predilection for allegorical at the expense of historical interpretations sets the Southampton gloss apart from the generality of Irish exegesis on the psalms which was predominantly Antiochene in its approach. Whatever the explanation for this departure from the main tradition it prob-

---

35) "sensus Iudeorum sequentium historiam tantum, et nesciebant intellectum"; Ó Néill, *Psalterium Suthantoniense*, p. 40, ll.97-98.
36) "semplices quibus historia sufecit"; Ó Néill, *Psalterium Suthantoniense*, p. 290, ll.123-124.
37) "altis sensibus", Ó Néill, *Psalterium Suthantoniense*, p. 272, l.53.
38) Ó Néill, *Psalterium Suthantoniense*, p. 272, ll.56-57.

ably owes much to the influence of the dominant source of the glosses, a commentary on the psalms composed in a monastery of southern Gaul in the early seventh century known as the *Glosa Psalmorum*.[39] That work, markedly monastic both in its origins and intended audience, was designed to make the psalms applicable to daily Christian life, and as such may have served as an interpretative model for the composer of the Southampton Psalter gloss.

B. The Psalter's Second Life (as a de-luxe manuscript)

What has been discussed so far refers to the "first life" of the Southampton Psalter when it was used in Ireland, initially as a display book and soon after as a glossed text of the Psalms intended for study. What follows is the story of its "second life," when it was brought to England, not as a working Psalter but as an object venerated for its sacred text, antiquity, visual art and perhaps strangeness, by the monastic custodians, Protestant bibliophiles, and professional librarians who have cared for it since, four of whom have left their mark on its pages. Using these latter entries I propose to sketch a broad timeline of the Psalter's history in England with a series of chronological milestones, while asking for the reader's tolerance in speculating about the gaps.

---

39) For evidence of that influence, see Ó Néill, *Psalterium Suthantoniense,* pp. lxx-lxxii.

Significant Dates in the "Second Life" of the Southampton Psalter :

c.1000	Written in Ireland (Armagh?)
12th c.	Corrected in England, perhaps at Christ Church Canterbury
c. 1140	Housed at Dover Priory for 400 years
1389	Catalogued by John Whitfield, the precentor of Dover Priory
16th	In possession of R. Benet
c.1610	In possession of W. Crashaw
1614/15	Assessed at 40 shillings
1615-35	In possession of the Earls of Southampton
1635	Donated to St John's, Cambridge
1705	Examined by Humphrey Wanley
1818	Rebound

The starting-point, of course, is Ireland, around 1000 AD. Unfortunately, we don't know where exactly in Ireland our Psalter was produced though some tenuous clues point to Armagh in the northeast, the primary ecclesiastical centre of Ulster.[40] The surest point on our timeline is the third one (1389) when the manuscript was certainly at St Martin's Priory, Dover, where it was catalogued in that year. So that fact naturally raises two related questions : how long had it been at Dover and how did it get there? Dover is a strategically located town through which many Irish ecclesiastics would have passed on their way to or from Rome, so it is tempting to imagine various scenarios in which a valuable Psalter somehow parted company with its Irish owners and ended up in the local Benedictine priory. But less romantic possibilities have to be considered as more likely. St Martin's was founded in 1130 on the site of a former Anglo-Saxon foundation donated by Henry I to Canterbury Cathedral, which established a community of Augustinian canons there. In 1139 it was appropriated by the pri-

---

40) See Ó Néill, *Psalterium Suthantoniense,* pp. xxxv-xxxvii.

ory of Christ Church Canterbury on the basis of a re-reading of Henry's charter, and handed over to Benedictine monks. This period coincides with Canterbury's cultivation of close ties with the Irish Church, which drew a steady flow of ambitious Irish ecclesiastics to Kent[41], a context that might explain how the Southampton Psalter came to England.

On the English side, Canterbury's appropriation of St Martin's during this same period would provide a plausible context for its donation of manuscripts (including, perhaps, a decorated Psalter) to the new foundation.[42] We know of at least six books probably written at Christ Church during the twelfth century that ended up in the Dover Priory Library.[43] More significantly, our Psalter bears evidence of English readership at about this date. At Ps 52 : 2 (fol. 39^v) the reading "SUIS" was added after "INIQUITATIBUS" in the main text, and at Ps 65 : 4 (fol. 45^v) "ALTISSIME" after "TUO," in what may be a twelfth-century hand. Both additions are readings from the *Romanum,* the version par excellence of the Latin Psalms used by the Anglo-Saxon Church (but not the Irish), one which although no longer official was still being copied at Christ Church Canterbury in the middle years of the twelfth century.[44] Perhaps most telling is the

---

[41] For example, the roll-copies of Canterbury episcopal professions for 1138 and 1139 contain those of Patrick and Maurice, bishop elects of the Irish dioceses of Limerick and Bangor, respectively.

[42] See C. R. Haines, "The Library of Dover Priory, its Catalogue and Extant Volumes", *The Library : Transactions of the Bibliographical Society,* new series 7 (1927), 73-118 at 87.

[43] See W. P. Stoneman (ed.), *Dover Priory,* Corpus of British Medieval Library Catalogues 5 (London, 1999), p. 5, who concludes that "[t]hese few extant books support what might have been taken for granted, namely that in the years following its foundation the priory was equipped with books from the parent house."

[44] For other possible evidence of English scribal interventions in the Southamptonn Psalter, see J. J. G. Flexander, *Insular Manuscripts 6th to the 9th Century,* (London, 1978), p. 88.

correction of a phrase from the third Canticle of our Psalter on fol. 37ʳ. The original reading, "A UESPERE" (Is 38 : 13), was corrected to "SPERABAM," a process which involved erasing "A UE", retaining the syllable "SPER" and adding the syllable *"bam"* above the line. The nature of the correction, whereby the original Old Latin reading was replaced by the corresponding Vulgate, is consonant with what we know of twelfth-century England where the Vulgate text of the Canticles had fully replaced the Old Latin text current before then.[45] These corrections imply a scriptorium engaged in the scholarly collating of the different versions of the Psalms (*Gallicanum, Romanum, Hebraicum*). For such activity we have ample evidence in the magnificent Eadwine Psalter produced at Christ Church monastery *c*.1160.[46]

The addition of *"bam"* is in a very different kind of script from the surrounding text; note the treatment of the end (or foot) of the vertical strokes (the minims) of the "m." According to N. Ker, finishing the vertical stroke of a letter was typical of eleventh-century English script from about 1040 onwards; but whereas for decades the foot received a horizontal stroke, by the second quarter of the twelfth century it takes on a pronounced curving stroke that was steeply angled.[47] From this cumulative

---

45) The Psalter of common use in Anglo-Saxon England at least until the late tenth century was the *Romanum* which normally had accompanying Canticles of the Roman Series in an Old Latin text. But it is unclear how the Old Latin reading, "A UESPERE," found its way into the Southampton Psalter whose text of this Canticle is otherwise *Gallicanum*.
46) See P. P. O'Neill, "The English Version", in M. Gibson *et al.* (edd.), *The Eadwine Psalter: text, image, and monastic culture in twelfth-century Canterbury* (London and University Park, 1992), pp. 123-38 at 137-8.
47) See N. R. Ker, *English Manuscripts in the Century after the Norman Conquest* (Oxford, 1960), p. 37. The profession of bishop-elect Patrick of Limerick, preserved in Canterbury Cathedral, MS C. 117, no. 38 (1138), has minims which bear a considerable resemblance ↗

evidence I would argue that the Southampton Psalter was being scrutinized and emended by readers in England around the mid-twelfth century, perhaps at Canterbury, before the Psalter was donated to the new Benedictine foundation at Dover.

Moving on to the third point in the timeline, we have a firm date of 1389, based on two entries made in the Southampton Psalter in that year by a member of the Dover community, John Whitfield. We don't know much about John's background, but he was Kentish, probably from the village to which he owed his surname. He was a contemporary of Geoffrey Chaucer, who was also living in Kent at this time, and would memorably satirize in the General Prologue to the *Canterbury Tales* one type of Benedictine monk. However, unlike Chaucer's monk who hated having to read and whose main interest was hunting, John's proclivities leaned towards maintaining and protecting the priory's books. He probably took a degree at Oxford; certainly he was a scholar (judging by the contents of the 22 books that he donated to Dover, as well as a commentary on the Rule of Benedict which he copied while at Rome in 1380-1). Our interest in him stems from his flair for organizing and cataloguing the priory's books (some 440 in all), which included the Southampton Psalter, a task which he undertook as precentor of the priory—one of the duties of that office was to act as custodian of the community's books. We are most fortunate not only that John's catalogue has survived, in Oxford, Bodleian Library, MS Bodley

---

⟍ to those of the *"bam"* addition in the Southampton Psalter; see Ker, Plate 18 a. On the other hand, the same addition lacks the "prickly angular appearance which is associated with S.E. English centres" of the first half of the twelfth century; see M. P. Brown, *A Guide to Western Historical Scripts from Antiquity to 1600* (Toronto & Buffalo, 1990), pp. 76-7.

920,[48] but also that corroborative evidence of his cataloguing activity is to be found in the Southampton Psalter.

John took his job seriously. His catalogue has three discrete parts, each with a particular audience in mind. Part 1 was designed primarily for the precentor, to allow him to check at a glance the status of each book in the library. In his Preface to Part I of the Catalogue—written, of course, in Latin—John describes how his system of cataloguing the library's books was devised so as "to prevent, as far as he could, future loss to his monastery—while impeding the malice of such as entertained the desire to steal and barter a precious object of this kind—and to establish a sound barrier of defence and resistance."[49] In other words, he planned to make it as difficult as possible to steal the priory's books. There were, of course, well-tried methods of protecting books from theft in place at this time, which John would have been familiar with, such as keeping books in a locked *armarium* (cupboard or chest); locking a reader into a carrel with the volume(s) he/she wished to read; chaining books to their shelves.[50] These draconian measures would hardly be necessary or appropriate for a small and stable community such as Dover, which in any case was cloistered. It's not as if a monk could brazenly walk out the gate with a valuable manuscript concealed on his person.

Besides, such measures for guarding the books from theft would inevi-

---

48) Edited in full by W. P. Stoneman, *Dover Priory*, Corpus of British Medieval Library Catalogues 5 (London, 1999).
49) My translation of the Latin text edited by Stoneman, *Dover Priory*, p. 16. For a full translation of John's Prefaces and an account of his system, see the next article, pp. 39-85.
50) See R. Gameson, "The Medieval Library (to *c.*1450)", in E. Leedham-Green and T. Webber, *The Cambridge History of Libraries in Britain and Ireland, vol.1 to 1640* (Cambridge, 2006), pp. 13-50 at 35-38.

tably come into conflict with John's other stated goal of encouraging the community to read more books more often. (The Dover monks were obligated by their Rule to borrow and read at least one book per year, but John evidently had greater ambitions for them.) His approach to reconciling these potentially conflicting goals of conservation and circulation was to devise a catalogue of the library's holdings whose first part would serve, as he himself put it, "to provide the precentor with information about the number and accurate location of the volumes." This is a polite way of referring to a system which, while allowing for the distribution of books, would involve a series of checks and controls so that the precentor could readily discover at any time the status, physical condition, and location of all the books under his charge by glancing at the first part of the catalogue.

For this purpose John employed the device of the *dicta/dictiones probatoria* (literally, 'testing words'). This was a way of identifying a volume from the opening words of the first line of a particular page (usually fol. 2^r). Unlike our printed books with their standardized pagination and text, each medieval manuscript has its own unique layout and spread of text, so that if the library contained several copies of a particular work it would be most unlikely that the words of their respective texts would exactly match in pagination, lineation, and head position. The system of the *dicta probatoria* seems to have been invented at the University of Paris; the earliest example comes from the Sorbonne around 1280. The first example in England comes from a collection of books on philosophy in the library of Merton College, Oxford, dating 1318 × 1334.[51] Indeed there is good reason to think

---

51) R. Sharpe, "The Medieval Librarian," in Leedham-Green and Webber, *The Cambridge History of Libraries*, pp. 218-62 at p. 227.

that this system originated in the college libraries of Oxford which, with their relatively free environment of fellows coming and going, and borrowing heavily, required a different system for controlling the circulation of books.

The practice of the *dicta probatoria* served two main purposes : it facilitated the checking of books being borrowed or returned ; an assistant (*succentor*) could read aloud the opening words of the designated folio of the book, while the precentor could check that what he heard tallied with what was recorded about the book in Part I of the Catalogue. By the same token if a book went missing, that too could be recorded. The *dicta probatoria* also forestalled another problem, a subtle form of theft whereby an inferior copy of a borrowed book might be substituted for a more valuable original.

We are fortunate to have direct evidence that John applied this technique of identification to the Southampton Psalter. Part 1 of the catalogue has the following entry for our Psalter :[52]

A. V. 1   Psalterium vetus glosatum   6   apprehendite disci-   105 1.

The first item is what we would call the shelf mark of the book ; then its title ('an ancient glossed psalter'), based on contents ; next the folio on which one should seek the "testing words" (folio 6^r) ; followed by the words themselves, "apprehendite disci<plinam>" ; then the number of folios in the manuscript (105) ; and finally the number of works it contains (1). A glance for confirmation at fol. 6^r of the Southampton Psalter (bottom margin) shows the following entry in John's hand, "A : V : .i. Psalterium

---

52) Stoneman, *Dover Priory*, p. 18.

An Irish Psalter with Two Lives: the Story of the Southampton Psalter

uetus glosatum ydiomate incognito . . . 'apprehendite disciplinam' . . . 105 . . . . 1," which offers the same information, except for omitting the reference to fol. 6 (which in the present context would be unnecessary) and adding the mention of "ydiomate incognito."[53] And for the hyper-skeptic reader a glance upwards to the first line of the page shows that the opening words are indeed "ADPREHENDITE DISCIPLINAM," thus confirming the validity of the testing words. By locating the *dicta probatoria* on the sixth folio, rather than the normal second, John was making it that much harder to counterfeit the volume, thereby adding an extra measure of security, perhaps in deference to the manuscript's value. As a final measure of security John entered the title and shelf-mark of the Southampton Psalter on its inside front cover (fol. (i^v)) where it survives to the present day.[54] The only item of John's protocol for each manuscript that is missing in our Psalter is the inscription of the shelf mark on the outside cover; this may have been lost when the manuscript was rebound in 1810.

In addition to serving as a form of identification, the shelf-mark ("A. V. 1.") also guided the reader to the physical location of the Southampton Psalter in the Dover library. Thus, the letter "A" indicated that the Psalter was in the first (of nine) bookcase, the one which in John's system of classification was reserved for the most prestigious books, Bibles and biblical concordances. The notation "V" indicated that within bookcase "A" the Psalter rested on the fifth shelf—there were seven shelves, the fifth of which was reserved for Psalters—and the final "1" that it occupied first place on that shelf, a choice position which likely indicates that the manu-

---

53) See Plate 1. One can only assume that John found the Irish minuscule script so unfamiliar as to imagine that it was written in "an unknown language."
54) See his entry on the upper middle part of Plate 3 (fol. (i^v)).

script was regarded as special both on account of its age and its de-luxe character. We don't know if it was much used or borrowed by the Dover community—neither seems likely. John's characterization of it as written in a strange language (*"idiomate incognito"*) would surely have discouraged most borrowers, and in any case a decorated psalter would presumably have been spared the wear and tear of ordinary use, since alternative, and more practical, copies of the psalms would have been available within the cloister.

For all his vigilance in guarding the books of Dover Library, John could hardly have foreseen the fate awaiting it some century and half later following Henry VIII's mandate to dissolve the monasteries. Shortly after 1534 the Prior of Dover subscribed to the Act of Supremacy and surrendered the house.[55] The inquisition and visitation that followed make no mention of a library, so presumably it had already been dispersed.[56] Out of a total collection of some 450 volumes only 24 have survived,[57] among them the Southampton Psalter. One of the early laymen who came into possession of our Psalter was a certain R. Benet whose name appears on fol. 4ᵛ above the illuminated picture of David and the Lion. According to M. R. James, the same name is recorded for a sixteenth-century mayor of Romney (one of the cinque-ports that included Dover),[58] so one could surmise that Mr.

---

55) D. Knowles and R. N. Hadcock, *Medieval Religious Houses : England and Wales* (London 1971), pp. 64 and 156.
56) For further speculations about the dispersal of the library, see C. R Haines, "The Library of Dover Priory : Its Catalogue and Extant Volumes," *The Library : Transations of Bibiographical Society,* new series 7(1927), 73-118 at 115-18.
57) See N. R. Ker, *Medieval Libraries of Great Britain, a list of surviving books* (2ⁿᵈ edn., London 1964), pp. 58-9, for a list of the twenty-four manuscripts that survived, including the Southampton Psalter.
58) I have not been able to verify this information, nor has the town clerk of Romney

Benet was well-positioned to profit from the breakup of St Martin's library. Almost certainly he was a collector, one with a special interest in religious works, as evident by the fact that St John's Library has six other manuscripts of a similar character that bear his signature, invariably entered on the flyleaf or the first folio.[59] That these manuscripts likely came from places other than Dover Priory[60] suggests that the seven books originally formed part of a collection assembled by Benet. Subsequently, in the early decades of the seventeenth century, they passed through at least two more sets of hands before eventually ending up in St John's Library.

Of these two more recent owners the first, William Crashaw (1572-c.1626), a Fellow of St John's since 1593/4, was the enabler, while the second, Henry Wriothesley, Third Earl of Southampton (1573-1624), was the donor, with the beneficiary being St John's Library. Crashaw, a noted Puritan divine and a bibliophile, had amassed an extensive library and was still acquiring manuscripts in 1611,[61] but a few years later his deteriorating financial situation led him to make several unsuccessful attempts to sell the collection. The Southampton Psalter seems to have been one of the books which he planned to sell, judging by the numeration "40 shillings" at the

---

  (Mrs Catherine Newcombe), who was kind enough to check the town's Mayoral Roll, which dates back to the 1400s, and the Clerk's Roll (personal communication, April 2, 2104).

59) The six manuscripts in question are C.18 ; D.2 ; D.13 ; D.22 ; D.26 ; and E.9 ; for descriptions, see M. R. James, *A Descriptive Catalogue of the Manuscripts in the Library of St John's College*, Cambridge (Cambridge, 1913) and its updated (online) version at http : //www.joh.cam.ac.uk/library/special_collections/manuscripts/ medieval_manuscripts/.

60) Since they are listed in John Whitfield's catalogue.

61) For example, St John's Library MS A. 12 has Crashaw's name and the date "Nov 17, 1609" ; A. 14 has "W. Crashawe 1611" ; A. 15 has a list of owners the last of which was "Wilhelmi Crashavi 1610." See James, *A Descriptive Catalogue*, pp. 16, 18 and 19.

27

upper margin of its flyleaf in a seventeenth-century hand. This entry probably represents an appraised value of the manuscript—at least 47 other manuscripts of the present St John's manuscript collection have a similar kind of numeration entered on their front leaves.[62] The obvious explanation for this activity is that the manuscripts were being priced with a view to selling them. That the seller was Crashaw and the prospective buyer Cambridge University,[63] is suggested by an item in the University accounts for 1614-1615 which records an expense of 20 shillings "pro itinere Stationariorum London' in examinanda bibliotheca Magistri Crashawe."[64] In other words, the University paid the travel expenses of professional booksellers from London who journeyed to Cambridge to appraise Crashaw's library.

In the event it was not Cambridge University but one of its alumni, the Third Earl of Southampton, who bought the collection. Like Crashaw, Wriothesley was a Johnian, but the two men more likely came in contact through their shared interest in a business venture, the Virginia plantation, rather than through College connections.[65] While the details of the contract between them is not known, two things seem clear : that the Earl bought the collection with a view to donating it to his alma mater, and that terms were agreed before March 23, 1614. On that date Crashaw wrote to Dr Gwyn, Master of St John's, about "that good motion his Lordship made to me for our librarye, mentioning that his collection had "some 500 manuscript volumes" of which some were "very ancient," a description that cer-

---

62) See Plate 3. I am grateful to Professor Richard Beadle for pointing this out to me.
63) Documented on the St John's website under "Old Library" at http : //www.joh.cam.ac.uk/history-old-library.
64) As first noted by James, *A Descriptive Catalogue*, p. viii.
65) As suggested by Stopes, *The Life of Henry*, p. 374.

tainly brings to mind the Southampton Psalter. Two months later Crashaw reported that "This noble Earl persists in his honourable intendment towards our Librarye," advising the Master "that you are like shortly to have a faire parcel of books," including "some ancient manuscripts . . . ." By June he was able to report to Gwyn that the transaction between himself and Wriothesley was well under way : "I have delivered alreadye into Southampton house almost 200 volumes of manuscripts in Greeke Lattine English and french."[66]

Despite this flurry of activity, the final step of transferring the collection to St John's did not occur—at least for another twenty years. The College was simply not prepared for this *embarras de richesses* ; it lacked adequate facilities to house such a large collection. This effectively meant that the books would have to remain with Southampton until such time as a suitable library was built. In June 1618 Crashaw wrote to Gwyn and informed him that Wriothesley had questioned him about progress on the building project, at the same time re-affirming his commitment to the original donation, while also promising to do even more for the new library. Unfortunately, building did not begin until late 1624, just weeks before Wriothesley (and his heir) died in Holland ; nor was it yet completed when Crashaw died two years later. Thus neither of the two Johnians lived to see the collection fully and properly housed in the new library which opened in 1628.

Despite this hiatus the close connection between the Southampton family, represented by the Third Earl's widow (Elizabeth née Vernon) and her second son, Thomas (now heir), was maintained. No doubt it was fur-

---

66) All three letters are conveniently printed in Stopes, *The Life of Henry,* pp. 371-72.

thered by Thomas's attendance as a student at St John's for a year (in 1625), but one gets the impression that it endured mainly because of Elizabeth's desire to fulfill her husband's wishes. As she wrote to the College in a letter of August, 1626, her endeavour was that "his name and memory [*sc.* her husband's] may forever live and be fresh amongst you." In the furtherance of that end she now sent them a consignment of "certaine bookes."[67] However, it does not appear that Crashaw's manuscripts (including the Southampton Psalter) formed part of this first round of donations, since there is no reference to manuscripts (as distinct from books) in the correspondence surrounding the transaction. It would take another decade for the manuscripts to become part of St John's Library, and when this happened in 1635, they now bore the mark of ownership, "Tho : C. S," that is, *"Thomas Comes Suthantoniensis"* ("Thomas, Earl of Southampton"). This mark is found in some 160 manuscripts that now survive at St John's, among them the Southampton Psalter, which has it at the top right corner of the flyleaf.[68] Directly below the notation, and apparently of a piece with it (at least spatially), is the numeration "A. 3. 13" (now erased). It probably represents an earlier shelf mark from the period when the psalter belonged to a library other than St John's. If so, that putative library must have been a large one to judge by the three layers of identification inherent in the shelf mark, perhaps the library of Southampton House. The marks of erasure through the entry were probably made when ownership was transferred to another library, perhaps when it reached St. John's and received the new shelf mark "C. 9," which appears twice on the same page.

As for the note of ownership, almost certainly it was not entered by

---

67) Stopes, *The Life of Henry,* p. 476.
68) See Plate 3.

Thomas, since it does not resemble in any way specimens of his later autograph.[69] Its presence nevertheless raises interesting questions about when and why it was entered. The Third Earl had died intestate, leaving his wife Elizabeth to serve as administratrix of the estate. And since Thomas's older brother (James) also died at that time, Thomas by default became heir in 1624, albeit as a minor (aged sixteen). In the following year he went up to St John's, Cambridge, and after a stay of about one year headed immediately for the Continent where he remained for more than eight years.[70] Given these circumstances it seems very unlikely that Thomas would have taken much interest during that period in the manuscripts still remaining from his father's incomplete donation, at least until such time as he returned to England in late 1634. It is surely more than a co-incidence (as implied by Stopes) that within months of his return that his mother sent the remainder of the promised collection (the manuscripts) to St John's. Legally, Thomas could now do with them as he pleased, and he may well have had them individually inscribed with his name at this time for that very reason. But as subsequent events suggest, his mother's single-minded desire to complete her husband's donation brought about an agreement whereby the manuscripts were sent "as a joint gift."[71] In acknowledging the gift the Master and Fellows of St. John's wrote separate letters in April 1635 to mother (in English)[72] and son (in Latin), thereby showing

---

69) In these later examples he invariably writes only the initial 'T' of his first name followed by "Southampton," with no mention of the title "Earl" ; furthermore, the ductus of these signatures is entirely different from that found in the Southampton Psalter and other manuscripts at St. John's.
70) Stopes, *The Life of Henry,* p. 478.
71) The conclusion of James, *A Descriptive Catalogue,* p. viii.
72) As recorded in the opening paragraph of the present paper ; see n. 1.

their awareness of a delicate situation in which the wishes of an adminstratrix were reconciled with the rights of an heir.

Finally, two other pieces of evidence on the flyleaf. The paper pastedown with the St John's crest and inscription confirms the library's acquisition of the Psalter. Another note on the same page (in Latin) describes the book's contents as "Psalms and Canticles," while also asserting that "This book was written around the year of our Lord 800." The dating, which is off by about two centuries, may be a misreading of Humphrey Wanley's verdict that "The book seem's to be 800 years old." Wanley, the father of English palaeography, examined the psalter *in situ* in 1705.[73] He was also the first person to recognize that among the Latin glosses were Irish words, a list of which he sent to the Welsh antiquarian Edward Lhwyd. Indeed, Wanley's professional approach to the Southampton Psalter could be said to have initiated for this fortunate book a "third life" as a valuable witness to early Irish learning and culture.

---

73) P. L. Heyworth, *Letters of H. Wanley, Palaeographer, Anglo-Saxonist, Librarian 1672-1726*, (Oxford, 1989), p. 198. Wanley seems to have been the first modern reader to recognise the presence of Irish words ; ibid., pp. 207-8.

An Irish Psalter with Two Lives : the Story of the Southampton Psalter

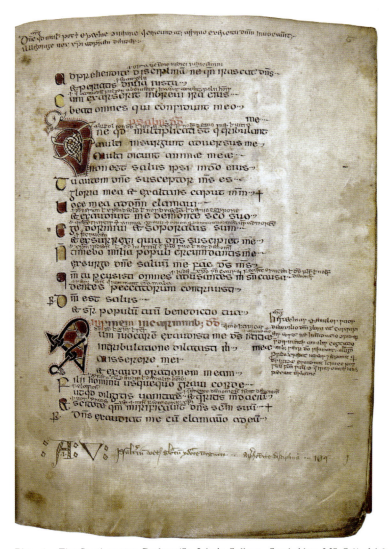

Plate 1 : The Southampton Psalter (St. John's College, Cambridge, MS C.9), fol.6r.

Plate 2 : The Southampton Psalter (St. John's College, Cambridge, MS C.9), fol.39ʳ.

An Irish Psalter with Two Lives: the Story of the Southampton Psalter

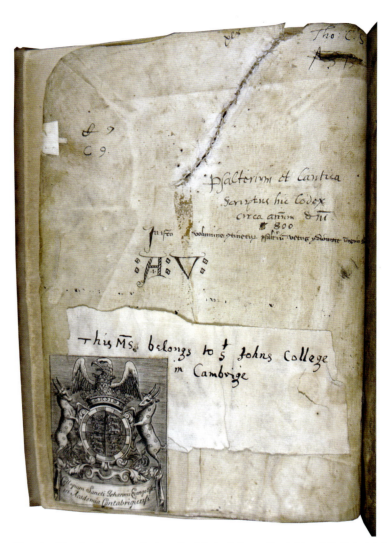

Plate 3: The Southampton Psalter (St. John's College, Cambridge, MS C.9), fol.(i)ᵛ

How to administer a late-fourteenth century monastic library : the case of Dover Priory[1]

Patrick P. O'Neill

Abstract:

A study of the library of the Benedictine foundation of St Martin's Priory, Dover, in the late fourteenth century, based mainly on the remarkably detailed catalogue prepared in 1389 by the librarian, John Whitfield. (The catalogue has survived as Oxford, Bodleian Library, Bodley MS 920.) Drawing on the contents of this tripartite catalogue, as well as the two prefaces appended by Whitfield, the present study examines how it was designed to balance the need for securing the library's books with the Benedictine ideal of encouraging the community to read and study them.

Keywords:

'Constitutions' of Pope Benedict XII ; *dicta probatoria* ; John Whitfield ; Lenten distribution of books ; Middle English works ; Oxford, Bodleian Library, MS Bodley 920 ; precentor ; Southampton Psalter ; St Augustine's, Canterbury ; St Martin's Priory, Dover

We are all familiar with certain officers of the medieval monastery :

---

1) This is a revised version of a paper originally read at the annual meeting of the Western Branch of the Japan Society for Medieval Studies, at Osaka University on June 8th, 2013. I wish to thank the Bodleian Libraries, The University of Oxford, for permission to reproduce the images of plates 2, 5, and 6 ; and the Master and Fellows of St. John's College, Cambridge, for permission to use the images of Plates 3 and 4.

39

the abbot and prior at the high end of the hierarchy and at the lower end the guest-master (*hospitarius*) and the bursar (*bursarius*). Less well known, perhaps because of his position in the middle, is the *precentor* (<Late Latin *prae* + *cantor*), literally "one who leads a choir or musical performance," a role which in an early medieval monastic context meant the officer who was in charge of the singing arrangements for the liturgy, notably the Mass and the Divine Office. In this latter role he would naturally have had control also of the various books used for the liturgy (e.g. calendars, missals, psalters) as well as responsibility for maintaining an adequate supply of such books.

By the eleventh century the role of the precentor had expanded so that he now assumed responsibility for *all* the books of his community. Indeed, in the larger monasteries he would have been so busy on various fronts as to require the assistance of a subordinate (the *succentor*) who ran the day-to-day business relating to the book collection, though the precentor alone retained the authority to distribute books. The precentor's job involved several important duties relating to the keeping and distribution of books and thus relevant to the present paper.[2]

(1) At a very mundane level he arranged for the copying, repair (including bookbinding), and proper storage of the books under his charge; for example, ensuring that the book-cupboards were kept in good repair.

(2) When a brother donated a book the precentor recorded the donor's name in it, adding a prayer for his soul.

---

[2] For other duties of the precentor, see R. Sharpe, "The Medieval Librarian," in E. Leedham-Green and T. Webber (eds.), *The Cambridge History of Libraries in Britain and Ireland, vol.1 to 1640* (Cambridge, 2006), pp. 218-41 at 220-22. The present article is heavily indebted to Sharpe's essay.

(3) He prepared an inventory of the library's collection (usually arranged by subject and author) for the annual audit.

(4) As part of the daily routine, with the assistance of young monks, "[w]henever the monks shall sit in the cloister, he must go round the cloister after the bell has been rung to put away any books that may have been forgotten through someone's lack of attention."[3]

(5) When a monk took out a book from the collection for personal study the precentor had to ensure that the borrowing was recorded: "no one shall take a book unless it is entered in his roll, nor shall anyone exchange books without an appropriate and sufficient memorandum which must be entered in his roll."[4] An example of such a roll containing the *electiones* (book choices) of the brethren of Thorney Abbey for the period 1324-30 has survived.[5] The list of names seems to be arranged according to seniority, beginning with the abbot and then the prior. One problem faced by the precentor of this community was the popularity of the name John among the brethren; this he solved by giving a different number to each John. Thus, the most junior John was identified as 'John 13' (he borrowed a copy of the Acts of the Apostles, a relatively easy text to read), while 'John 11' borrowed a glossed psalter (presumably for the sake of its interpretative notes on the psalms). But the precentor in his role as custodian of the books would face more serious challenges. In 1345 at the mandatory episcopal visitation of Thorney Abbey a problem was uncovered involving a

---

3) Cited by Sharpe, "The Medieval Librarian," p. 223, based on a fourteenth-century custumal from Evesham.
4) Loc. cit.
5) See R. Sharpe, J. P. Carley, R. M. Thomson and A. G. Watson (eds.), *English Benedictine Libraries: the Shorter Catalogues,* Corpus of British Medieval Library Catalogues 4 (London, 1996), pp. 598-604 [B 100].

scandalous book that was circulating among the community. The book was characterized as a series of writings that were *inordinata et pudenda* '('unlawful and 'shameful'—in a sexual sense), full of *oblocuciones et scandala* ('slanders and scandals'). This combination of the sexual and the scandalous suggests that the book in question contained satirical writings about sexual misconduct among religious orders, perhaps along the lines of the Middle English poem, *the Land of Cokaygne,* and other satires in Latin of monastic life (such as *The Abbot of Glastonbury's Feast*) found in the roughly contemporary manuscript, British Library, Harley 913. Alternatively, it might have contained fabliaux in which monks or friars played prominent roles as seducers. The offending book was last seen in the possession of Prior John, who had concealed it at the head of his bed, presumably as an act of confiscation, before it subsequently went missing. The episcopal visitor pronounced excommunication on the thief unless within six days he burned it and any copies. Despite this threat the scandalous book (and perhaps its progeny) did not go away. A visitation two years later reported that it was stolen by Brother William of Sutton and Brother Robert of Corby who circulated it among the other monks. The bishop ordered the immediate burning of the book (and any copies made) and forbade any mention of it thereafter. No doubt all this commotion kept the precentor busy.

(6) Probably the most important function of the precentor, at least in a Benedictine monastery, was his role in the annual Lenten distribution. This practice was meant to fufill a requirement of the *Rule of Benedict,* ch. 48, verses 14-16, which prescribed that

> In the days of Lent, however, let them [*sc.* the monks] leave free for their readings the period from early morning to the end of the third hour. . . . In which days of Lent let them all accept from the library

their own particular book which they should read through in its entirety. These books are to be distributed at the beginning of Lent.[6]
Thus, every year at the beginning of Lent the community assembled in the chapter-room, each monk returning the book he had borrowed in the previous year and collecting a new one for the coming year.

Fortunately, we have a detailed account of the process in the *Constitutiones* of Archbishop Lanfranc of Canterbury. It was drawn up in 1077 for the monks of Christ Church, and is therefore likely to have been also used at Dover, which was a daughter house of the Canterbury foundation.

On the first Monday of Lent, before the brethren go in to chapter, the custodian of the books should have all the books gathered and spread out on a carpet in the chapter-house, except for those that were distributed for reading the previous year—these books should be carried in by the brethren who then had them. The custodian should read out summarily a list of the books which the brethren had during the previous year. When each brother hears his name read out, let him return the book which was assigned to him for that previous year. And anyone who is conscious that he has not read in full the book he received shall prostrate himself, confess his fault, and seek pardon. Then the aforesaid custodian shall give to each of the brethren another book to read; and when the books have been distributed in proper order, he shall at the same chapter record in writing the names of the books and of those who received them.[7]

---

6) *The Rule of St Benedict,* ed. and trans. by B. L. Venarde (Cambridge MA & London, 2011), pp. 162-3.
7) *Monastic Constitutions of Lanfranc*; ed. D. Knowles, revd. by C. N. L. Brooke (Oxford, 2002), pp. 29-31.

The "custodian of the books" was none other than the precentor. And as evident from this description, he presided over a process which involved on his part the minute control of all the library's books, by recording each year at Lent the names of the brethren with the titles of the books that they had just returned, as well as the ones they were newly borrowing. All this activity required record-keeping, rather similar to that of an accountant who must constantly juggle debits and credits—in this case books borrowed and books returned. We catch a glimpse from a fourteenth-century Evesham Abbey document of how this process was carried out: "No one shall take a book unless it is entered in his [sc. the precentor's] roll, nor shall anyone exchange books without an appropriate and sufficient memorandum, which must be entered in his roll."[8] One such roll, as noted above, has survived from Thorney Abbey.

Being the realistic legislator that he was, Benedict foresaw that there would likely be monks who failed to observe the daily reading requirement and so provided remedies for the offense in his Rule. Likewise, Lanfranc's legislation addressed the problem of certain monks who failed to meet the requirement in Benedict's Rule that each book borrowed in this manner should be read in its entirety. The problem seems to have been widespread in England all through the high Middle Ages. Geoffrey Chaucer addressed it in the General Prologue to the Canterbury Tales, where he portrayed a pilgrim monk confiding to Chaucer (the pilgrim) that this compulsory reading drove him crazy: "Why should he study and drive himself crazy/ constantly poring over a book in the cloister."[9]

---

8) Cited by Sharpe, "The Medieval Librarian," p. 223.
9) *"What sholde he studie and make hymselven wood/ Upon a book in cloystre alwey to poure"* ; ed. L. D. Benson et al., *The Riveside Chaucer* (Boston, 1987), p. 26, lines 184-85.

The well-documented activities and professional responsibilities of the precentor provide a context for the work of John Whitfield, whose catalogue is the main subject of the present paper. John occupied the post of precentor at the Benedictine house of Dover in the last quarter of the fourteenth century. Despite its strategic location Dover Priory was not a major foundation ; it never had more than 12-16 monks in its community. Moreover, for the first two centuries of its existence it had fought a losing battle against a powerful neighbour, the Benedictine Abbey of Christ Church, Canterbury, which claimed it as a daughter house. Dover had a library of some 440 books (in 1389) which, while seemingly insignificant when compared to the 1,800 listed for St Augustine's Canterbury or the 2,100 reconstructed for Bury St Edmunds,[10] would have been proportionally impressive for a community of its size. Even more impressive was that it had a remarkable custodian of its books in the person of John Whitfield. Little is known about John's background other than that he was Kentish, most likely from the village (located some three miles north of Dover) that matches the second part of his name. He may have studied at Oxford, where the Benedictine Order had a house of study for members from all over England.[11] Certainly, his interests and his work demonstrate telling signs of a scholar ; thus, he donated twenty-two academic books to Dover Library, he entered glosses and notes in its books, and while at Rome in 1380-81 he copied a commentary on the Rule of Benedict.

Much more relevant for present purposes is that John also had a flair

---

10) Sharpe, "The Medieval Librarian," pp. 229-30.
11) As noted by A. Coates, *English Medieval Books : The Reading Abbey Collections from Foundation to Dispersal* (Oxford, 1999), pp. 88-89, a Benedictine monk going to Oxford (at least after 1363) would not necessarily take a degree.

for organizing and cataloguing. For example, in 1372 he compiled a Cartulary of Dover Priory which documented its various charters, muniments and other titles of ownership. And in a spirit of vigilant guardianship he ordered that this manuscript be chained in a secret place where only professed members of the community could consult it. He also made a similar record for the muniments and possessions of the Hospital of St Bartholomew for poor Lepers, a dependent foundation of Dover Priory. But his finest piece of work would be a three-part catalogue of Dover Library, now preserved in Oxford, Bodleian Library, Bodley MS 920.[12] As precentor and custodian of Dover Priory's library, John was well aware of his duty to protect the collection under his charge from damage and theft. It was uppermost in his mind, as evident from the statement in his Preface to Part I of the Catalogue, where he outlined an elaborate system for cataloguing and controlling the Priory's books, one so designed "to prevent, as far as he could, future loss to his monastery—while impeding the malice of such as entertained the desire to carry off and barter a precious object of this kind —and to establish, as a safeguard, a barrier of defence and resistance."[13] In other words, he planned to make it as difficult as possible to steal a book.

There were, of course, well-tried methods of protecting books from theft in place at that time, which John would have been familiar with. Among the most common measures were: (1) the *armarium* with triple locks; (2) the locked compartment; and (3) the chaining of books. In the first system, commonly found in college libraries at Oxford and Cambridge,

---

12) The excellent edition by W. P. Stoneman, *Dover Priory*, Corpus of British Medieval Library Catalogues 5 (London, 1999), supersedes that by M. R. James, *The Ancient Libraries of Canterbury and Dover* (Cambridge, 1903).
13) See Appendix, p. 26.

books were kept in an *armarium* (cupboard or chest) that had three locks ; each fellow had a key to one lock, but the other two locks could only be opened by the Master and Dean, respectively. So, borrowing a book involved the combined presence of all three and thus made theft less likely. The second system was the locked carrel (Lat. *carola*), a small private compartment for study in which a reader would be locked in with the book(s) he wished to read ; this ensured that he could not leave without verifcation that no books had been removed. However, from a practical point of view neither of these two methods would be necessary or suitable at Dover Priory, where control could be maintained easily over its small community of a dozen or so monks who, in any case, were already locked into a cloistered institution. The third measure of securing a library's books was that of chaining them to their shelves in order to prevent their removal, while allowing enough slack on the chains to enable readers to place the book they wished to read on the desks underneath the shelves.[14] Evidently, John decided that this tactic, which was routinely employed in college libraries for reference books,[15] would be applied at Dover only in a single extreme case, that of the Priory's cartulary (collection of property documents) which, as a further measure of security, was chained in a secret place.

Instead of employing these draconian measures for guarding the library's holdings, John devised a catalogue which would be so detailed and precise that it would serve, as he put it, "to provide the precentor with in-

---

14) A notable example survives in Hereford Cathedral.
15) See R. Gameson, "The Medieval Library (to c. 1450)," in Leedham-Green and Webber, *The Cambridge History of Libraries,* pp. 13-50 at 35-38.

formation about the number and accurate location of the books."[16] This is a polite way of referring to a formidable system of checks and controls that would allow the precentor to know at any time the status, condition,[17] and location of all the books under his charge. In creating this kind of catalogue John was moving away from the conventional catalogues of the previous centuries, which merely provided an inventory of a library's holdings arranged by subject and author, as illustrated by the mid-fourteenth-century catalogue of the library of Ramsey Abbey.[18] The drawback with the earlier system was that it offered no means of connecting these entries to the physical books which they recorded; consequently, this type of catalogue was of very limited use in tracking the movement of books.[19] An effort towards solving this problem was made by introducing the technique of the *dicta probatoria* (literally, 'testing words'). This was a way of identifying a book from the opening words of a particular page (usually fol. 2^r). Unlike our printed books with their standardized pagination and text, each medieval manuscript had its own unique layout and spread of text, so that if a library had several copies of a particular work it would be most unlikely that

---

16) See Appendix, p. 69.
17) For example, in Part 2 of his Catalogue John labelled five books as *moustardier,* a French-derived term which seems to mean that they were in such poor condition as to be "fit only to wrap up mustard" (M. R. James, *The Ancient Libraries,* p. xciii). The books in question are A.III.6, B.II.5, H.V.3, H.V.4 and H.V.5.
18) See Sharp *et al., English Benedictine Libraries,* Plate 9.
19) See Sharpe, "The Medieval Librarian," p. 227: "Many booklists from the twelfth century onwards therefore make an attempt to list subsidiary contents of a book. . . . A refinement of this type of list makes a more serious attempt to record every text in each book, but these catalogues, particularly from the twelfth and thirteenth centuries, still offer no way of working from the physical book to its entry in the catalogue or indeed vice versa."

their respective texts would exactly match in pagination, much less the lines of a particular page. The technique of the *dicta probatoria* seems to have been invented at the University of Paris ; the earliest example comes from the Sorbonne around 1280. The first example in England comes from a collection of books on philosophy in the library of Merton College, Oxford, dating 1318 x 1334.[20] Indeed, there is good reason to believe that this system originated in the university colleges which, with their relatively free and unhampered environment of fellows coming and going in the library, while also borrowing heavily, required a different method for controlling the circulation of books.

The system of *dicta probatoria* served several purposes : it allowed for easy checking of books being borrowed or returned since an assistant (*succentor*) could read aloud the opening words of the designated folio (usually 2^r) while the precentor could check that they tallied with what was recorded about the book in the Catalogue. The *dicta probatoria* also forestalled another problem, a subtle form of theft whereby an inferior copy of a borrowed book might be returned in place of a more valuable one. Since books were handwritten it was most unlikely that the inferior copy would exactly match the original in the location (page, line, and position on the line) of one or two particular words. As already noted, the normal testing point was the opening word(s) of fol. 2^r but in quite a number of cases John chose other folios, one reaching as far as fol. 48^r.

An obvious method for keeping track of books was to make an inventory while imparting to its contents some system of classification.[21] Classi-

---

20) Ibid., pp. 227-28.
21) See Gameson, "The Medieval Library (to c. 1450)," pp. 23-27.

fying books by author,[22] subject matter,[23] location,[24] or even donor[25] were all used for this purpose. A more promising method was to classify the books based on their physical location within the book-room. The Cistercian house of Rievaulx provides the earliest example from England of this system, recording its library's books under a sequence of classes (A-Q) which probably reflected their physical arrangement in the book-room according to shelves. By the second half of the fourteenth century catalogues using this system were evidently much in use, though by this time content rather than physical location had become the primary factor in determining their arrangement—no doubt the crucial factor in this change would have been the tendency to assemble books of a single author or of related subjects on the same shelf. Correspondingly, the sequence of letter classes that had once been used simply to mark the location of bookcases was now made to represent the books in a hierarchy of importance based on their contents. Thus Bibles were marked by "A," Biblical studies by "B," Patristica by "C," other Religious Subjects by "D," Canon Law by "E," and the secular *artes* by "F," where the sequence of letters reflects the descending order of importance of the books so classified.

About the same time (fourteenth century) we find these location

---

22) For example, a catalogue of Rochester Cathedral library (dated 1202) opens with sections for copies of Augustine, Gregory, Ambrose, Jerome and Bede; see A. Coates, *English Medieval Books: The Reading Abbey Collections from Foundation to Dispersal* (Oxford, 1999), p. 22.
23) An example is the catalogue of the library of Burton-on-Trent Abbey (*c.*1175); ed. Sharp *et al.*, *English Benedictine Libraries* [B 11], pp. 33-42.
24) An example is the second part of the Rochester catalogue; ed. Sharp *et al.*, *English Benedictine Libraries* [B 79], pp. 497-526.
25) An example is the catalogue of the library of Ramsey Abbey (mid-fourteenth century); see Sharpe, "The Medieval Librarian," p. 225.

marks recording the bookcase (and shelf) being added to the books themselves by the librarian. In this way the book-room, its furniture and the way that the books were arranged could be coordinated and carefully recorded. Here is John's description of how he arranged the Dover library:

> ... this library is divided into nine separate bookcases (*Distincciones*), following the first nine letters of the alphabet, which are clearly affixed to the bookcases themselves, so that to the person entering the room, 'A' indicates the first bookcase, 'B' the second, 'C' the third, and so on in alphabetical order. Each of the above-mentioned bookcases (it will be seen) is further divided into seven separate shelves (*gradus*), which are themselves highlighted by the addition of Roman numerals after the letters denoting the seven separate bookcases. One begins counting the shelves from the bottom, ascending in such a way that the bottom shelf is marked 'I,' the second 'II,' the third 'III' and so on, up to 'VII.'[26] Moreover, all the books of this library, to make it easier to get to know their contents, have their individual folios (*folia*) numbered with Arabic numerals. ... Furthermore, the individual books themselves, not only on the outside cover, but also inside, adjacent to the Table of Contents, at the beginning of each book, have their unique bookcase letter and shelf-mark added. And within each bookcase letter is included the small Arabic numeral by means of which is more precisely revealed what numerical position that book holds in the order of placement on the relevant shelf.[27]

---

26) See Plate 1.
27) See Appendix, pp. 69-70.

Unfortunately, it is not possible to ascertain from John's description how the bookcases were physically arranged since he merely mentions that "the person entering the room" would immediately perceive their large letters. A contemporary catalogue from Titchfield Abbey describes its library of some 220 books as having four presses (Bookcases) ". . . of which two . . . are on the east wall; on the south wall is the third; and on the north wall is the fourth; and each of them has eight shelves (*gradus*) marked with a letter and number."[28] It is possible that the nine bookcases at Dover were similarly disposed in being placed against the walls.

Although John does not expressly say so, it is evident from the contents of his Catalogue that he followed the traditional hierarchy in assigning the letters of the alphabet to the nine bookcases (A-I) according to the level of the importance which they would have carried for a monastic audience. Thus, the disposition of books was as follows:

A. Bibles and concordances;

B. Commentaries and Glosses on the Bible;

C. Theology, Homilies, Tracts on religious topics; Plato, Cicero, Sermons;

D. Hagiography; the Seven Deadly Sins;

E. Sermons, Rules;

F. Roman Law;

G. English Law; Canon Law;

H. Logic, Philosophy, Rhetoric, Mathematics, Medicine, Vernacular (French) Literature (Chronicles, Romance);

I. Schoolbooks, including the Latin Classics (Virgil, Ovid, Horace, Statius— many of them glossed); Grammars (Boethius, Donatus, Priscian), and Dic-

---

28) Cited by Gameson, "The Medieval Library (to c. 1450)," p. 27.

tionaries (especially Hugotio of Pisa's etymological dictionary).

As one might expect in a book collection from a Benedictine monastery, Scripture and religious works occupy the five highest categories. Two whole bookcases dedicated to Law might seem a bit odd. Certainly, John personally was interested in matters legal to judge by the books on that subject which he donated to Dover. But there seems to be more at stake here, a hint perhaps that Dover Priory had a very immediate interest in secular law and the ways of the world. Recall that for over two hundred years (1136-1356) the Priory fought a complicated legal battle with Christ Church Canterbury over the issue of its independence from that institution, so it would have needed all the legal information it could get from books and documents. In last position are books on the liberal arts. Although lowest in the hierarchy, secular subjects get two bookcases (H and I), an impressive number. In this respect Dover was surely complying with the *Constitutions* of Pope Benedict XII in 1336 which mandated that each Benedictine monastery provide within its walls instruction in the 'primitive sciences' (presumably the first four liberal arts, arithmetic, geometry, music and astronomy), in grammar, in logic and in philosophy.[29]

John entered the unique case- and shelf-number not only on the outside cover but also on the flyleaf of each book. That on the outside cover would have helped him to find a book quickly; that on the inside frontispiece was intended as another of a series of security measures.[30] John also added to each book continuing pagination in arabic numerals.[31] Although by no means a recent technology—it was already in place in western Europe

---

29) Dover Priory had at least three copies of this work; see Stoneman, *Dover Priory*, p. 283.
30) Discussed below, p. 56.
31) See the number "6" on the top right corner of Plate 3 (discussed below, p. 56).

by *c.*1200—pagination was hardly universal. As will be seen below, it was an essential component of John's plan that readers should be able to locate precisely within a manuscript containing multiple works where a particular text began and ended.

Having considered in outline John's plans for organizing the library and securing its books, one naturally moves to examining how he implemented them. Although most of the books of Dover Priory have long since disappeared, we are fortunate that John's catalogue of them has survived (in his own hand), preserved in Oxford, Bodleian Library, Bodley MS 920. The work is divided into three discrete parts, each with its own function. Looking first at Part I: the catalogue of books has nine divisions corresponding to the nine bookcases of the library, each of which, in turn, is subdivided into shelves and then the numbered books on each shelf. For every book six pieces of information are provided, in six columns, each with its proper heading as follows:[32]

(1) The first column (heading written vertically) provides the **ORDO LOCACIONIS**, the location of the book in relation to the other 8 on the shelf, in a sequence of Arabic numerals from 1 to 9.[33]

(2) The second column (heading written horizontally) gives the **NOMINA VOLUMINUM** ('the titles of the books'); thus shelf V begins with three copies of "Isidorus *De summo bono*," then "*Liber florum* Michaelis" (C.V.4), "Flores in contemplacione Augustini," Flores in contemplacione beati Augustini," "Meditacione Bernardi," "Liber Cassiodori de vera amicicia," and ends with "Hugo de sancto Victore de claustro anime" (C.V.9).

---

32) See Plate 2, which covers shelves V and VI of bookcase "C."
33) Because of the manuscript's tight binding, the numbers for shelf V are scarcely visible in Plate 2.

(3) The third column (heading written vertically) gives the **LOCUS PRO-BACIONIS**, 'the location of the *dicta probatoria* or "testing words"' within the book, based on the pagination supplied by John. Within the books contained on shelf V, their location ranges from the second to the sixth folio—always recto, presumably to facilitate the precentor (or his assistant) when searching for the initial words on the page.

(4) The fourth column (heading written horizontally) gives the **DICTIONES PROBACIONUM**, the actual 'testing words'; correspondingly, in the first copy of Isidore's book on shelf V of the "C" bookcase (thus C.V.1) the opening words on folio 2^r were "dici possit quam," whereas those for the second copy of Isidore (on fol. 3^r) were "reuertatur quibusdam."

(5) The fifth column (heading written vertically) is entitled **SUMMA FOLIORUM** ('the sum total of folios'). Thus, the first book of Isidore had 226 folios; and the unique copy of Hugh of St Victor's work had 177 folios.

(6) The sixth column (heading written vertically) indicates the **NUMERUS CONTENTORUM**, the number of discrete works contained in the book. Thus, the first copy of Isidore had 13 different works (actually, 12), whereas the second copy had only one, which gave its name to the book's title.

The key piece of information in Part 1, at least for purposes of security, was that contained in column (4) because, as indicated by its very name, it required that its wording be matched with that of the actual book. As an example of how this matching method worked in practice, take the Southampton Psalter, a highly decorated manuscript of Irish origin from *c.*1000, which belonged to Dover Priory (now at St John's College Library, Cambridge, as MS C. 9). In Part 1 of his catalogue, John assigned this manuscript the shelf-number number "A. V. 1" (column 1); identified its title as "Psalterium uetus glosatum" (column 2); gave its *locus probacionis* as fol. 6 (column 3), its *dictio probacionis* as "apprehendite disci- (column 4)," the number of its folios as "105" (column 5), and the number of works it contained as "1" (column 6).[34] A glance at the first line of fol. 6^r of this psalter shows that the opening words are "ADPREHENDITE DISCIPLINAM," thus confirming the *dictio probacionis*.[35] Lest there be any misunderstanding about the 'testing words,' John wrote an entry at the bottom margin of fol. 6^r, "A : V : .i. Psalterium uetus glosatum ydiomate incognito. . . . apprehendite disciplinam . . . 105. . . .1," which matches the entry in Part 1 (except that he omitted column (3) which was self-evident, and added the information that the psalter was written in "ydiomate incognito", 'an unfamiliar language'). As to why John chose his testing words from fol. 6^r rather than the conventional location (fol. 2^r), one can only speculate that knowing that copies of the psalms abounded in the Middle Ages, he wished to make it harder to simulate this precious Irish psalter with an inferior copy. The book was evidently a treasured possession of St Martin's, since it occupied first place (.i.) on the fifth shelf ('V') of its class ('A'), the highest in John's system of classification. Finally, to make assurances doubly sure, John entered on the flyleaf (fol. (i)^v) the following note "in isto uolumine continetur psalterium uetus ydiomate incognito glo<sa>t<um>" and underneath it in bold letters "A.V" with the Arabic numeral '1' inserted within the arms of the "A."[36] In content and script the note closely resemble John's inscription on fol. 6^r. The same treatment was, presumably, con-

---

34) Text from Stoneman, *Dover Priory,* p. 18.
35) See Plate 3.
36) See Plate 4.

fessed on every book of the library.[37]

Another advantage of Part 1, from the precentor's point of view, was that its details allowed him to identify readily a particular book—especially useful when the library had several copies of a work—while also keeping tabs on its current location and, if on special loan,[38] identifying the name of the borrower. Take, for example, the following entries, where slanting strokes indicate notes added by John :[39]

A. V. 5   *Sermones super Psalterio* \de habet/ \Th. Langle/

B. VI. 1   *Scolastice historie* Iohannis Fabri \Iohannis Wysbard doctor ecclesie Christi/.[40]

In the case of the *Sermones* it appears that the book was borrowed by Thomas Langle but was last in the possession of "de" (note the present tense, *habet*). The *Scolastice historie* (authored by Peter Comestor, and donated by John Faber) was borrowed by Dr John Wysbard, but evidently also by the prior of Dover, since the corresponding entry on this book in Part 2 of the Catalogue, which normally did not record book locations, has the additional notation, "\\Prior habet//."[41]

In certain cases where a book left the precincts of the priory, John also noted its extramural location ; thus,

G. VII. 3   *Liber sextus glosatus* \Ox'/

---

37) For an example of the same procedure in another surviving book from the Dover Library, see Stoneman, *Dover Priory*, plate 5.
38) That is, a loan outside of the customary annual borrowing dictated by the Benedictine Rule.
39) The single slants represent additions entered between the lines by John in the text, following the editorial policy of Stoneman *Dover Priory*, p. x.
40) Text from Stoneman, *Dover Priory*, pp. 18 and 21.
41) Stoneman, *Dover Priory*, p. 58. The double slanted lines indicate an addition on the margin.

H. III. 13   Fhisinomia aristotilis \\Ox'// /perditur per I. Chiltoun\.[42]

The notation "Ox'" probably refers to Oxford, the university attended by students of the Benedictine Order, which by 1336 had a house of studies there known as Gloucester College.[43] Presumably members of Dover Priory who were studying there borrowed books from their home library.[44] John Chilton may have been one such student, who lost a copy of Aristotle while at Oxford. Perhaps less serious were other cases noted by John Whitfield where a book was deemed missing rather than lost; for example,

I. III. 11   Virgilius in bucolicis \\I. Hede caret//

I. III. 5   Epistule Horacii \\I. Hede caret//.[45]

It appears that John Hede was a student of the classics, perhaps at Oxford. In the case of the Horace book at least, it seems to have been retrieved, since it survives as Cambridge, Trinity College MS R.3.51.

So far what we have seen in Part 1 is a system designed mainly to track books and to safeguard them. But as John's second preface indicates, he was well aware that this approach represented only one aspect of his job. As an expert himself on the Benedictine Rule he well understood that monks were expected not only to borrow at least one book per year but were also encouraged to read privately (*legere sibi*) every day. In other words these same books that he zealously guarded needed to be readily

---

42) Stoneman, *Dover Priory*, pp. 37 and 38.

43) On the Benedictine presence at Oxford, see Coates, *English Medieval Books : The Reading Abbey Collections*, pp. 87-90.

44) Pope Benedict XII's *Constitutions* emphasized the obligation of monasteries to make their books available to members studying at university. See P. J. Lucas, "Borrowing and reference : access to libraries in the late middle ages," in Leedham-Green and Webber, *The Cambridge History of Libraries*, pp. 242-62 at 254.

45) Stoneman, *Dover Priory*, p. 43.

available to the community. It was to facilitate this objective that John composed a second Catalogue (Part 2).

It has five columns, the first of which repeats the information found in the first column of Part 1,[46]

(1) the **ORDO LOCACIONIS** (heading written vertically).
Just as John had arranged in Part 1 to supply this column for his own convenience so that he could immediately hone in on a book's shelf-mark, so too readers would need the same information, which would allow them not only to identify a particular book but also to find it on the shelves. Thus, the first book listed on fol. 27^r of the Catalogue, Isidore's "De summo bono" (second of three copies) comes from case "C," shelf V, and is number 2.

(2) the **NOMINA VOLUMINUM** (heading written horizontally). Although this column has the same wording as the corresponding one in Part 1, the notion of *nomina uoluminum* differs between them. In Part 1 the word *nomina* denotes the 'official' title of a book (thought of as a single unit), whereas in Part 2 it effectively covers also any other titles of works contained in that book. The distinction becomes clear when one compares the corresponding entries for each; for example, in Part 1 manuscript C.V.3 has a single title, "Isidorus de summo bono," probably its traditional title. But in Part 2 the entry for the same manuscript contains five titles (*nomina*)—each title somehow squeezed into a single line—for the five different works that it contained: (1) Isidore's *De summo bono*; (2) a "tabula" (probably a list of chapters) of (1), supplied by John Whitfield; (3) *Liber scintillarum*; (4) *Interpretaciones diccionum theologicarum*; and (5) *Textus*

---

46) See Plate 5, which covers the same shelves (and books) listed on fol. 8^r (Plate 2) as entries for Part 1.

quarundam decretalium. The explanation for the difference in treatment between the entries of Parts 1 and 2 for the same manuscript is one of emphasis. In Part 1, which was designed for John's personal use, the title of a book as given on the outside cover was all that he needed to know; it served as an 'official' shorthand for identifying the book and its location. And most likely John would have known what its full contents were. By contrast, in Part 2 the focus was less on identifying the book than it was on revealing exactly how many works it contained; otherwise, these latter might well lie concealed from potential monastic readers and therefore remain unread.

(3) The third column (heading written vertically), **NOTACIO INCHOANCIUM** (literally 'the registering of the incipits') identifies the folio on which each of the individual works, identified in (2), began. Thus, the first book, copy 2 of "Isidorus de summo bono" (C. v. 2), has no notation because it is a single text occupying the whole manuscript; by contrast, copy 3 of Isidore (C. v. 3) has four *notaciones* (fols. 1, 55, 71 and 78) because it contains five separate works each beginning at one of these places.[47]

(4) the fourth column (heading written vertically), **LATERA FOLIORUM** ('the sides of the folios'), offers a refinement of the information in (3), by distinguishing on which side of the folio listed in the previous column the work begins. As explained by John in his Preface to Part 2, it employs the letters 'a' and 'b,' respectively for this purpose.[48]

(5) the fifth column (heading written horizontally), **PRINCIPIA TRAC-**

---

47) The second item, "Tabula Iohannis Whit<field>," does not have a *notacio* probably because it was treated as an integral part of Isidore's work rather than a separate item. Significantly, it lacks an entry in column 5.

48) See Appendix, pp. 72-73.

TATUUM, provides what we would call the incipit of each work. Thus, to take the example given in (3) above, copy 2 of Isidore's "De summo bono" (C.V.2) has only the incipit of that work ("Summum bonum Deus est") because it is a book with a single text; by contrast, copy 3 of Isidore (C.V.3) has four incipits corresponding to the four main works which it contains, as given in (2) above (under *Nomina Voluminum*).

To understand John's modus operandi one could hardly do better than quote his own words in the Preface which he wrote to Part 2.[49]

Part 2 of the Catalogue (which follows) is here arranged in the same way as Part 1 in having inscribed in columns the bookcases, shelves, numbers of the books (as well as their order), references and assigning of names, and the allotment of spaces. However, certain books have further (and maybe more valuable) contents beyond what their name or title denotes, which would lie concealed, to the serious detriment of students, unless they can be revealed through the goodwill of those precentors who are more especially concerned with this Catalogue. In view of this situation, there is prefixed to each such book—the main title and notation being added as in Part 1—a mark resembling 'CC' to make finding them clearer and easier, and to separate and distinguish them more fully from the other contents of that book—other than the single work that gives its title to the whole book—which are to be supplied directly below. These individual books and their contents, under separate and individual titles—though in some cases the titles assigned to them by our very own predecessors were not always correctly chosen—are spelled out in sequence in the space that follows

---

49) Full translation below in Appendix, pp. 72-73.

after the previously mentioned enumerations. To each individual title we attach a number which indicates precisely on which folio each tract begins, while the letters in the next column immediately following this number point out on which side of the folio it begins; thus, in every case by 'a' is meant the first page (recto) and by 'b' the second (verso).

Moreover, in our anxiety to avoid being labelled presumptuous, we have nowhere changed the existing titles of books and their contents (even when ineptly assigned), while in the final column of that page we resolved to make clear the original incipit of each work or treatise through reference to its first two or three words. And so the discerning reader endowed with wisdom, when he has noted the titles and incipits of the books and the other works they contain, and carefully scrutinized them, will be able at suitable times and places to apply to them the file of textual emendation and give his attention to the better naming of the treatises—or at least to devising more accurate titles for them—for the betterment of students.

Broadly speaking, while Part 1 was designed by John for the precentor in his role as custodian of the books, with the 'testing words' as its centerpiece, Part 2 was intended for what he calls the discerning reader (*lector discretus*) of the same books, and its centerpiece was the full listing of the titles of works to be found within a particular book (the *Nomina Voluminum* of column 2). Although he does not expressly say so, John seems to have had in mind confreres who would read a book (or part thereof) not out of a mere sense of obligation to the rule but with genuine intellectual curiosity. That curiosity (he believed) would be best aroused by identifying (under *Nomina Volumina* of Part 2) every work contained in a particular manuscript, supplying where possible the author's name and the subject matter; and it would be further accommodated by pointing the reader to the exact spot in the manuscript where the work began. This latter cue was surely intended to anticipate the reader who might glance through a large book with multiple tracts of potential interest but then decide to ignore them, either because he did not recognize the work for what it was, or because he was unwilling to track down the point within the book where it began. No doubt John was well aware that traditional, old-fashioned catalogues, by giving only the general title of a book, normally based on the first work (or the main work), led to the neglect of the other works which it often contained. As a result intellectually curious students were losing the opportunity of broadening their knowledge. For example, the book with shelf mark C. v. 5 is described succinctly in Part 1 as "Flores in contemplacione Augustini," whereas in Part 2 (under *Nomina Volumina*) the curious reader would learn that it actually contained 35 discrete works attributed to such notables as Augustine, Anselm, Bernard of Clairvaux, and Bonaventure ; and that it included such prestigious works as the Pseudo-Clement *Recognitiones,* the Pseudo-Augustine *De duodecim abusiuis saeculi,* and Bonaventure's *Itinerarium mentis in Deum.*[50]

One might have thought that with Parts 1 and 2 in place John would have considered his task completed, since he had achieved a balance between the precentor's need to maintain constant control over the collection on the one hand and his duty on the other hand of encouraging confreres to search out the treasures hidden within these manuscripts. But John was also a scholar, and as such he envisaged another class of reader, those en-

---

50) For the full list, see Stoneman, *Dover Priory,* pp. 71-73.

gaged in research. For this group he composed Part 3. Although it has no separate preface, its raison d'être is implied in its layout. Put simply, it is an alphabetical list of all the works contained in the full complement of manuscripts, as revealed in Part 2 (under *Nomina Voluminum*), arranged by title. And although it has five columns the information can be captured at a glance, unlike that of Parts 1 and 2. It consists simply of the book case (*distinctio*), the shelf within the bookcase (*gradus distinctionis*), the book number (*quoto libro*), the folio on which the work begins (*quo to folio incipium*), and which side of that folio (*quo latere folii*). For example, under the letter 'F' the first entry (on fol. 75^r line 1) of the Bodleian manuscript reads: "Fleobotmie tractatus H V 7 36 b,"[51] indicating that a treatise on plebotomy can be found in bookcase "H," shelf "V," book number "7," and that the work begins on fol. 36^v of that book.

Yet for all John's demonstrated thoroughness there is some evidence to suggest that Part 3 of the Catalogue was a work in progress. On the same fol. 75^r (lines 10-12) occur the following three consecutive entries:[52]

Florum liber Augustini	C V 4
Florum *manipulus*	/C VI\[53]
Flores *Manfredi* super decretales	--------

Of these three listings, the first has an incorrect shelf mark which, when checked against Part 1,[54] is found to refer to "Liber Florum Michaelis" (the correct information is "C V 5 6 a"). In the second entry the shelf-mark information (which was added later) remains incomplete; it should read "C

---

51) See Plate 6 and Stoneman, *Dover Priory*, p. 200.
52) See Plate 6 and Stoneman, *Dover Priory*, p. 201.
53) The slanting lines indicate an addition on the writing line.
54) Stoneman, *Dover Priory*, p. 24.

VI 8 1 a."[55] Finally, the location information on the third listing is entirely lacking (it should read "G II 1 165 a").[56]

Modern readers of John's Catalogue who are interested in Middle English literature may be disappointed at the almost total absence of any reference to works of that category . Whereas the Catalogue (Part 2) lists some 43 books containing works in French and covering a great variety of genres (including four romances, *Ferrumbras, Charlemagne, The Romaunt de la Rose* and *Athys and Prophilias*), Middle English is represented by only two works, both in the same manuscript (D. VII. 7), which also has nine works in French.[57] The first ME work is "Fabula de Wlpe medici (read 'medico') in anglice"[58] and we are given in Part 2 its incipit, "Hit byful whylem" ('It happened once upon a time'). The reference to a *fabula* with a fox as its main character certainly suggests the Beast fable, a proposition supported by the presence of a text of Aesop's fables immediately following in the same manuscript. Unfortunately, no work about a fox playing the role of doctor is known in Middle English. Indeed, as noted by Wilson, the number of known works in Middle English about Reynard the Fox comes to a mere two, "The Fox and the Wolf" and Chaucer's "Nun's Priest's Tale." Wilson also pointed out that the reference to the fox as physician recalls one of the Anglo-Norman 'Fables' of Marie de France where the fox prescribes the heart of a hare as a cure for the sick lion.[59] The other ME work listed in

---

55) Stoneman, *Dover Priory*, p. 81.
56) Stoneman, *Dover Priory*, p. 121. I take the liberty of suggesting these corrections in the spirit of John's own preface to Part 1, where he encourages others to improve his catalogue ; see Appendix, p. 73.
57) Stoneman, *Dover Priory*, p. 99 (nos. 170 d and 170 e). The manuscript has not survived.
58) Although Stoneman, loc. cit., reads "Tabula," it seems more likely that "Fabula" was originally intended.
59) R. M. Wilson, "More Lost Literature in Old and Middle English," *Leeds Studies in*

the same Dover manuscript is Hending's *Proverbs*, which has the incipit, "Jhesu Crist al þys. . . ." As noted by Max Förster, this incipit agrees with that of the copy of *Proverbs* in Digby 86, as against the two other surviving versions which have 'Jesu Crist al folkis rede'.[60]

This lack of books in the native English vernacular at Dover, as evidenced by John's catalogue, should not come as a surprise. Although English was beginning to assert itself in the late fourteenth century as a sophisticated literary medium—thanks mainly to Chaucer—and by the fifteenth century as a language well adapted to all kinds of genres, including theology and spirituality, progress on the latter front was slower in the religious houses. Moreover, within the cloister it was uneven ; for example, nuns were far more advanced than their male counterparts in cultivating the vernacular over Latin for their religious literature. So, the fact that Dover Priory had only two Middle English works in its library *c.*1380 should not necessarily be seen as evidence of backwardness. After all, as late as the early decades of the fifteenth century the enormously wealthy library of Syon Abbey (Brigettine-Augustinians) near London had only 26 titles in English out of a total collection of 1,421 books.[61]

Scholars have been unanimous in their praise of John's catalogue, though R. Sharpe has expressed mild criticism that so much talent and expertise was expended on "an undistinguished collection."[62] While one can hardly rebut his assessment of Dover library, some mitigating factors

---

    English, vol.5 (1930), 1-49 at 27.
60) *Archiv für das Studium der neueren Sprachen und Literaturen* 115 (1905), 165-7, at 166.
61) See D. N. Bell, "The libraries of religious houses in the late middle ages," in Leedham-Green and Webber, *The Cambridge History of Libraries,* pp. 126-51 at 134.
62) Sharpe, 'The Medieval Librarian', p. 229.

should be considered. As a small community the priory did not have the motivation, much less the means, to build up a large library. Not only was it always under the shadow of its mother house, Christ Church, Canterbury, but its modest size meant that it could not fully avail of the reforms of intellectual life in the monasteries that had been mandated by Pope Benedict XII in his *Constitutions* of 1336. For example, in an effort to raise intellectual standards among the religious orders the Pope had stipulated that at least one monk in twenty of a community should attend university, a requirement which if taken literally would not apply to Dover where the community never reached that number. Whether another requirement of the same papal document, that all monasteries should have a master in grammar, logic and philosophy, was met at Dover Priory is a moot point.[63] Certainly, in his numerous references to himself, John never uses the title "magister"—much less "doctor." At the same time it seems plausible that he served as master of studies at Dover; his numerous written interventions in the books under his charge, where he often supplied glosses and tables of contents ("tabula"), as well as the scholarly character of the books which he bequeathed to his monastery says as much. Of particular significance for a possible pedagogical role for John are those books in the library which he glossed. Dover not only had three copies of Gratian's *Decretum*, the core text for the study of canon law at the universities, but one of them was glossed by John.[64] Although the book with its gloss has not survived, it may well have been intended for teaching purposes; its presence would certainly be compatible with a 1247 decree of the Benedictine General Chapter which mandated that monks were to attend a daily lecture on

---

63) On this requirement, see Bell, "The libraries of religious houses," p. 129.
64) "Decreta cum glosa Iohannis"; Stoneman, *Dover Priory*, pp. 117-18.

canon law or theology.[65]

Speaking of the fourteenth and fifteenth centuries David N. Bell makes the generalization that the monastic orders in England "were generally receptive rather than creative in the realm of university studies" and "preferred the works of authors who belonged to an earlier tradition."[66] While this characterization might not altogether apply to a larger Benedictine house such as Reading Abbey, whose library *c.*1300 seems to reflect "the widening of the intellectual interests of the monks,"[67] it aptly fits Dover library where almost half of the books consisted of patristica (Augustine, Bernard of Clairvaux, Ambrose, Jerome etc.), in marked contrast to the scant number of books from more recent theological authorities such as Grosseteste (6) and Aquinas (3). Moreover, in the case of these latter two, as well as other notable university lecturers such as Stephen Langton and Robert Holcot, one finds that the works of these scholars possessed by Dover library were generally not the ones studied at university level. For example, Dover had no copy of Aquinas's *Summa Theologica* or his commentary on the fourth book of Peter Lombard's *Sententiae*; nor of Langton's gloss on the *Cantica Canticorum,* nor Holcot's commentary on Ecclesiasticus or Wisdom.[68] However masterfully John Whitfield dissected, catalogued and glossed the books of Dover library, he could not alter their contents.

---

65) Coates, *English Medieval Books : The Reading Abbey Collections,* pp. 67-68.
66) Bell, "The libraries of religious houses," p. 127.
67) Coates, *English Medieval Books : The Reading Abbey Collections,* pp. 77-78.
68) According to John's Catalogue (Part 2), the library had Holcot's "Tractatus de penitencia" (Stoneman, *Dover Priory,* p. 96, no.152 d) and an (unidentified) "Liber Roberti Holcote" (Stoneman, *Dover Priory,* p. 101, no.176).

Appendix

The following texts are translated from the original Latin of John Whitfield (Oxford, Bodleian Library, MS 920, fols. 1^r-2^v and 19^v), edited by William P. Stoneman, *Dover Priory,* Corpus of British Medieval Library Catalogues vol.5 (London, 1999), pp. 15-16 and 47.

PREFACE 1

The present catalogue of the library of Dover Priory assembled in A.D. 1389 under the leadership of Brother John Newenham, prior [1372-92] and professed member of the same church, can be found divided into three main parts. The aim of Part 1 is to provide the precentor with information about the number and accurate location of the books ; of Part 2 to encourage studious brethren to study them carefully and frequently ; and of Part 3 to point out to scholars convenient ways of finding individual works. And although there is placed before each part, to make understanding it easier, a short specific preface, yet to Part 1 in particular are prefixed, for a clearer comprehension of the whole Catalogue, certain comments of a general nature.

First, that this library is divided into nine separate bookcases (*Distinciones*), following the first nine letters of the alphabet, which are clearly affixed to the bookcases themselves, so that to the person entering the room, 'A' indicates the first bookcase, 'B' the second, 'C' the third, and so on in alphabetical order. Each of the above-mentioned bookcases (it will be seen) is further divided into seven separate shelves (*gradus*), which are themselves highlighted by the addition of

Roman numerals after the letters denoting the seven separate bookcases. One begins counting the shelves from the bottom, ascending in such a way that the bottom shelf is marked 'I', the second 'II', the third 'III' and so on, up to 'VII'.

Moreover, all the books of this library, to make it easier to get to know their contents, have their individual leaves (*folia*) numbered with Arabic numerals. And because it so happens that many of the books contain a number of works, the titles of these works (although they have not always been correctly named) are entered under their respective book and, immediately after, an Arabic numeral identifying on which folio the actual work begins, with 'a' or 'b' directly added to mark the first [recto] and second [verso] page of the leaf, respectively. Furthermore, the individual books themselves, not only on the outside cover, but also inside, adjacent to the Table of Contents, at the beginning of each book, have their unique bookcase letter and shelf-mark added. And within each bookcase letter is included the small Arabic numeral by means of which is more precisely revealed what numerical position that book holds in the order of placement on the relevant shelf.

On the second or third or fourth folio (or somewhere close) of each book, its title is entered on the bottom margin, preceded by the relevant bookcase letter and shelf-mark and, after a small space, the opening words of that folio are directly entered, which may be termed 'the testing of identification' (*probatorium cognicionis*). The next Arabic numeral that follows reveals the number of folios in that particular book. And finally, another Arabic number, placed immediately after the previous one, indicates clearly the number of works contained in the book.

When the preceding information, therefore, has been firmly committed to memory, it will be abundantly clear in what bookcase, shelf, place, and sequence the individual books of the entire library ought to be stored; and on which folios (and sides of folios) can be found the beginning of individual works.

For by expressly supplying a variety of designations and notations for bookcases, shelves, sequences, references, works and books, the compiler of the present catalogue and library wanted to prevent as far as he could, future loss to his monastery—while impeding the malice of such as entertained the desire to steal and barter a precious object of this kind—and to establish a sound barrier of defence and resistance. And, truly, that person who more efficiently organizes this Catalogue, which is still defective in all kinds of ways, will not offend the compiler, but rather will clearly demonstrate affection for him—even if he wants to appropriate the whole credit of the enterprise to himself.

So, in Part 1 of the Catalogue, at the upper margin between the black lines which are ruled horizontally throughout, comes first the bookcase letter in red, followed by the shelf-mark in black. But between the other red lines, from top to bottom—taking first those which are ruled on the left—is placed first a numeral, showing what is the place of the book in its sequence on the Shelf (*ordo locacionis*); secondly, is added the title of the book (*nomina voluminum*); thirdly, the number of the identitifying page (*loca probacionum*); fourthly, the identifying words (*dictiones probatorie*) which, incidentally, must refer to the text and not to a gloss; fifthly, the number of folios in the whole book (*summa foliorum*); and finally, the number of works which it contains (*numerus contentorum*)—inscribed on the lines we have mentioned. Moreover, within each shelf of this part of the Catalogue some vacant spaces should be left at the end, where the names of books that will be acquired in the future may be placed.

PREFACE 2

Part 2 of the Catalogue (which follows) is here arranged in the same way as Part 1 in having inscribed in columns the bookcases, shelves, numbers of the books (as well as their order), references and assigning of names, and the allotment of spaces. However, certain books have further (and maybe more valuable) contents beyond what their name or title denotes, which would lie concealed, to the serious detriment of students, unless they can be revealed through the goodwill of those precentors who are more especially concerned with this Catalogue. In view of this situation, there is prefixed to each such book—the main title and notation being added as in Part 1—a mark resembling 'CC' to make finding them clearer and easier, and to separate and distinguish them more fully from the other contents of that book—other than the single work that gives its title to the whole book—which are to be supplied directly below. These individual books and their contents, under separate and individual titles—though in some cases the titles assigned to them by our very own predecessors were not always correctly chosen—are spelled out in sequence in the space that follows after the previously mentioned enumerations. To each individual title we attach a number which indicates precisely on which folio each tract begins, while the letters in the next column immediately following this number point out on which side of the folio it begins; thus, in every case by 'a' is meant the first page (recto) and by 'b' the second (verso).

Moreover, in our anxiety to avoid being labelled presumptuous, we have nowhere changed the existing titles of books and their contents (even when ineptly assigned), while in the final column of that page we resolved to make clear the original incipit of each work or treatise through reference to its first two or three words. And so the discerning reader endowed with wisdom, when he has noted the titles and incipits of the books and the other works they contain, and carefully scrutinized them, will be able at suitable times and places to apply to them the file of textual emendation and give his attention to the better naming of the treatises—or at least to devising more accurate titles for them—for the betterment of students.

How to administer a late-fourteenth century monastic library: the case of Dover Priory

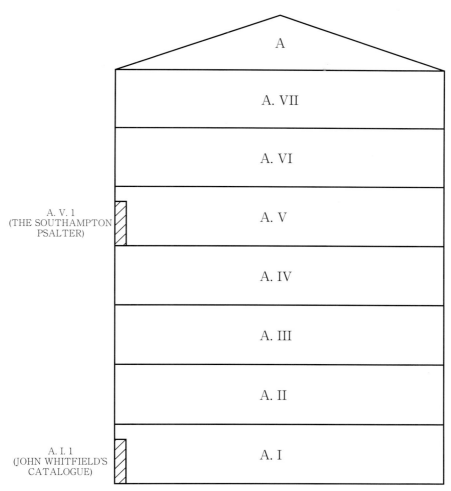

Plate 1: reconstruction of the first bookcase ("A"), based on John Whitfield's description.

How to administer a late-fourteenth century monastic library: the case of Dover Priory

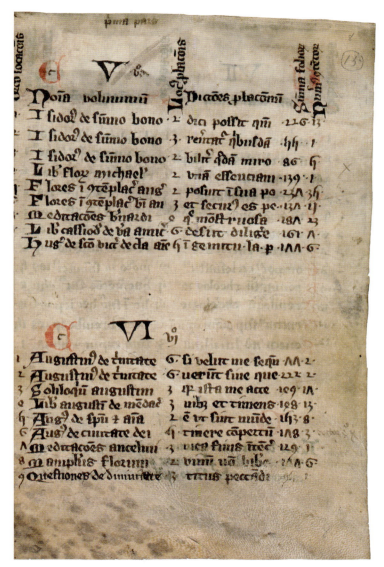

Plate 2 : Oxford, Bodleian Library, MS Bodley 920, fol. 8ʳ.

How to administer a late-fourteenth century monastic library : the case of Dover Priory

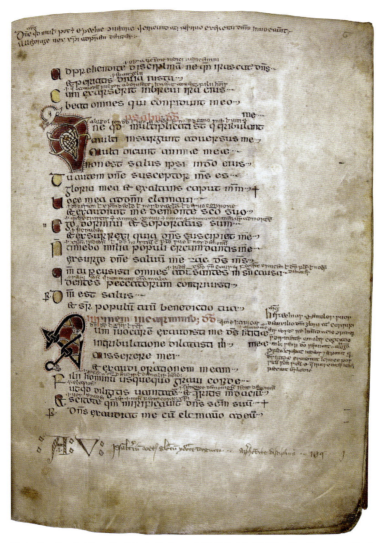

Plate 3 : Cambridge, St. John's College, MS C.9, fol. 6ʳ (The Southampton Psalter).

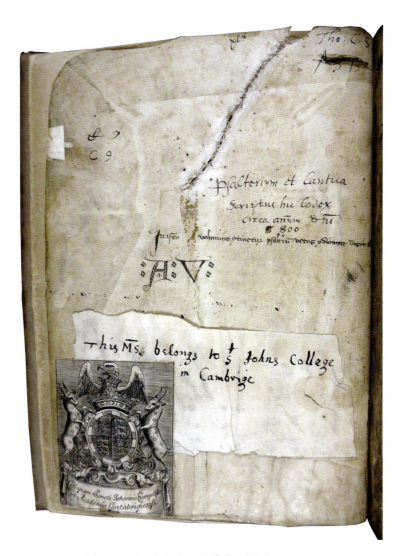

Plate 4 : Cambridge, St. John's College, MS C.9, fol. (i^v)

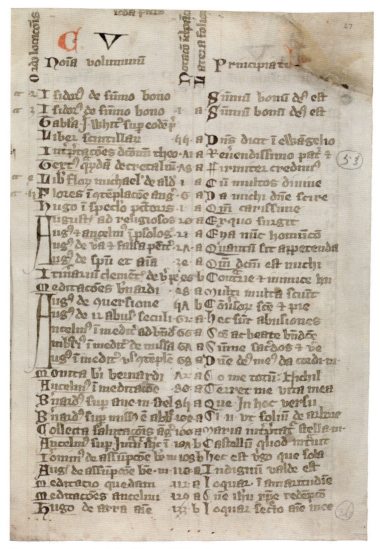

Plate 5 : Oxford, Bodleian Library, MS Bodley 920, fol. 27ʳ.

How to administer a late-fourteenth century monastic library : the case of Dover Priory

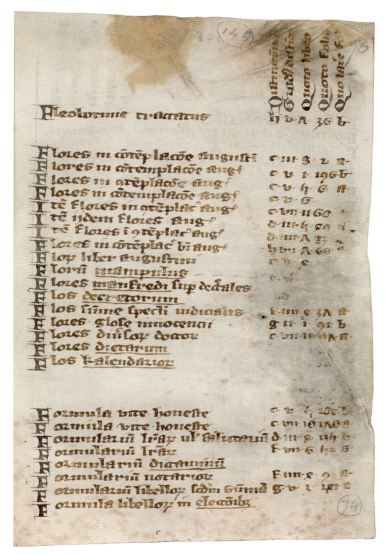

Plate 6 : Oxford, Bodleian Library, MS Bodley 920, fol. 75ʳ.

The relationship between two Anglo-Norman alliterating verses in London, British Library, MS Harley 913

Yoko WADA

Abstract:

London, British Library, MS Harley 913, written in Ireland in about 1330, contains two short poems in Anglo-Norman which are remarkable (among other things) for their heavy alliteration. This paper investigates the relationship between these two poems and discusses the significance of the title "Proverbia Comitis Desmonie" which was entered between them in the manuscript.

Keywords:

Harley 913, Anglo-Norman, Earl of Desmond, alliteration, proverbs, Ireland

London, British Library, MS Harley 913, written in Latin, English and Anglo-Norman French, probably in Waterford, Ireland, about 1330,[1] contains two short works in Anglo-Norman.[2] With the exception of "The Walling of New Ross," a poem about how the inhabitants built defences to pro-

---

1) Alan Fletcher, "The date of London, British Library, Harley MS 913 ('The Kildare Poems'), *Medium Ævum* 79 (2010), 306-10.
2) Thorlac Turville-Petre (ed.), *Poems from BL MS Harley 913 "The Kildare Manuscript"*, EETS o.s.345 (2015), pp.21-22 and 107 ; John D. Seymour, *Anglo-Irish Literature, 1200-1582* (Cambridge : Cambridge University Press 1929), pp.91-2 ; Thomas Wright and James Orchard Halliwell-Phillipps (edd.), *Reliquiae Antiquae* 2 (London : Smith, 1845), 256.

tect their town, the present two works are the only French texts surviving in the manuscript.[3] They start at the top of fol 15v and occupy the upper half of the page—the remaining lower half of the page, as well as the previous page, fol 15r, were originally left blank.[4] A stylistic peculiarity shared by both works is their hyperalliteration with a single letter (sound) "f" in the first and "s" in the second.[5] The first work appears to be a collection of four proverbs, each of which is not only joined by alliteration of "f", but also by cross-rhyme (*ababcdcd*) which has the effect of suggesting a single work of poetry.[6] The proverbs concern aspects of human folly with mention of the role of fortune, common themes in medieval verse. The second

---

3) Hugh Shields, "The Walling of New Ross: a Thirteenth-Century Poem in French", *Long Room* (Dublin), 12-13 (1975-6), 24-33.
4) Metrical proverbs in Latin are written on fol 15r, the top margin of fol 15v and the top margin of fol 16r. A Latin proverb on the top of fol 16r is copied on the foot of fol 15v by a later hand. Below the proverb a recipe is written (Turvill-Petre, *Poems,* p.22).
5) The choice of the two letters, "F" and "S", might have something to do with their accepted mystical meanings, as explained in a tract (the first of two) on the letters of the alphabet on fols 1v-2r of Harley 913. According to the first tract, the letter "F" signifies "fluxit, quando sedem in aquilone ponere uoluit ("he decayed when he desired to place his throne in the north [of Heaven]"), while "S" signifies "salus" ("state of well-being", or "salvation"). The explanation of "F", which refers to Satan's military rebellion (his "force") and consequent downfall (compare "funder"), correlates neatly with the maxims enunciated in the first poem; however, the explanation of "S" as "well-being" would only be applicable to the second poem as the state for which the speaker longs. (Personal communication from Professor Patrick O'Neill, November 1, 2016).
6) Ruth J. Dean and Maureeen B. M. Boulton describe the two alliterative verses as two groups of proverbs (Dean and Boulton, *Anglo-Norman Literature: A Guide to Texts and Manuscripts,* Anglo-Norman Text Society, Occasional Publications Series 3 (London: Anglo-Norman Text Society 1999), p.152), but, as I shall argue in the present paper, the second "group", entitled "Proverbs of Earl of Desmond", clearly does not consist of proverbial pieces, much less four of them.

item, while having the appearance of a continuous prose passage, can also be resolved into an eight-line poem, in which the author laments the misery of his loneliness. However, unlike the first item, its tone is not proverbial, but rather expresses a personal lament.

The following table shows in parallel columns the two works, first as entered in the manuscript (left column), and secondly as edited and arranged in verse format (right column). The bold initials in this edited text represent red capital letters in the manuscript.

Folie fet · qe en force sa fie ; fortune fet force failire. **F**iaux funt fort folie, fere en fauelons flatire. **F**ere force fest fiaux fuir faux fiers fount feble fameler. **F**ausyne fest feble fremir. feie ferme fra fausyn fundre.	**F**olie fet qe en force sa fie, Fortune fet force failire. **F**iaux funt fort folie, Fere en fauelons flatire. **F**ere force fest fiaux fuir. Faux fiers fount feble fameler. **F**ausyne fest feble fremir, Feie ferme fra fausyn fundre.
Proverbia comitis Desmonie	
Soule su simple · e saunz solas seignury me somount soiorner. **S**i suppris sei de moune solas · sagesse deit soul solacer. **S**oule ne solai soiorner · ne solein estre de petit solas. **S**ouereyn se est de se sola cer qe se sent soule e saunz solas.	**Proverbia comitis Desmonie** **S**oule su, simple e saunz solas, Seignury me somount soiorner ; **S**i suppris sei de moune solas, Sagesse deit soul solacer. **S**oule ne solai soiorner, Ne solein estre de petit solas ; **S**ouereyn se est de se solacer, Qe se sent soule e saunz solas.

(He who puts his trust in brute force behaves foolishly; Fortune causes such force to fail. **F**alsehoods strengthen folly, induce flattering with sweet talking. **B**rute force makes violent deceivers flee; violent deceivers make the weak suffer hunger. **D**eceit makes the weak tremble, but steady trust will confound deceit.

PROVERBS OF THE EARL OF DESMOND

Alone am I, single and without solace; nobility calls on me to remain. **E**ven if I am bereft of my comfort, wisdom alone ought to console me. **I** was not used to remaining alone, or being deprived of the smallest comfort. **W**hat is most important is that he who feels himself abandoned and without comfort finds consolation in himself.)

A striking feature of the manuscript is that the title, "**Proverbia Comitis Desmonie**," in red is located between the first item and the second. This layout is potentially ambiguous: does the title, "Proverbs of the Earl of Desmond", belongs to the first item or the second? Curiously, scholars traditionally attribute both pieces to the Earl of Desmond.[7] One wonders if

---

7) For example, Marc Caball says, "The *Proverbie* [sic.] comprise two short poems which have been attributed to Maurice fitz Thomas, created first earl of Desmond in 1329" ("The literature of later medieval Ireland, 1200-1600: from the Normans to the Tudors, part 1: Poetry" edited by Margaret Kelleher and Philop O'Leary, *The Cambridge History of Irish Literature* 1 (Cambridge: Cambridge University Press 2006), p.87). Turville-Petre reads the rubric to mean that "the second [poem] is a lament by the 1st Earl of Desmond, while also suggesting that "Desmond may indeed be the author of one or both [poems]" (*Poems,* p.21); however, his comment on authorship in the Introduction (p. xxxv) is more guarded.

this is because the Latin word, "proverbia", is plural,[8] and therefore could be read as referring to the aggregate of the two items, or because they are arranged in a very similar fashion so as to convey the impression of a unity. One piece of evidence in support of the latter view is that the two items are enclosed with a red line which appears at both the top and the bottom. If we accept this view then it would seem that they should be read as a set, each item closely related to the other.

At first glance certain prosodic similarities are evident. Both pieces, although entered as prose, actually consist of eight lines each of verse, divided into four units, each of the latter marked by red capitals. Both are hyperalliterative pieces, on the letters "f" and "s" respectively ; and both also have octosyllabic lines with alternating rhymes, the first *ababcdcd,* the second *ababbaba.* That said, there are equally obvious differences in genre. The first item could be read as a conscious imitation of Anglo-Norman "folies" poems associated with human conduct and transactions which take their place in a vigorous Anglo-Norman tradition of didactic and sententious poetry.[9] In most "folies" poems every line starts with the same word but it does not set off a chain of alliteration. Here is one example :

Ke nul ben seit e nul vot aprendre
Ke mwt acreit e n'at dunt rendre
Ke tant dune ke ren ne retent

---

8) Incidentally, Dean and Boulton mistranslate *comitis Desmoniae* in the title as "of a Countess Desmonia" (*Anglo-Norman Literature,* pp.152-3), as pointed out by Geert De Wilde, "The origins and stanza form tradition of the Vernon/Simeon Lyrics", *Leeds Studies in English* 41 (2010), 74.
9) Tony Hunt, "The Anglo-Norman 'Folies' poems", *Pluteus* 3 (1985), 15.

> Ke mut promet e ne dune neient
> Ke tant parole ke nul ne le escute
> Ke tant manace ke nul ne le dute
> Ke tant jure ke nul le creit
> Ke demande kanke il vayt
> Ke a enfaunt e a fol son consel cunte
> Ke pur autre hunir se meymes mette a hunte
> (Cambridge, Gonville and Caius College, MS 408 (414), p. 323.)[10]

Individually, the two items of Harley 913 have alternating rhymes (with a single exception), whereas Gonville and Caius College 408 has rhyming couplets. Yet if we isolate the last sound of each of the four "proverbs" of item 1, and combine them with the corresponding sound of each couplet in item 2, the pattern which emerges is: *-ire, -ire, -er, -er (re) / -er, -er, -as, -as*. This is the same pattern of rhyming couplets as that of the "folies" poem of Gonville and Caius College 408 which has *-re, -re, -ent, -ent, -ute, -ute, -it, -yt, -unte, -unte*. But the Harley poet goes further, embellishing his work with heavy alliteration that enhances the sound effect while also, perhaps, displaying prosodic and verbal prowess.

Unlike the first item, the second is starkly personal and elegiac. As first pointed out by Heuser[11] the sad situation described by its first-person speaker most likely refers to the first Earl of Desmond, the same one mentioned in the rubric, otherwise known as Maurice fitz Thomas Fitzgerald

---

10) Hunt, "The Anglo-Norman 'Folies' poems", 24.
11) Wilhelm Heuser, *Die Kildare-Gedichte. Die ältesten mittelenglischen Denkmäler in anglo-irischer Überlieferung. Bonner Beiträge zur Anglistik* 14 (Bonn: P. Hanstein, 1904), pp.17-18.

(c.1293-1356). A magnate and great landowner in the province of Munster, he also held the office of Justiciar of Ireland for a period.[12] He was created the first Earl of Desmond in 1329, but among the minor landowners and townsmen of Anglo-Norman Munster who came under his sway he had a bad reputation as a tyrant, a traitor, and a felon. Evidently, this extremely ambitious lord did not much care about the ruthless means he employed to achieve his objectives. Desmond trusted in, and exercised, brutal force to fulfil his ambitions, savagely exploiting the people of his territory—just like the man in the first piece "who put his trust in brute force" and "made the weak suffer hunger".[13] Again, the first piece's general warning that Fortune eventually brings about the failure of such brute force, can be seen as readily applicable to Desmond who, at the zenith of his enforced power, was overturned by the wheel of Fortune. Having rebelled against the Crown and come under suspicion of plotting to become King of Ireland, he was arrested and sent to Dublin Castle in August, 1331. Just a few months later, his first wife, Katherine, whom he had married in 1312, died while he

---

12) No verse allegedly composed by Desmond has survived except that of MS Harley 913, whereas his younger son, the third Earl of Desmond, Gerald Fitz Maurice Fitzgerald (c.1338-1398) was well known as Gerald the Rhymer since he composed very good bardic poems in Irish. For example, a copy of *Duanaire Ghearóid Iarla* (The Poetry-book of Earl Gerald) is preserved in a fifteenth-century manuscript (see G. Mac Niocaill, *"Duanaire Ghearóid Iarla", Studia Hibernica* 3 (1963), 7-59). We know that Gerald had many native Irish friends and loved Irish literature. (Gerald fitz Maurice Fitzgerald, *Oxford Dictionary of National Biography* online (http://www.oxforddnb.com/)). That is certainly why the author of our verse of MS Harley 913 is sometimes mistaken for Gerald Fitzgerald. Since his father, Desmond, in fact, employed an Irish court poet, he must have been interested in bardic poems in Irish.
13) *Oxford Dictionary of National Biography*.

was in prison.[14] It is likely that the second item describes his predicament at this very time in 1331 or 1332 since he was imprisoned for eighteen months.[15]

In this way, these two Anglo-Norman French poems of Harley 913 can be seen to have a complementary relationship : the first is a collection of proverbs whose theme is the abuse of power ("force"), while the second is a real-life story or exemplum which teaches a lesson based on the maxims of the first.[16] At the same time, since the second poem is a lament in which a speaker (Desmond) describes his personal feelings of utter despair and absolute loneliness, the title "Proverbia comitis Demonie", which hovers above it in the manuscript, would seem to be entirely inappropriate. However, it is just possible that the author of the two poems might have maliciously intended the title to apply to the second poem, thereby implying that Desmond's wretched life was a living set of proverbs, didactic in its real-life situation and sentiments. That might explain why the layout of the second poem with four red capitals and so on is visually arranged exactly like the first item, the formal set of proverbs.

I should also like to point out the potential significance of having the second item related in a first-person voice. It makes the poem sound very much as if composed by Desmond himself. Interestingly, Desmond was on

---

14) J. S. Brewer and William Bullen (edd), *Calendar of the Carew Manuscripts, preserved in the Archiepiscopal Library at Lambeth* (Lonodn : Longman and Trübner, 1871), p.328 ; Douglas Richards, *Magna Carta Ancestry : A Study in Colonial and Medieval Families* 1 (Salt Lake City, UT : Genealogical Publishing Company, 2005), p.174.
15) *Oxford Dictionary of National Biography.*
16) The second item might contain echoes of Boethius' "Consolation of Philosophy".

one occasion referred to as a poet by his enemy, Arnold le Poer, at an assembly in 1327. The term used on that occasion was "rhymer", a word of Norman-French origin which in the present context was intended not as a compliment but rather an accusation to irritate him. The term "rhymer" in fourteenth-century Ireland was a disparaging one, applied by the Anglo-Normans to Gaelic poets who were regarded as potentially dangerous, along with harpers, drummers, fiddlers, gamblers, story tellers and bards, since all of them were suspected of acting as instigators and spies working on behalf of the Irish enemy.[17]

The two poetic pieces of Harley 913 written in Anglo-Norman belong together as a complementary couple, the first proverbial, the second personal. Although the second item concerns Desmond's personal grief, it is visually presented in the manuscript as a mirror image of the first item. In this way, the author might have wanted to show that Desmond's way of life should be read as constituting real-life didactic material, replete with implied warnings and lessons. By implying that Desmond was the speaker (and composer) of the second poem, its real composer may have intended to bring to mind once more Le Poer's charge that Desmond was a mere "rhymer", an accusation which would likely still be remembered when the present poem was composed.

I should like to thank Professor Patrick O'Neill for his useful suggestions and comments. This paper was financially supported by Grant-in-Aid for Scientific Research of MEXT/JSPS for 2016 (Grant Number : 15 K 02327).

---

17) Richard Butler (ed. and trans.), *Jacobi Grace, Kilkenniensis, Annales Hiberniae* (Dublin for the Irish Archaeological Society, 1842), pp.104-5 and the footnote.

SELECT BIBLIOGRAPHY

Alan Bliss and Joseph Long, "Literature in Norman-French and English" in *A New History of Ireland ; ii, Medieval Ireland 1169-1534* edited by Art Cosgrove (Oxford : Oxford University Press, 1987), pp.708-36.

J. S. Brewer and William Bullen (edd), *Calendar of the Carew Manuscripts, preserved in the Archiepiscopal Library at Lambeth* (London : Longman and Trübner, 1871).

Carleton Fairchild Brown, *Religious Lyrics of the Thirteenth Century* (Oxford : Oxford University Press, 1932).

Richard Butler (ed. and trans.), *Jacobi Grace, Kilkenniensis, Annales Hiberniae* (Dublin, for the Irish Archaeological Society, 1842).

Ruth J. Dean and Maureeen B. M. Boulton, *Anglo-Norman Literature : A Guide to Texts and Manuscripts,* Anglo-Norman Text Society, Occasional Publications Series 3 (London : Anglo-Norman Text Society, 1999), pp.152-3.

Geert De Wild, "The origins and stanza form tradition of the Vernon/Simeon Lyrics", *Leeds Studies in English* 41 (2010), 66-75.

Susanna Greer Fein, "*Somer Soneday* : Kingship, sainthood, and fortune in Oxford, Bodleian Library, MS Laud Misc. 108", *The Texts and Contexts of Oxford, Bodleian Library, MS Laud Misc. 108 : The Shaping of English Vernacular Narrative* edited by Kimberly Bell and Julie Nelson Couch (Leiden NL : Brill, 2010), pp.275-97.

Susanna Greer Fein, "The early thirteen-line stanza : style and metrics reconsidered", *Parergon* 18 (2000), 97-126.

Alan Fletcher, "The date of London, British Library, Harley MS 913 ('The Kildare Poems')", *Medium Ævum* 79 (2010), 306-10.

Helen Fulton, "The theory of Celtic influence on the Harley Lyrics", *Modern Philology* 82 (1985), 239-54.

Wilhelm Heuser, *Die Kildare-Gedichte. Die ältesten mittelenglischen Denkmäler in anglo-irischer Überlieferung.* Bonner Beiträge zur Anglistik 14 (Bonn : P. Hanstein,

1904).

Tony Hunt, "The Anglo-Norman 'Folies' poems", *Pluteus* 3 (1985), 14-32.

Margaret Laing, *Catalogue of Sources for a Linguistic Atlas of Early Medieval English* (Cambridge : D. S. Brewer, 1993).

Margaret Kelleher and Philip O'Leary (edd), *The Cambridge History of Irish Literature* 1 (Cambridge : Cambridge University Press, 2006).

Angela M. Lucas (ed.), *Anglo-Irish Poems of the Middle Ages* (Dublin : the Columba Press 1995).

A. T. E. Matonis, "An investigation of Celtic influences on MS Harley 2253", *Modern Philology* 70 (1972), 91-108.

Hilda M. R. Murray (ed.), *The Middle English Poem* Erthe upon Erthe, *printed from 24 manuscripts. EETS* o.s.141 (1911; repr. 1964).

G. Mac Niocaill, *"Duanaire Ghearóid Iarla'*, *Studia Hibernica* 3 (1963), 7-59.

Annette Jocelyn Otway-Ruthven, *A History of Medieval Ireland* (London, 2nd edn, 1980).

O. S. Pickering, "Newly discovered secular lyrics from later thirteenth-century Cheshire", *Review of English Studies* 43 (1992), 157-80.

Douglas Richards, *Magna Carta Ancestry : A Study in Colonial and Medieval Families* 1 (Salt Lake City UT : Genealogical Publishing Company, 2005).

John D. Seymour, *Anglo-Irish Literature, 1200-1582* (Cambridge : Cambridge University Press, 1929), pp.91-2.

Thorlac Turville-Petre (ed.), *Poems from BL MS Harley 913 "The Kildare Manuscript"*, EETS o.s.345 (2015), pp.21-22 and 107.

Yoko Wada, "The bilingual poem *Erth* in London, British Library, MS Harley 913 : possible relationships between the Latin and the vernacular parts", *Journal of Faculty of Foreign Language Studies, Kansai University* 11 (2014), 43-59.

Alfred Webb, *A Compendium of Irish Biography : Comprising Sketches of Distin-*

guished Irishmen, and of Eminent Persons Connected with Ireland by Office or by Their Writings (Dublin : M. H. Gill and Son, 1878).

Thomas Wright (with a new introduction by Peter Coss), *Thomas Wright's Political Songs of England from the Reign of John to that of Edward II* (Cambridge : Cambridge University Press, 1996).

Thomas Wright and James Orchard Halliwell-Phillipps (edd.), *Reliquiae Antiquae*. 2 vols. (London : John Russell Smith, 1845).

Ветла и образ собора в романе Достоевского «Преступление и наказание»

"White willows and the image of the church in *Crime and Punishment* by Dostoevsky"

Масао Кондо
Masao KONDO

Abstract:

At the beginning of *Crime and Punishment*, Raskolnikov suffers from a delirium in which he imagines that he is in a small town "without a white willow" overlooking a wood in the distance. This paper shows that the town and the wood of his nightmare represent Sennaya Square and Siberia (since white willows grow there), and that in the epilogue Dostoevsky used the image of a church in the background because white willows are holy trees associated with Palm Sunday.

Keywords:

Dostoevsky, *Crime and Punishment*, white willow, Sennaya Square, Siberia, Palm Sunday, church

 Роман «Преступление и наказание» был основан на двух замыслах : на вопросе о пьянстве и на рассмотрении психологии убийцы.

 Достоевский в письме к редакторам представил роман

«Пьяненькие», где разъясняет вопрос о пьянстве, которое приносило вредные и серьёзные проблемы в общество и семейную жизнь того времени.[1] Но на это не обратили внимания из-за экономических вопросов. Кроме того, в то время у Достоевского был другой замысел : описать психологический конфликт одного убийцы в форме признания от первого лица. Принявшись за это, сразу понял, что нужна точка зрения третьего лица, чтобы тщательно и глубоко описать внутренний мир преступника. И вот первый замысел снова привлёк внимание писателя.

При разъяснении проблемы пьянства Достоевский чётко различает водку от пива. В кабаке, где Раскольников увидел Мармеладова, пьяницу, какие спиртные напитки они пили? Мармеладов выпивал водку, а Раскольников – пиво. Раскольников пил пиво не только от жары.

Мармеладов, находившийся в падении и глубоком отчаянии, кончает жизнь самоубийством, а Раскольников оживляется, выпив стакан пива.

> Ему захотелось выпить холодного пива, тем более что внезапную слабость свою он относил и к тому, что был голоден. Он уселся в темном и грязном углу, за липким столиком, спросил пива и с жадностью выпил первый стакан.

---

1) Достоевский писал издателю «Отечественных записок» Краевскому 8 июня 1865 г. : «Роман мой называется "Пьяненькие" и будет в связи с теперешним вопросом о пьянстве. Разбирается не только вопрос, но представляются и все его разветвления, преимущественно картины семейств, воспитание детей в этой обстановке и проч. и проч.» (Достоевский Ф.М. Пол. Соб. Соч. в 30-ти томах. Т.7. – Л., 1973. С.309)

> Тотчас же всё отлегло, и мысли его прояснели. "Всё это вздор, – сказал он с надеждой, – и нечем тут было смущаться! Просто физическое расстройство! Один какой-нибудь стакан пива, кусок сухаря, – и вот, в один миг, крепнет ум, яснеет мысль, твердеют намерения!"[2]

Сопоставление пива с водкой и дальше продолжается. Прочитав письмо от матери, Раскольников хотел воздуха, пространства и зелени. И он пошёл на Петроградский остров, и там, в харчевне, выпил рюмку водки, которой он не пил очень давно. Она привела его к богатому намёками на убийство страшному сну.

Сопоставление не кончается на этом. После четырёхдневной лихорадки Раскольников опять пьёт пиво.

> Он схватил бутылку, в которой еще оставалось пива на целый стакан, и с наслаждением выпил залпом, как будто потушая огонь в груди. Но не прошло и минуты, как пиво стукнуло ему в голову, а по спине пошел легкий и даже приятный озноб.[3]

Таким образом, Достоевский относился к водке, одному из основных налогов государства, отрицательно, а к пиву – положительно. Он считал пиво так же, как и хрен, едой.

Раньше в праздники варили и выпивали пиво или квас. Они

---

[2] Достоевский Ф.М. Преступление и наказание.// Достоевский Ф.М. Пол. Соб. Соч. в 30-ти томах. Т.6. —Л., 1973. С.10–11.

[3] Достоевский Ф.М. Преступление и наказание. Указ. соч. С.100.

были необходимыми «как воздух» хмельными.

XXXV.

В день Троицын, когда народ
Зевая слушает молебен,
Умильно на пучок зари
Они роняли слезки три ;
Им квас как воздух был потребен,
И за столом у них гостям
Носили блюда по чинам.

(Пушкин «Евгений Онегин». Глава II)[4]

Пиво, которое придавало Раскольникову свежесть, силу и оживлённость, приводит его в Троицу-семик, когда православный и языческий праздники, русалье слились сравнительно смирно.[5] И с этого места Свидригайлов начинает играть важную роль. Он тоже пьяница. Но он больше любит женщин.

Недаром в Троицын день развратный Свидригайлов, двойник и "хороший выход" Раскольникова, видел во сне утопленницу, изнасилованную им девушку. По русской мифологии, она переродится в русалку и отомстит ему. После того, как он видел

---

4) Пушкин А. П. Евгений Онегин.// Соб. Соч. в 10-ти томах. Т.4. —М., 1975. С.45.
5) Тульцева Л. А. Календарные праздники и обряды. // Русские, М.: Наука, 1999. С.638. А по Афанасьеву, «в христианскую эпоху он приурочен к Троицыну и Духову дням». Афанасьев А. Н. Поэтические воззрения славян на природу. М., 1865. Т.3. С.141.

во сне наводнение, ему приснилась пятилетняя мокрая девочка. Она как продажная камелия из француженок стала искушать его. Оба глаза у неё обводили Свидригайлова огненным и бесстыдным взглядом, они звали его, смеялись. . . Потом Свидригайлов промок под деревом в парке на острове Петровском и покончил жизнь самоубийством, как будто его соблазнила русалка.

А на Раскольникова, который во сне жадно пил воду в оазисе, русалка оказала благотворное влияние. В народе было поверье, что у русалок двойственный характер и что они раз в год бегают в поле и обеспечивают хорошим урожаем.

Для Раскольникова такой же положительный образ несёт Соня. Ей 18 лет. Но она выглядит моложе, чем она есть. У неё «личико всегда бледненькое, худенькое», рука «совсем прозрачная», «пальцы как у мертвой». И ходит в зелёном платке. Русалке, в общем, семь лет[6], и у неё зелёные волосы.

И зеленый, влажный волос
В нем сушить и отряхать. (Пушкин «Русалка»)[7]

Как русалка поливкой водой приводит к богатому урожаю на земле, так и Соня любовью оживляет Раскольникова на перекрёстке.

---

[6] Афанасьев А. Н. Указ. соч. С.126.
[7] Пушкин А. П., Русалка. // Соб. Соч. в 10-ти томах. Т.3. —М., 1975. С.345.

Он вдруг вспомнил слова Сони: «Поди на перекресток, поклонись народу, поцелуй землю, потому что ты и пред ней согрешил, и скажи всему миру вслух: "Я убийца!". Он весь задрожал, припомнив это. И до того уже задавила его безвыходная тоска и тревога всего этого времени, но особенно последних часов, что он так и ринулся в возможность этого цельного, нового, полного ощущения. Каким-то припадком оно к нему вдруг подступило: загорелось в душе одною искрой и вдруг, как огонь, охватило всего. Всё разом в нем размягчилось, и хлынули слезы. Как стоял, так и упал он на землю...

Он стал на колени среди площади, поклонился до земли и поцеловал эту грязную землю, с наслаждением и счастием. Он встал и поклонился в другой раз.[8]

Когда Раскольников поцеловал землю, пьяненький мещанин сказал: «Это он в Иерусалим идет». Здесь пьяненький служит заупокойную службу, то есть намекает на то, что Раскольников вновь оживёт.

Двойник Раскольникова, Свидригайлов, «не смог вырваться за пределы Петербурга и погиб физически и душевно, а Раскольников покаялся, покинул Петербург, отправился на восток, в Сибирь, в направлении, противоположном Свидригайлову, и там нашёл свое спасение: сидя на высоком берегу реки, он читает Евангелие»[9].

---

8) Достоевский Ф.М. Преступление и наказание. Указ. соч. С.405.
9) Беневолененская Н.П. Образ Петербурга в русской литературе XIX ↗

Ветла и образ собора в романе Достоевского «Преступление и наказание»

Сопоставление Запада с Востоком напоминает страшный сон Раскольникова. Сон намекает не только на убийство, но и на пространство и структуру романа.

> Городок стоит открыто, как на ладони, кругом ни ветлы; где-то очень далеко, на самом краю неба, чернеется лесок. В нескольких шагах от последнего городского огорода стоит кабак, большой кабак, всегда производивший на него неприятнейшее впечатление и даже страх, когда он проходил мимо его, гуляя с отцом. Там всегда была такая толпа, так орали, хохотали, ругались, так безобразно и сипло пели и так часто дрались; кругом кабака шлялись всегда такие пьяные и страшные рожи... «...» Возле кабака дорога, проселок, всегда пыльная, и пыль на ней всегда такая черная. Идет она, извиваясь, далее и шагах в трехстах огибает вправо городское кладбище. Среди кладбища каменная церковь с зеленым куполом, в которую он раза два в год ходил с отцом и с матерью к обедне, когда служились панихиды по его бабушке, умершей уже давно, и которую он никогда не видал.[10)]

Городок во сне топографически совпадает со Сенной площадью: большой кабак, шум, пьяные и церковь. На площади был собор Успения Пресвятой Богородицы. И собор с зеленым куполом напоминает Соню в зелёном платке и дом, где она живёт. Дом

века. 2003. С.26.
10) Достоевский Ф.М. Преступление и наказание. Указ. соч. С.46.

был зелёного цвета и принадлежал портному Капернаумову.[11]

Тогда где находится очень далёкий чёрный лесок? Он находится там, где есть ветла, то есть в Западной Сибири. Ареал ветла —Европа (за исключением Крайнего Севера), Малая Азия, Иран и Западная Сибирь.

Таким образом, пространство во сне сопоставляется с Сенной площадью (западом) и Сибирью (востоком).[12]

Как в центре Иерусалима находится источник Гихон (источник Девы Марии), так и в Сибири, на берегу, где Соня и Раскольников сидят, течёт река Иртыш. И за рекой распространяется божий мир. Это тот же самый пейзаж, который видел Горянчков, герой «Записок из мёртого дома».

> Я, впрочем, любил таскать кирпичи не за то только, что от этой работы укрепляется тело, а за то еще, что работа производилась на берегу Иртыша. Я потому так часто говорю об этом береге, что единственно только с него и был виден мир божий, чистая, ясная даль, незаселенные, вольные степи,

---

[11] Иисус Христос проповедовал в синагоге Капернаума и совершил в этом городе много чудес.

[12] «Ива белая, ветла (S. alba), —дерево выс. до 20—30 м, диам. ствола до 1,5 м. Кора тёмно-серая, с глубокими трещинами. Листья узколанцетные, на верхушке заострённые, по краям мелкозубчатые. Цветёт одновременно с появлением листьев. Распространена в Европе (кроме Скандинавии), М. и Ср. Азии, сев.-зап. части Африки, в СССР —в лесной и лесо-степной зонах Европейской части (кроме С.), в Сев. Казахстане и на юге Зап. Сибири, на Кавказе, Юж. Урале». (Лесная энциклопедия : В 2-х т. Т.1. М. : Сов. энциклопедия, 1985. С.361)

производившие на меня странное впечатление своею пустынностью.¹³⁾

Берег в старину означал гору. Раскольников дошёл до символичного берега через Урал, самый старый горный хребет в мире. Значит, Раскольников поднимался на гору, то есть дошёл до церкви, или дошёл до пустыни, то есть до монастыря.

Река – место крещения. Она связывает верхний мир (гору) с низким миром (морем) и вода, упавшая в море, испарится и льётся в гору. Не возможно ли считать реку Иртыш символом иконостаса, который вечно связывает два мира ; Ветхий и Новый заветы и одновременно перегородит два мира : средняя и алтарь. Средняя символизирует этот свет‹7›, а алтарь тот свет‹8›, восточный край которого называется горним местом. А Соня напоминает Марию, и Евангелие ассоциируется с Иоанной. Перед Раскольниковым, который умер символически, тускло виден Деисус иконостаса.

Недаром в конце эпилога, то есть седьмая часть романа, Раскольников считает семь лет семью днями.

Она тоже весь этот день была в волнении, а в ночь даже опять захворала. Но она была до того счастлива, что почти испугалась своего счастья. Семь лет, только семь лет! В начале своего счастия, в иные мгновения, они оба готовы

---

13) Достоевский Ф.М.С. Записки из мёртого дома.// Достоевский Ф.М. Пол. Соб. Соч. в 30–ти томах.Т.4. –Л., 1972. С.178.

были смотреть на эти семь лет, как на семь дней. Он даже и не знал того, что новая жизнь не даром же ему достается, что ее надо еще дорого купить, заплатить за нее великим, будущим подвигом...[14]

Хотя новая жизнь будет трудной, однако здесь они оба воспринимают вечность.

Таким образом, Достоевский построил огромный собор, входом которого является Сенная площадь, а горним местом – Сибирь, чтобы показать исход разрушенных семей.

---

[14] Достоевский Ф.М. Преступление и наказание. Указ. соч. С.422.

ラモンの『サーカス』に「日本人」が登場するまで
―― ジャポニスムのスペイン伝播について ――

"How Japanese acrobats came to appear in Ramón Goméz de la Serna's *El Circo*. —an influence of Japonism on Spanish Literature"

平田　渡

Wataru HIRATA

Abstract:

Almost all the works of the Spanish writer, Ramón Gómez de la Serna, including *El Circo*, are composed in *greguería*, his own style of prose formulated as short verses. The present paper argues that this literature is replete with Japonisms, because *greguería* was influenced by Japanese *haikai* poetry via England and France.

Keywords:

William George Aston, *A History of Japanese Literature* (1899), Basil Hall Chagremberlain, *Bashô and the Japanese Poetical Epigram* (1902), Paul-Louis Couchoud, *Le Haïkaï Les Épigrammes poétiques [lyliques] du Japon* (1906), Joseph Carner and Eugeni (Eugenio) D'ors, Antonio Machado, Juan Ramón Jiménez, Federico García Lorca, Ramón Gómez de la Serna, *El Circo* (1917). Greguería. Japonism. *Haikai*.

ユウェナリスの「パンとサーカス」と近代サーカスの誕生

　ローマの詩人ユウェナリスが、『風刺詩集』の中で、政治に関心を示さなくな

り、もっぱら「パンとサーカス」にのみ現を抜かす民衆のことを揶揄している話は有名である。

けれども、この場合の「サーカス」circenses は、わたしたちが知るサーカスではない。もともとは、古代ローマ時代に、勇壮な戦車競争がおこなわれていた会場の馬場を指していたのだが、そこから意味が広がり、剣闘士の試合などを含んだ見世物、娯楽一般を指すようになったのである。

為政者にすれば、民衆に、パン（食糧）とサーカス（娯楽）を与えて、政治意識を持たせないようにすれば、おのれの権威の座の安泰を図ることができたのである。そのように、「パンとサーカス」は、いわゆる愚民政策の手立てとしてうまく利用されていたのだった。

現在のかたちのサーカスが登場するのは、それから気が遠くなるように永い歳月が流れた18世紀半ばのイギリスにおいてであった。

阿久根巌『サーカスの歴史』によれば、「1768年になると、イギリスの退役軍人フィリップ・アストレーが、曲馬と軽業の演目から始めたショーを発展させた、近代サーカスが誕生していた。新しい見世物であるサーカスは、やがてイギリスからフランスやロシアなどのヨーロッパ諸国に広がり、魅力ある娯楽として受け入れられていった」[1]。

1862年には、ロンドン万国博覧会がひらかれたが、その頃、日本の陶器や置物に対する関心が高まり、ロセッティを中心としたラファエル前派の画家たちは、美術に深い興味を抱くようになった。そして、1867年のパリ万国博覧会と1868年の明治維新の頃には、日本人の軽業師や手品師がパリやロンドンに渡り、興行を打つまでになる。

「幕末から明治にかけて、じつに多くの芸人が見知らぬ外国に飛び出していったことには驚かせられる。彼らの足どりを丹念に辿った記録としては、宮岡謙二著『（異国遍路）旅芸人始末書』が知られているが、何が芸人をかりたてたのであろうか。加藤秀俊著『見世物からテレビへ』では、旅が唯一の生活スタイルで

1）阿久根巌『サーカスの歴史』西田書店、1977、39-40頁。

ある河原ものと呼ばれる芸人 – 旅芸人の伝統こそが、異国への芸能人の進出を支えた」[2] 原動力なのだ、という見方が示されている。

ともかくも、明治維新の1871年（明治4年）と1874年（同7年）に、フランスからスーリエという曲馬団 Cirque Soulié が来日して、横浜や京都や新潟でヨーロッパ風のサーカス芸を披露している。じつは、それに先立つこと7年の1864年（元治元年）に、中天竺舶来之軽業という外国の一座が日本に初めてやってきているのだが、それについて、バレエ、シャンソン、演劇、サーカス研究の泰斗である蘆原英了は、以下のように指摘している。

「1864年（元治元年）の中天竺軽業が、シルク・スーリエであるかもしれないのは、錦絵に馬の芸がのっていること、つまり曲馬団であることが確実なこと、そして1866年（慶応2年）にパリへ戻ったとき、日本からトリカタという曲芸師を連れていっているという事実から考えられる。

たしかに鳥潟小三吉は、1866年にフランスに渡り、パリのシルク・ナポレオンに出演している」[3] からである。

つまり、日本に到来した最初の外国のサーカスは、中天竺軽業ということになっていたけれど、その正体はフランスのスーリエ曲馬団だったというのだ。そして帰国したときに、綱渡り芸を得意とする、秋田県大館市生まれの、鳥潟小三吉が同行していった。

綱渡り師、鳥潟小三吉のパリとロンドンでの活躍

鳥潟小三吉（トリカタ コ サンキチ）は、パリで高い評価をうけたあと、イギリス人興行師と契約を交わしロンドンに渡った。さらに、のちに、みずから軽業師の一座を立ちあげて、イギリス、フランス、オランダ、ドイツを巡業して廻った。その間、知り合ったドイツ娘を妻に迎えたが、本業の方はおおむね好評を博した。

二度目の渡欧のさいには、当時のドイツ皇帝ヴィルヘルム1世に招かれ、宮廷

2）『前掲書』37頁。
3）蘆原英了「サーカス渡来」丸善PR誌『學燈』71巻 12号所収。

で妙技を披露するに及んでいる。

　このように、鳥潟小三吉は、幕末から明治時代初期にかけて、ヨーロッパで活躍し国際的な名声をえた最初の日本人サーカス芸人であった。

ラモンの『サーカス』に登場する「日本人」と「大和撫子」

　ラモン・ゴメス・デ・ラ・セルナは、『サーカス』の中の「日本人」の章を、「日本人は、比肩するものがない、理想的なところがあって、サーカスにみごとな展望と将来性をもたらしている」[4]という絶讃の言葉から始めている。

　続いて、綱渡り師、鳥潟小三吉を想わせるような芸人が姿をあらわす。もちろん、ゴメス・デ・ラ・セルナが描いている芸人は、パリやロンドンで見たであろう、さまざまな日本人を総合したものに違いないけれど、以下のように好意的な捉え方が際立っている。

　「（日本の）サーカスでは、前代未聞のことがおこなわれている。野外のサーカスにおいては、芸人が、彩りあざやかな提灯がぶら下がった、長い竿をもって、ピーンと張られた綱の上を渡って、高いところまでするすると登っていくのである。川や森の上に斜めに張られた綱の上を渡ると、影法師が、空自体の淡い光のみならず、素晴らしい月の光に照らされて、澄みきった空にくっきりと浮かびあがるのだ」[5]。

　このくだりの日本人は、規模が違うはずだが、秋田の竿燈まつりらしき曲芸を、綱渡りをしながらおこなうという放れ技を披露している。おまけに、美しい影法師まで計算して、観客を唸らせているから驚かざるをえない。

　この引用に続くくだりで、サーカスの演し物に伴う音楽も申し分がないと述べたあと、

　「そうしたすべては、サーカスの神様、〈千位楠智〉に捧げられている。さらに、それぞれの芸人が、その神よりも小さな神、仕事の神様に、第二の供物を捧

4）ラモン・ゴメス・デ・ラ・セルナ『サーカス』関西大学出版部、拙訳、2016、151頁。
5）『前掲書』152頁。

げる。というのも、日本には、曲芸師の神や道化師の神といった神神が存在するのである。

それが分かると、とうてい本当とは思えないことがじっさいにおこなわれていることに対して納得がゆく。そう、神神が日本人を手助けしているのである。そのことは、生きていく上では、少なくとも多神教であるべきだということを示している。そうすれば、すべてが有利に働くし、りっぱな演技ができるのだ」[6]。

日本の芸人が大胆きわまりない、命がけの演技に挑む背景には、八百万の神神のご加護があるという見解には、苦笑を禁じえないけれど、いまなお自然崇拝は珍しくないし、日本人の心には、神道、仏教、それにキリスト教が共生していることは、ご承知のとおりである。

もっとも、拙訳では、el dios del circo Tix-Chi というスペイン語は、サーカスの神様〈千位楠智〉としたが、この正体を突き止めることはできなかった。おそらく、ゴメス・デ・ラ・セルナがひねり出した造語ではないかと踏んでいる。ともかくも、その疑問については、追い追い明らかにしていきたい。

次に、日本の芸人が使う道具類と皿まわし芸については、ラモンはこう述べている。

「彼らが使うすべての道具類、仕事に必要なすべての用品、たとえば、手裏剣、小体な花瓶、ボール、くさぐさの奇術用品は、まったく非の打ちどころがない。

日本人が、軽い竹竿の先でまわす皿は、まぎれもなく観客を魅了してやまないものである。皿が落ちないように、運命の神神が指で留めてくれている、としか言いようがない。日本人は、すべての仕事に対して、魔法の扇子を使って風を送る。というのも、彼らは、魔法の杖の代わりに、魔法の扇子をそなえており、それで空中に、魔法のかかった、かすかな風を起こしているのである」[7]。

もともと手先が器用な日本人ならではの、繊細な造りの小道具を操りながら、皿まわしはおこなわれるけれど、これもまた神がかり的だと言う。魔法の杖なら

---

6)『前掲書』152 頁。
7)『前掲書』154 頁。

ぬ、魔法の扇子が送る風が作用しているという見立てである。

　『サーカス』が上梓された、1917年頃の、スペイン女性の正装は、ペイネータ peineta と呼ばれる大きめの櫛を髪につけ、その上にマンティーリャ mantilla という黒い絹のレースをかぶり、派手な模様の扇子を手にしているのがふつうであった。とくに、闘牛見物に出かけるとき、婦人によく見られる服装だった。また、扇子はフラメンコを踊るさいに小道具として使われることもめずらしくなかった。そんなわけで、ゴメス・デ・ラ・セルナが、日本人芸人が使う扇子に注目したのも、自然のなりゆきであろう。

　『サーカス』全体を通して、ラモンは日本贔屓(びいき)を貫いているといって構わない。これは、あとで取り上げる、彼の短詩型の散文、グレゲリーアの根本に、俳諧の思想が横たわっていることと繋がりがあるようだ。

　それはともかく、ラモンの日本人の容貌や体形の描き方は面白くて、微苦笑を誘われる。たとえば、

　「日本人の顔は、ひどく眠気をもよおす体(てい)のものである。瞼は、泣きはらしたかのようだが、そこから、小さい目の先端がのぞいている。けれども、手裏剣を投げると、その可愛い目でしっかりと的を捉えるのだ。そして、それぞれの物の勘所を、寸分も違わぬ正確さで見抜き、隠された秘密を暴き、それぞれの物が立てられるべき刃(やいば)を見据えるのである」[8]とか、「日本人はもともと敏捷だけれど、腕が細くて脚が短いせいで、そのぶん動きがにぶくなっている」[9]とか……。

　さらに、髪については、こうである。

　「日本人の髪は、植物から採られたような黒色をしているけれど、それが最大の特徴になっている。すべてのものを超越する特徴、と言ってもいいかもしれない。ああ、そうそう、たとえば、もしぼくたちが大和撫子の板前を抱えていたとして、料理に髪の毛が入っているのを見つけたら、彼女は言いわけはしないだろうし、ほかの方のものですわ、とシラを切ることもないであろう。大和撫子の髪

---

[8] 『前掲書』155頁。
[9] 『前掲書』158頁。

は、思わず見とれるくらい素晴らしいのである」[10]。

　日本人の黒髪は、欧米人にとって、こよなく蠱惑(こわく)的だとは耳にしていたが、今から百年前の1917年（大正6年）の、この『サーカス』という作品に、はっきりとした言葉で記録されているとは思わなかった。それも、「すべてのものを超越する」日本人の特徴だと言い切っているのである。茶髪や金髪に染めたまま欧米に出かけてゆく、今日日(きょうび)の若者に聴かせてやりたい、言葉ではないだろうか。ついでながら、これは、大和撫子の髪のみならず、日本男児の髪もまたしかりであるらしいので付け加えておきたい。

　ともかくも、ゴメス・デ・ラ・セルナは、日本人、とりわけ大和撫子にぞっこんのご様子である。それは、次のくだりを読んでいただければ一目瞭然である。

　「しかしながら、日本人が演技をするところを見ていて、何かもの足りなさを感じるのも確かである。それは、ふつう、大和撫子を登場させて演技の手助けをさせようとはしないせいかもしれない。大和撫子の流し目に心を奪われた観客が、すっかり惚れこんでしまって、身動きできなくなることを恐れているのであろうか。それとも、大和撫子が恋に落ちることを怖がっているだろうか。どうやら、大和撫子はだいじに匿(かくま)われているように見える」[11]。

　けれども、ラモンが大和撫子に捧げたいちばん優れた作品は、『乳房抄』の掉尾(とうび)を飾るような位置にそっと挿入されているので、へたをすると見落としかねない。

　「大和撫子の乳房は可愛い乳房である。時として孔雀石(マラカイト)か翡翠(ひすい)製で、また時として薄衣(うすぎぬ)か睡蓮、もしくは椿で出来ているように見える。大和撫子の乳房は、大きな人形に付けてある、ふくらみ染めたばかりの乳房である。そうなったわけは色色と考えられるけれど、ひとつには、黎明(れいめい)の恩恵をいちばんに享受する国、日本は、日出(い)ずる国であるのみならず、乳出る国でもあるからに違いない」[12]。

---

10) 『前掲書』155頁。
11) 『前掲書』157頁。
12) ラモン・ゴメス・デ・ラ・セルナ『乳房抄』関西大学出版部、拙訳、2008、208頁。

ゴメス・デ・ラ・セルナは、グレゲリーアとは、〈諧謔＋隠喩〉だと定義しているが、「大和撫子の乳房」は、その定義をもののみごとに実現しているのではないだろうか。小粒ながら、このように馥郁たる文学の薫りをただよわせた、印象あざやかな作品に仕立てあげられた背景には、19世紀後半に英仏を中心にヨーロッパ諸国に広がったジャポネズリー（日本趣味）、ひいてはジャポニスム（日本美術や文学が及ぼした影響）が作用しているように思われる。

ジャポニスム（俳諧）のスペイン伝播
　このテーマについては、2015年、田澤佳子の手になる『俳句とスペインの詩人たち－マチャード、ヒメネス、ロルカとカタルーニャの詩人－』（思文閣出版）という好著が出た。今までに看過されていた、カタルーニャの詩人による新しい視点を導入し、スペインにおけるジャポニスム事情を深く掘り下げることに成功している。以下は主に、それをひもとくことによって得た情報に寄りかかっていることをお断わりしておく。
　俳諧がイギリスとフランス、ひいてはスペインに導入されるに際して、火付け役を果たしたのは、アーネスト・サトウとともに、イギリス人の日本研究家として知られるウィリアム・ジョージ・アストン（1841-1911）が、1899年に、ロンドンで上梓した『日本文学史』だったと見られている。
　田澤佳子『俳句とスペインの詩人たち』とほぼ同じ2015年に上梓された、金子美都子の労作『フランス二〇世紀詩と俳句　ジャポニスムから前衛へ』（平凡社、2015、87頁）によれば、ヘンリー＝D・デイヴレーが仏訳した『アストン日本文学史』（1902）を参照すると、「四章には、〈17世紀の詩：俳諧または発句・俳文・狂歌〉として、俳諧の記述がおよそ8頁にまとめられ、山崎宗鑑（16世紀）から松尾芭蕉（1644-94）に至る簡単な俳諧の歴史、特徴などを略述し、17句（うち芭蕉8句）の例句を挙げている」。芭蕉は、「〈俳諧を洗練し、改良し、短歌にとって恐るべきライバルに押し上げた〉とあるのを見れば、ここで初めて俳諧が短歌に並びうるものとして認識される基盤」ができたことが分かる。

以下は、田澤佳子の本に依拠しているけれど、「詩人の考えをできるだけ短く表現したいという日本人の願いが、俳諧(ハイカイ)を生み出した」として、俳諧が紹介されているのはいいが、俳諧の文字数が和歌の三十一文字(みそひともじ)と間違えられたり、芭蕉がバチョーと表記されたりしており、苦笑させられる。けれども、そうした些事をあげつらうよりも、ヨーロッパにおける俳諧に関する情報の嚆矢(こうし)となったという事実の方が重要である。

そして、原著の『日本文学史』に関する情報は、1899年末になると、当時としては驚くべき早さで、マドリードの〈モダン・スペイン〉*La España Moderna* という総合誌(発刊期間：1889-1914。スペイン人富豪ホセ・ラサロ・ガルデイアーノが発行人)に掲載された。それは、フランスの〈両世界評論〉*La Revue des deux mondes* に似た雑誌であった。〈モダン・スペイン〉を通して、日本起源の新しい詩のかたちをめぐる情報がスペインをはじめ、ヒスパニック・アメリカ諸国に広まることになったのである。

①アントニオ・マチャード(1875-1939)

1899年といえば、アントニオ・マチャードがパリに赴き、ガルニエ兄弟社で翻訳家として働き始めた年にほかならない。以後。1902年、1910年にもパリを訪れている。

マチャードは、1903年に処女詩集『孤独』を、1907年にその増補版『孤独、回廊、そのほかの詩』を出したが、後者には、前者に含まれていない、俳諧を想わせる三行詩が収められている。面白いことに、マチャードは俳諧という言葉を極力、使おうとしなかったけれど、『新しい歌』(1924)には、俳諧から受けた影響がはっきりと見てとれる。したがって、スペインの詩人で文芸批評家のエンリケ・ディエス・カネード(1879-1944)は、作者を「日本の詩人」と呼び、そこに発表された三行詩には、「日本の詩の完璧で目を見張るような経済性」が認められると指摘したのである。

そこで、田澤佳子は、マチャードが1903年から1907年の間に俳句を知ったの

ではないかと推測し、アナトール・フランスの友人で詩人の、ポール゠ルイ・クーシュー Paul-Louis Couchoud（1879-1959）が、1906年に〈レ・レットル Les Lettres〉誌に発表した、「俳諧　日本の抒情的なエピグラム」 *Le haïkaï LES ÉPIGRAMMES LYRIQUES DU JAPON* という論文を読んで刺戟を受けたのかもしれないと見ている。

そのほか、アーネスト・サトウ、それにウィリアム・ジョージ・アストンと並ぶ、英国人の日本研究家、バジル゠ホール・チェンバレン（1850-1935）の「芭蕉と日本の詩的なエピグラム」 *Bashô and the Japanese Poetical Epigram* や、アストンの『日本文学史』に着想を得たことも考えられるとしている[13]。

②フアン・ラモン・ヒメネス（1881-1958）

一方、フアン・ラモン・ヒメネスがマチャードの知遇を得たのは、マチャードが1899年にパリから当時住んでいたマドリードに帰った翌年1900年のことであ

---

13) 田澤佳子『俳句とスペインの詩人たち―マチャード、ヒメネス、ロルカとカタルーニャの詩人―』思文閣出版、2015、31頁。
　　金子美都子は、『フランス二〇世紀詩と俳句　ジャポニスムから前衛へ』（平凡社、2015）の88頁で、「俳諧　日本の抒情的なエピグラム」は、「例句157句を含む、フランスの読者に向けた本格的な俳句論。（中略）総合文芸誌『レ・レットル』 Les Lettres 1906年4・6・7・8月号に」掲載されたと述べている。
　　また、バジル゠ホール・チェンバレン（1850-1935）の「芭蕉と日本の詩的なエピグラム」 *Bashô and the Japanese Poetical Epigram* （1902）については、91-92頁で、
　　「乾昌幸氏はすでに、チェンバレンが1889年『日本口語案内』で其角作とされる〈赤とんぼ〉の句や千代女の〈朝顔や〉の句を含む4句を紹介しているが、それ以外は、（中略）俳句はほとんど黙殺されていたに近いジャンルだった。ところが、〈日本アジア協会紀要〉掲載の『芭蕉と日本の詩的エピグラム』では、俳諧の形式、歴史、特徴について詳述し、貞門から千代女までの作品を206句挙げて、それぞれに解説を付している。これらの句、および挿入されたエピソードから見て、この書は、以後の欧米のにおけるすべての俳句研究の源となったと言っていいほどの影響を与えている。
　　じじつ、クーシュー自身、『アジアの賢人と詩人』のなかでチェンバレンの前掲論文の名を挙げ、〈私はチェンバレン氏から芭蕉に関する歴史的な情報ともっとも美しい作品例を使わせていただいた〉と断っている。
　　このように、当時の俳諧のヨーロッパへの紹介に関しては、ほとんどイギリス人が先行し、フランス人が追随するかたちになっているので、金子美都子にしきりに嘆息をつかせている。

ラモンの『サーカス』に「日本人」が登場するまで

った。

　それ以降、ヒメネスは、フランスの〈メルキュール・ド・フランス Mercure de France〉誌を購読するようになった。また、1920年に、俳諧特集を組むことになる〈ヌーヴェル・ルヴュー・フランセーズ La Nouvelle Revue Française〉誌も当然視野に入っていたことだろう。両誌は、俳諧がフランス、ひいてはヨーロッパ諸国に伝播してゆくうえで、一役買った文芸誌であった。

　ヒメネスとマチャードは、同じアンダルシア地方の出身（ヒメネスはウエルバ県モゲール、マチャードはセビリア県セビリアの生まれ）ということもあって、おたがいにフランス語の詩集の貸借をし合う親しい間柄になった。

　1900年は、ヒメネスの父親が急逝した年でもあった。ヒメネスは大きな衝撃を受け、病に取り憑かれる。医者の勧めもあって、最初はフランスのボルドー近郊の療養所、のちにマドリードのサナトリウムに入った。前者においては、フランス国内を旅行したり、所内の図書館でヴェルレーヌやボードレールなどの象徴派の詩に親しんだりした。

　1912年、体調が恢復したヒメネスは、1910年にマドリードのフォルトゥニー街に創立されてまもない学生寮 Residencia de Estudiantes（ドイツ人哲学者クラウゼの思想にもとづき、教育や社会の革新をめざすために創設された、自由教育学院 Institución Libre de Enseñanza 経営）に入った。

　この寮は、1915年、究極の落ち着き先である〈アルトス・デル・イポードロモ街（「競馬場の丘」の意）〉に移るが、そのときヒメネス自らが〈コリーナ・ロス・チョポス（「ポプラの丘」の意）〉と名づけたことで知られている。けれども、何よりもまず初期にヒメネスをはじめ、ルイス・ブニュエル（映画監督）、フェデリコ・ガルシア・ロルカ（詩人）、サルバドール・ダリ（画家）といった著名人を輩出した揺籃の地であったことを指摘しておかなければならない。

　ヒメネスは、この学生寮で、講演会を聴きにやってきたセノビアという女性とめぐり会い、恋に落ち、やがてニュー・ヨークでめでたく結ばれることになる。カタルーニャ人の父とプエルト・リコ人の母のあいだに生まれたセノビアは、ア

メリカのコロンビア大学でスペイン文学と英文学を学んだあと、スペイン語と英語で小説を書いたり、アイルランドの劇作家シングやインドの詩人タゴールの作品をスペイン語に翻訳したりしていた才媛であった。

そうしたセノビアの文学趣味がヒメネスに影響を及ぼすことになった。その点に関して、田澤佳子はこう述べている。

「1913年にヒメネスがタゴールの『新月』を西訳したことは、ヒメネスと俳諧の関係を考える上で重要である。つまり、俳諧の影響を受けたタゴールの作品の翻訳を通して、ヒメネスはあらためて俳諧を意識するようになったのではないか。また、セノビアを介して、イマジズムの詩にいっそう親しむようになった」[14)]という事情もあった。

ヒメネスは、『新婚詩人の日記』（1917）以降、詩から装飾的なものや挿話に類するものを剝ぎ取り、抒情的な本質だけを残す、いわゆる〈裸の詩〉を書き始めた。すなわち、新境地の短詩に向かって大きく舵を切ったのである。『新婚詩人の日記』に続く、『永遠』（1916-17）、さらに『石と空』（1917-18）、これら三冊が、俳諧からの影響が比較的はっきりと窺われる詩集だと言われている。

そして、ヒメネスが最終的にめざしたものは、俳諧がヒントになったとも考えられなくもない純粋詩の確立であった。

③フェデリコ・ガルシア・ロルカ（1898-1936）

フェデリコ・ガルシア・ロルカは、スペインが米西戦争に敗れ、最後に残った植民地だったキューバ、フィリピン、グアムを手放した1898年に生まれ、スペイン内乱が勃発した1936年に反乱軍の国民派側に捕らえられ、銃殺刑に処された。いずれも、スペインを揺るがす歴史的な事件が起きた年であり、ロルカはそれを象徴する悲劇の中心的な人物と見られている。そして、彼もマチャードとヒメネス同様、アンダルシア地方（グラナダ県フエンテ・バケーロス）の出身だっ

---

14)『前掲書』98-99頁。

た。

　ロルカと俳諧との関わりが取りざたされる詩集といえば、『組曲』、『カンテ・ホンドの歌』、『歌集』である。この三冊が完成したとき、ロルカは、私信において、次のような感想を洩らしている。

　「これらは、奇妙なことに、ひとつの魂(かたまり)なのだ。だから、三冊いっしょに上梓しなければならない。それぞれが互いに補い合い、第一級の詩を作りあげているのである」[15]。

　ロルカがそう述べるのも不思議はない。いずれもが、一篇ないしは一連が、三行か四行のほどの短詩で埋め尽くされており、俳諧を想わせるにじゅうぶんだからである。

　加えて、1920年頃に書かれたらしい注目すべき資料が存在する。すなわち、「ママに捧げるお祝いの俳諧(ハイカイ)」という詩、そしてそれに付されたとおぼしい「俳諧(ハイカイ)についての注釈」と「俳諧(ハイカイ)批評」という書簡にほかならない。この中でいちばん興味深いのは、「俳諧(ハイカイ)についての注釈」であろう。以下にそれを引用してみる。

　「俳諧(ハイカイ)は、フランスの新しい詩人たちがヨーロッパに持ちこんだ、すぐれて日本的な歌です。僕は特に新しいものが好きなので、それを試作して愉しんでいます。

　俳諧(ハイカイ)は、二行か三行で心の中にあるものをまとめ、ひとを感動させなければならないのです。

　したがって、僕はいちばん現代的で、いちばん甘美なかたちでママにお祝いの言葉を述べていることになります。

　これらの俳諧(ハイカイ)は、僕がママに贈る、抒情的なチョコレート・ボンボンの小箱なのです。そこには、僕のいちばん新しい、出来立ての、心からの言葉が納められています」[16]。

---

[15] 『前掲書』128 頁。
[16] 『前掲書』149 頁。

ロルカは、1919年から28年まで、マドリードの学生寮で暮らした。その10年になんなんとする間に、俳諧に関わりのある、さまざまな人物に出会っている。

　「まず、カタルーニャの作家で評論家の（アウジェニ・）ドルースを挙げることができる。彼は、早くも1904年に、〈カタルーニャの声〉というバルセロナの日刊紙で俳諧(ハイカイ)を取り上げたばかりか、実作を試みたことがあった。また、フアン・ラモン・ヒメネスが学生寮に住んだのは、1913年から16年に結婚するまでであるが、その後も学生寮に出入りし、ロルカをはじめ、多くの寮生にいい影響を与えている。寮長の右腕的な存在だったホセ・モレーノ・ビリャは、当時、出た俳諧(ハイカイ)の手引書について書評をものした。さらに、アドリアーノ・デル・バリェは、熱心な日本研究者でロルカの親友であった」[17]。

　ついでながら、アウジェニ・ドルースとは、日本では、『プラド美術館の三時間』や『バロック論』といった美術評論の翻訳を通して、比較的よく知られているエウヘニオ・ドールスのことにほかならない。アウジェニ Eugeni は、スペイン語のエウヘニオ Eugenio のカタルーニャ語読みである。彼については、後述することになっている。

④ジョセップ・カルネー（1884-1970）とアウジェニ（エウヘニオ）・ドルース（1881-1954）

　フランスで俳諧が流行するきっかけになったのは、ポール゠ルイ・クーシューが書いた『俳諧　日本の抒情的なエピグラム』という論文であった。これは、〈レ・レットル〉誌に、1906年4月から四回にわたって掲載されたものだった。

　それを読んだバルセロナ出身の詩人でジャーナリスト、ヒメネスと親交のあったジョセップ・カルネーは、〈カタルーニャの声〉 *La Veu de Catalunya* という新聞（1906年6月15日付）に、いち早くその内容を紹介する記事を書いたのであ

---

17)『前掲書』155頁。

る。それに触発されて興味を示したのが、当時、同じ新聞のパリ特派員をしていた、若き日のアウジェニ・ドルースにほかならなかった。

　彼は、なんとわずか八日後に、自ら一種の俳諧と呼んでいる作品を含んだコラム記事を〈カタルーニャの声〉に載せたのだ。というのも、じつは、以前から〈時事解説〉 *Glosari* というコラムを担当しており、そこで取り上げることができたからだった。

　〈時事解説〉はむろん、カタルーニャ語で書かれていたが、マドリードを中心とするほかの地域の知識人にも読まれていた。その証拠に、哲学者ホセ・オルテガ・イ・ガセーは、〈時事解説〉を「文化の発展のために日日放たれている弓矢」にたとえて高く評価していた。

　結局、このコラムは、16年間、4000回にわたって書き続けられ、好評を博したばかりか、ドルースの思想をつぶさに伝える手段となった。本人の意図したとおり、時事的な問題について深く掘り下げられ、時代の鼓動を捉えることに成功したと言われている。

　1920年、マドリードに転居したあとも、発表紙を全国紙のABC新聞に変えて執筆を続けた。それとともに、言葉はカタルーニャ語からスペイン語になったことは言うまでもない。

　話をもとに戻すと、ドルースの記事には、〈聖ヨハネ祭の夜に打ち上げられる花火〉という見出しが付けられていた。そして、西洋のソネットとは異なる基準に従って作られる魅力的な短詩だと紹介されたのだった。

　一方、ポール゠ルイ・クーシューの方は、俳諧は独特の詩のジャンルであって、いわば気まぐれな小さな骨董品、極端なまでに素朴で繊細なところがあり、まるで現代人の好みに合わせて作られたかのようだ、と説明している。

　エウヘニオ・ドルースは、マドリードに引っ越した頃がちょうど円熟期に当たる。代表作の『プラド美術館の三時間』(1922)や戯曲『ウィリアム・テル』(1926)、『ゴヤの生涯』(1928)をものした。そして、学生寮で講演会をひらいたり、いわばマドリード版のベル・エポックを現出させた感がある、ラモン・ゴメ

ス・デ・ラ・セルナが主宰する文学カフェ・ポンボの会に顔を出たりするようになった。そのあと、宮仕えをするために、しばらくフランスのパリで暮らすことになったけれど、その間の成果が『ポール・セザンヌ』(1930)、『パブロ・ピカソ』(1930)、『バロック論』(1935)といったすぐれた美術評論である。

⑤エンリケ・ゴメス・カリーリョ (1873-1927)

　エンリケ・ゴメス・カリーリョは、若き日に母国グアテマラの首都で、当時そこに住んでいたニカラグア人の詩人ルベン・ダリーオ (1867-1916) に出会い、その推輓を受けてマドリードに公費留学した。けれども、じっさいにはパリに定住し、事実上、半生以上をそこですごした、今でいう国際派のジャーナリストで、作家、外交官である。ルベン・ダリーオは、19世紀末にスペイン語圏おける詩の改革めざすモデルニスモ modernismo 運動を展開したことで知られるが、ゴメス・カリーリョにとっては、まさにかけがえのない恩師と言ってよかった。

　パリでは、フランス人のポール・ヴェルレーヌ、ジャン・モレアス、ルコント・ド・リール、そしてアイルランド人のオスカー・ワイルド、スペイン人のマチャード、ヒメネス、ミゲル・デ・ウナムーノなどと親交を深めた。

　とくにマチャードは、翻訳家として務めたガルニエ兄弟社において、やがて同社から、次次に本を出すことになる、ゴメス・カリーリョと知り合う幸運に恵まれた。そして彼の口利きで、ルベン・ダリーオをはじめ、ジャン・モレアス、オスカー・ワイルド、アナトール・フランスと交遊関係を結ぶことができた。残念ながら、のちにマチャードが耽読することになるヴェルレーヌは、すでに鬼籍に入っていた。

　ゴメス・カリーリョが出す本とは、日露戦争が勃発している最中の、ニコラス二世統治下のロシアの不正を鋭く暴いたルポルタージュ『現今のロシア』(1906)、訪れた国国の政治や社会、風俗習慣を伝えるとともに、日露戦争に勝利した日本の現状を報告した『マルセイユから東京まで：エジプト、インド、中国、日本の印象』(同前)、それに、前作と同様、フランスの新聞や雑誌で讃辞を

浴びた『日本の魂』(1907) のことである。

　この『日本の魂』の中に、「詩の心」と題された章があり、俳諧についての解説と作品が4首、収められている。「詩の心」は、1907年、ゴメス・カリーリョが主宰する〈新メルキュール〉*El Nuevo Mercurio* 誌にも、マドリードのナシミエント社から出す『誇り高く優雅な国、日本』(1912) にも転載された。これに、仏訳の『日本の魂』に載ったものを加えると、「詩の心」は通算4回発表されたことになるので、それなりに宣伝効果はあったはずである。

　田澤佳子によれば、収録されている俳諧というのは、荒木田守武の「落花枝にかへると見れば胡蝶哉」、松永貞徳の「みな人の昼寝の種や秋の月」、それに松尾芭蕉の「花の雲鐘は上野か浅草か」が下敷きになっているようだ。そして、すべてがアストンの『日本文学史』に取り上げられたものと重なっていると指摘している。

　このように、パリに在住しながらスペイン語で作品を書き続けたゴメス・カリーリョが、俳諧の伝播のために果たした貢献も少なくないであろう。

ジャポニスムとラモン

　すでに述べたように、ラモン・ゴメス・デ・ラ・セルナの場合、『乳房抄』において〈諧謔＋隠喩＝グレゲリーア〉の定義どおりに、大和撫子の乳房をみごとに捉えて忘れがたい逸品に仕上げたし、『サーカス』の中では「日本人」という章をもうけ、並並ならぬ日本贔屓であることを示した。

　では、俳諧(ハイカイ)と関わりがあるようなものは見られないだろうか。答えは大ありである。

　何よりも、1908年、わが子を思う父親ハビエルの肝煎りで創刊された〈プロメテウス〉*Prometeo, revista social y literaria* という文芸誌 (1912年まで4年間に全38号刊行。スペインの前衛誌と、1923年に創刊される、哲学者ホセ・オルテガ・イ・ガセー主宰の〈西欧評論〉*Revista de Occidente* という文芸・思想誌の先駆的な存在) に発表された頃から、1950年代半ばまで、ほぼ半世紀にわたって書き続けられた、短

詩型の散文、グレゲリーアを挙げなければならないであろう。

〈プロメテウス〉創刊号の裏表紙に、ひとまとまりのグレゲリーアが掲載されているけれど、その中に

騾馬の鼻面に浮かぶ哀しみかな
¡Qué tristes son las narices de las mulas!

臍(へそ)から太陽までに小蜥蜴(とかげ)が顔をのぞかせている
Del ombligo al sol nos sale una lagartija

という2句[18]が混じっている。

松浦明編『大辞林　第三版』(三省堂、2006)によれば、俳諧は、以下のように説明されている。

「はいかい【俳諧・誹諧】〔たわむれ、おどけ、諧謔の意〕①〔「俳諧の連歌」の略。日本独自の短詩形文芸形式の一。「座(共同体)」の意識のもとに成立し、「滑稽」を本質とする文芸。発句・連句・前句付・俳文などより成る。室町末期の山崎宗鑑・荒木田守武らによる滑稽・卑俗な作風を受け、江戸時代に松永貞徳が出て独自なジャンルとして確立。談林俳諧を経て松尾芭蕉の蕉風に至って文学的に高められた。→俳句。

---

18) Ramón Gómez de la Serna‒*Antología cincuenta años de literatura,* Selección y prólogo de Guillermo de Torre, Buenos Aires : Editorial Losada, Espasa-Calpe Argentina, Editorial Poseidón, Emecé Editores, Editorial Sudamericana, 1955所収の「グレゲリーア理論」*Teoría de las greguerías* に付けられたラモンの自註によれば、〈プロメテウス〉創刊号の裏表紙に掲載された中にある2句のうちのひとつは、
　「臍(へそ)から太陽までに小蜥蜴(とかげ)が顔をのぞかせている」Del ombligo al sol nos sale una lagartija ではなく、「わが臍の上でひなたぼっこをしようと静けさが訪れるのを待つ美しい小蜥蜴かな」Qué hermosa lagartija espera el silencio en mi ombligo para tomar el sol だと述べている。
　この件に関しては、〈プロメテウス〉創刊号未見のために、真偽のほどは分からない。ただし、〈プロメテウス〉創刊号の発行年を1910年としているのは、ラモンの記憶違いだと思われる。1908年が正しい。

②「俳諧歌」の略」。

　ここでは、俳諧とは本来、〔たわむれ、おどけ、諧謔の意〕で、「滑稽」を本質とする文芸であるという点に注目したい。というのも、ゴメス・デ・ラ・セルナが言うグレゲリーアの〈諧謔＋隠喩＝グレゲリーア〉という定義と重なっている部分があるからである。そして、上記に挙げた二首には、軽妙さという点でじゅうぶん俳諧味が感じられるように思われるのだ。

　あるいは、前掲書の談林派の項目に、西山宗因を中心とした一派は、「奇抜な着想・見立てと軽妙な言い回しを特色とする」というくだりが見られるが、こちらの説明の方がぴったりするかもしれない。

　いずれにしても、ラモンのグレゲリーアとっては、「たわむれ、おどけ、諧謔」もしくは「滑稽」は不可欠な要素であることは間違いない。その意味では、どちらかというと、近代的な俳句ではなく、古風な江戸俳諧か、古川柳の流れを汲んでいるように見える点が、はなはだ興味深い。

　ゴメス・デ・ラ・セルナの「グレゲリーア理論」 *Teoría de las greguerías*[19] を読むと、松尾芭蕉や、蕉門十哲の第一の門弟、宝井其角の名前が唐突に登場するくだりがある。そこでは、其角が詠んだ「赤とんぼ羽をとったら唐がらし」という句に対して、芭蕉が「あまりにも残酷だ」と評して、「唐がらし羽を付けたら赤とんぼ」と「御仏の慈悲によって」朱を入れて返したという有名な逸話が紹介されている。

　じつは、この種本は、すでに取り上げたものだが、俳諧がフランスからヨーロッパ諸国に伝播するとき、大きなバネの役割を果たした、ポール＝ルイ・クーシューが書いた『俳諧　日本の抒情的なエピグラム』（1906）という論文にほかならない。

　フランスかぶれと言ってもいいラモンは、おそらくパリの詩人のあいだで評判

---

19) Ramón Gómez de la Serna – *Antología cincuenta años de literatura,* Selección y prólogo de Guillermo de Torre, Buenos Aires : Editorial Losada, Espasa-Calpe Argentina, Editorial Poseidón, Emecé Editores, Editorial Sudamericana, 1955, pp.124-158.

になっていた、この論文を通して芭蕉と其角のこぼれ話を知ったものと思われる[20]。とすると、彼が俳諧と出会った時期は、1906年以降ということになる。もちろん、ジョセップ・カルネーが、バルセロナの〈カタルーニャの声〉新聞に、いち早く発表した紹介記事や、アウジェニ・ドールスの人気コラム〈時事解説〉を読んだ可能性もなしとはしないけれど。

さらに、クーシューやカルネー、ドールスの論文や記事よりも早く、本格的な俳諧紹介をおこなった、バジル゠ホール・チェンバレンの「芭蕉と日本の詩的なエピグラム」(1902) を手に入れて読んだ可能性も排除できないであろう。

それはともかく、ここで、ラモン自身の言葉を借りれば、「グレゲリーアが何かの影響をうけているとすれば、俳諧の影響であろう。けれども、グレゲリーアは散文による俳諧なのだ（中略）。グレゲリーアの中では、東洋と西洋が抱擁し合っているのである」[21]ということになる。

それにもかかわらず、『サーカス』と『乳房（抄）』と同様、1917年に、ラモンが上梓した最初の『グレゲリーア（抄）』をひもとけば、俳諧というには長すぎる、四、五行から半頁に及ぶような作品が目につく。この版は、初期にあちこちの新聞や雑誌に発表したものを集成したものなので、まだ試作の段階にあり、まとまりに欠けていたせいに違いない。

---

20) 金子美都子『前掲書』に付された註釈（＊15、447頁）によれば、チェンバレン『日本口語案内』*A Hand-Book of Colloquial Japanese,* London : Trûbner Co. ; Tokyo : The Hakubunsha, 1884 には、

「芭蕉と其角が馬で街道を通っていた際に、赤とんぼを見て其角が詠んだ句を、芭蕉が〈あまりにも残酷だ〉と非難して添削したエピソードが紹介されている。〈赤とんぼ／羽をとったら／唐がらし〉〈唐がらし／羽を付けたら／赤とんぼ〉という2句がローマ字表記で記載されている。チェンバレンはこの句をさらに、論文『芭蕉と日本の詩的エピグラム』のなかに取り入れた。以来、これは、芭蕉の動物への優しさを表すエピソードとして、欧文俳句紹介書のなかに必ずと言ってよいほど採用され、誤伝されている。クーシェーも『俳諧　日本の抒情的なエピグラム』のなかで、〈起よ起よ我友にせんぬる胡蝶〉（芭蕉）の原注として取り上げているが、それがこの誤伝に関連するか否かは定かではない。この2句は其角の句でも芭蕉の句でもない。チェンバレンが『日本口語案内』に採録し解説している残りの2句は、千代女の〈朝顔に釣瓶とられてもらい水〉、芭蕉〈一声は月がないたかほととぎす〉（正しくは〈一声の江に横ふやほとゝぎす〉である）。

21) Ibid., *op. cit.,* p.136.

ちなみに、拙訳『グレゲリーア抄』（関西大学出版部）を見ていただければお分かりのように、ほとんどの作品が一行あれば事足りる長さまで凝縮されている。そればかりか、切れ味も鋭いものに変わっていることに気づかれるはずだ。1954年、ゴメス・デ・ラ・セルナが最後に出す『全グレゲリーア』 *Total de Greguerías* に至るまで、ひたすら俳諧の簡潔さをめざして、諧謔と隠喩の腕を磨いていった感がある。

　ギリェルモ・デ・トーレ（1900-71）といえば、アルゼンチンの作家ホルヘ・ルイス・ボルヘスの妹である画家ノラ・ボルヘスと結婚した、スペインの詩人で文芸批評家だが、彼は、ゴメス・デ・ラ・セルナのグレゲリーアについて、こう述べている。

　「グレゲリーアを発見して以来、ラモンが書く作品の大半は、グレゲリーアといえば語弊があるだろうけれど、グレゲリーアの精神に支配されていることはまぎれもない」[22]。その「グレゲリーアの精神」とはつまり、ラモン主義 Ramonismo ということになるが、「それは、結局のところ、ほかのジャンルを破壊するジャンルを意味している」[23]。

　言い換えれば、「散文による俳諧」の精神というか、ジャポニスムの精神が、ラモン・ゴメス・デ・ラ・セルナの文学を包みこんでいると言って差し支えないのである。その意味では、彼の文学はスペインやヒスパニック・アメリカ諸国のみならず、ヨーロッパ諸国にも類例を見ない、まことに貴重な存在と言わなければならない。

---

22) Guillermo de Torre - *Prólogo en op. cit.*, p.21.
23) Guillermo de Torre - *Prólogo en op. cit.*, p.21.

ニューヨークの詩人──ビセンテ・ウイドブロの映画／小説『魔術師の鏡』もしくは『カリオストロ』の成立

A Chilean Poet in New York : Vicente Huidobro's Itinerancy for the novel-film, *Mirror of a Mage* or *Cagliostro*

鼓 宗
Shu TSUZUMI

Abstract:

Vicente Huidobro (1893-1948), a candidate for the Nobel Prize for Literature (1926), visited New York in 1927 and stayed there until spring of the following year. In the metropolis of the United States, he received an award for best novel that could be made into a film ; the script was initially written in French in the early years of the 1920s, but after its failure to be realized as a film it was published in English as *Mirror of a Mage* (1931), and, finally, in Spanish (his mother language) as *Cagliostro* (1934). In the present article, we retrace the steps of this Chilean avant-garde poet in New York, and reveal the circumstances surrounding the publication of the novel, whose protagonist was a famous European magician of the 18th century.

Keywords:

Vicente Huidobro, *Cagliostro* (1934), *Mirror of a Mage* (1931), Latin-American literature, Chilean literature, Avant-garde literature, novel-film

1927年7月23日付のニューヨーク・タイムズ紙[1]に、「チリ人が映画賞を獲得」と題する記事が掲載された。ここにある「チリ人」とは、小見出しで「ウイドブロが映画化の可能性を持つ本へ送られる一万ドルを受賞」と示されているように、『四角い地平線』や『アルタソル』といった詩集で知られる詩人、ビセンテ・ウイドブロを指している。スペイン語圏の詩に前衛主義の息吹を吹き込んだウイドブロが、映画化を前提とした小説に与えられる賞を、映画にかける情熱のあふれる地、アメリカ合衆国で受賞したという事実はまことに興味深い。それはいったいどのような作品だったのだろうか。記事は出来事を次のように伝えている。

　　優良映画同盟[2]が、映画の原作となる可能性がもっとも高い今年の本に対して提供する一万ドルの受賞者として、昨日、チリの若い詩人・小説家、ビセンテ・ウイドブロの名前が発表された。いまだ原稿のままパリの出版業者の手に置かれたその本は『カリオストロ』と題されており、十八世紀の魔術師で人々によく知られた神秘主義者の生涯に基づいている。
　　賞はコンデ・ナスト・パブリケーションズ社のオフィスで授与されたが、リリアン・アタル嬢、ベネディクト・ダーロン、チャールズ・ノーマン[3]ら

---

1) 'Chilean gets Film Prize.' en 'New York Times', 23, July, 1927, p.11. 2011年にカテドラ社から出たガブリエーレ・モレッリによる注釈本の解題（Gabriele Morelli, 'Introducción' en Huidobro, Vicente, *Cagliostro*（2011）Madrid, Cátedra, p.13）では、「1927年6月23日付」とされているが、誤り。
2) League for Better Pictures　詳細は不明。*Picturegoer*. 19, May, 1920：568 や、The San Bernardino County Sun', 6, February, 1921, p.8 の記事などによれば、文学に対して悪徳弾圧協会 Society for the Suppression of Vice がすでにしていたのと同じことを行うのを目的に設立された団体であり、遅くとも1920年か1921年の頃には活動していた。映画の内容——ことに道徳に関わる問題——に干渉しようというこうした動きは、当時の映画界で繰り返された不祥事への反動だと思われる。もっとも大きな同種の組織として、アメリカ映画製作配給業者協会（MPPDA）、後のアメリカ映画協会 Motion Picture Association of America（MPAA）を挙げられるが、これは各映画会社が1922年に協同して設立したもので、映画に倫理的な制約を課そうというその意図は、1934年以降のヘイズ・コードによる検閲の実施に結びついた。
3) Chirles Norman（生没年不詳）アメリカ合衆国の詩人。e.e. カミングスやパウンドの評伝の作者でもある。後述するように、ウイドブロはその詩を高く評価した。

の審査員が列席。「ヴァニティ・フェア」誌の編集者、フランク・クラウニンシールド[4]が授与を行った。

連盟の書記であるアタル嬢は、賞を寄贈した四名の名前を明かすことはできないと告げた。彼女の言によれば、四人のうちの一人は最大級の映画製作会社の社長であり、「映画におけるその理想主義でもって知られている」という。

ウイドブロ氏はアメリカの飛行士たちの記念碑を建立するための基金に五万フランを寄贈すると発言した。氏の語るところでは、陸軍省次官補F・トゥルビー・デイヴィソン[5]とこの計画について協議することになっている。

主催者による受賞者の発表は式の前日に、つまり7月22日に行われたようだが、ウイドブロにはそれ以前の7月20日に受賞を知らせる書留郵便が届いていた。上の記事は作品の内容にはごくわずかしか触れておらず、それが十八世紀にヨーロッパをまたにかけて活躍した稀代の魔術師、カリオストロ[6]にまつわるも

4）Frank Crowninshield（1872-1947）アメリカ合衆国のジャーナリスト、批評家。
5）Frederick Trubee Davison（1896-1974）アメリカ合衆国の政治家。第一次世界大戦中はパイロットだったが、事故で負傷、引退した。
6）Conde Alessandro di Cagliostro（1743-95）伯爵を僭称した魔術師、錬金術師、治療師、フリーメイソン。その正体は、イタリアはシチリア島北西岸の街、パレルモ出身のジゼッペ・バルサモ Giuseppe Balsamo であるというのが定説となっている。自らの悪事のせいで故郷を追われてカイロやマディーナなど東方を放浪するうちに、魔術師アルタトスに邂逅、教えを請うたという。1768年、ローマで妻となるロレンツァ・フェリチアーニ Lorenza Feliciani と出会う。二人は巡礼者を装う詐欺を働き、途中、カザノヴァと接点を持つなどしながら、各地を転々とする。1776年、ロンドンに着いたバルサモは、伯父の爵位を騙るようになった。サン・ジェルマン伯爵に倣い、次第にオカルト的な雰囲気を身にまとっていく。1777年にフリーメイソンリーに入会するや、幹部の地位を手に入れる。東欧の小公国で降霊術によって得た信用を携えて、1779年、サンクトペテルブルクに到着。薔薇十字団員を名乗り、人々の治療を行うが、エカチェリーナ二世の不興を買う。翌年、ポーランドを経て、たどり着いたストラスブールでは、大コプトを自称し、ロアン枢機卿に取り入った。サロンの生活を享受していたカリオストロは、1785年、王妃マリー・アントワネットも巻き込んだスキャンダル、首飾り事件の容疑者として妻や枢機卿とともに逮捕された。翌年、三人には無罪判決が下り、夫妻はイギリスへと渡る。エジプト派フリーメイソンリーの活動や治療行為にいそしむが、新聞記者に正体を明かされて名声を失い、アルプス山麓まで逃げのびる。しかし、反カリオストロ派の攻勢はスイスまで及び、最↗

のであることだけを明かしている。

　それで十分だということだろう。誰が審査し、誰が賞金を渡したのか、記者はむしろ受賞の状況に限られた字数を割いている。授与を行ったクラウニンシールドは海軍提督や下院議員を世に送っているアメリカの名家の出身で、記事にもある通り「ヴァニティ・フェア」誌の名編集長として知られる。サッカレーの小説と同名のこの雑誌は、「ヴォーグ」（後に同誌を吸収する）や「ザ・ニューヨーカー」と並ぶコンデ・ナスト・パブリケーションズの看板雑誌であったが、クラウニンシールドの編集のもとで文学、美術、そして映画などの文化を幅広く扱い、部数を拡大していた[7]。

　最後に触れられている「飛行士たちの記念碑」の詳細は不明だが、この年の5月21日から22日にかけてチャールズ・リンドバーグが愛機スピリット・オブ・

↘　終的にローマに落ち着く。ところが、1789年、裏切った妻の告発により異端審問にかけられ、2年にわたる裁判の末、終身刑を言い渡された。カリオストロは、サン・レオ要塞の恐ろしい独房で52年の生涯を閉じる。
　　ウイドブロの描くカリオストロは、登場の時点ですでに稀代の魔術師であり、詐欺師バルサモの顔は一切のぞかせない。映画に基づく小説は、フランスだけを舞台に「嵐のなかの序奏」、「より高みへ」、「絶頂と闇（英語版では「絶頂にて」）」の三部からなり、モンタージュやクローズアップなど、映画的手法を凝らして構成されている。サン・ジェルマン伯爵率いる薔薇十字団への入団、貧しい人々に施す治療の奇跡、ストラスブールの社交界での成功、彼を憎む医者との毒薬を用いた決闘、警視総監の執拗な追跡、王子の横恋慕を成就させるために使われる妖術、催眠術をかけられた妻ロレンツァの操る幻視術、ロシアの大公父娘の危機からの救出、エジプト・ロッジの設立、アルタトスの試練、ヴェルサイユ宮でマリー・アントワネットに披露する降霊術、忠実なエジプト人召使に命じる暗殺、白魔術との対決、ロレンツァの悲劇的な自害など、実在のカリオストロにまつわる歴史的事件を独自の解釈で脚色しながら、伝説の魔術師の物語を仕立てている。
　　ウイドブロの企画以外にもカリオストロを題材にした映画は多数あり、サイレント映画の時代に公開されたものとして、*Le miroir de Cagliostro*（仏1899）、*Cagliostro, aventurier, chimiste et magicien*（仏1910）、*The Legend of Cagliostro*（仏1912）、*Cagliostros Totenhand*（独1919）、*Der Graf von Cagliostro*（オーストリア1920）、*Cagliostro/ Cagliostro – Liebe und Leben eines großen Abenteurers*（仏独1929）などが記録に残る。トーキー作品では、アレクサンドル・デュマ『王妃の首飾り』を原作とする、オーソン・ウェルズが主演した *Black Magic*（1949）がある。

7）「ヴァニティ・フェア」の1927年10月号に、ウイドブロも 'The Executioner of France. A Sketch of the Present Master of the Guillotine Who is Known by the Name of Monsieur de Paris' という記事を寄せている。主題から推して、『カリオストロ』の執筆に際しての成果だろう。

セントルイス号を駆って大西洋単独無着陸横断飛行を達成している。ウイドブロはこの快挙にいたく感動し、「リンドバーグに捧げる歌」[8]という詩編をものしている。おそらくそれと同じ動機から、飛行士たちへの慈善に駆り立てられたのだろう。

ところで、同日付の「ブルックリン・シチズン」紙[9]もウイドブロの受賞を「小説は映画に適す──一万ドルを受賞」の見出しで報じており、詩人が残した記事の切り抜きには、この時の様子を伝える写真が掲載されている[10]。そこには先述のウタルやクラウニンシールドと並んで、ニューヨークで発行されていた合衆国で最大規模のスペイン語紙「ラ・プレンサ」の共同発行者であり編集人であったホセ・M・トーレス＝ペローナ[11]が、小切手を手にした詩人を囲んで写っている。「ラ・プレンサ」は、すでに7月7日、汎アメリカ主義をめぐるウイドブロへのインタヴューを掲載していた。

続報もある。「チリの詩人・作家、ビセンテ・ウイドブロが受賞」と報じる「ニューヨーク・タイムズ」の1927年7月30日付の短信である。

　　チリの詩人であり作家であるビセンテ・ウイドブロは先週、著書『カリオストロ』により優良映画連盟が映画のシナリオにもっともふさわしい今年の書籍に提供する一万ドルの賞金を獲得したが、昨日、連盟が西40丁目のレ

---

8) 'Canto a Lindbergh' (1927). スペイン語で執筆され、その後、英語版が書かれたと思われる。当時は未刊行。後に詩誌 'Poesía' 30-31-32 (1988-1989) pp.256-258 に、現存する英語版からのスペイン語訳が収載される。
9) *The Brooklyn Citizen* (1886-1947) ニューヨークで発行された日刊紙。
10) Morelli, G., 'Introducción' en Huidobro, V., *Cagliostro* (2011), p.13, p.15.
11) スペイン内戦が開始して間もない時期にペルーのメキシコ大使館が、トーレス・ペローナはフランコ派の活動家であり、スペインのファシズム勢力のためにニューヨークの「ラ・プレンサ」の他、リマの「ラ・プレンサ」、メキシコの「エクセルシオル」、ハバナの「ディアリオ・デ・マニャーナ」を買収する任を負っているものと見なしていたとする記録が残っている。('Archivo de la Secretaría de Relaciones Exteriores, México. Carta del embajador mexicano en Lima, Sr. Sáenz, a la Secretaría de RR. EE. 8 de diciembre de 1936. Carta de Francisco Castillo Nájera, Washington, a Eduardo Hay, 25 de enero de 1939' en Geroid Gino Baumann, *Los voluntarios latinoamericanos en la guerra civil española*, (2009) Cuenca, la Universidad de Castilla−La Mancha, p.151)

ストラン・ボザールで催した午餐会の主賓となった。会の同席者には、映画女優のリア・デ・プッティ[12]やチリの副領事アカリオ・コタポス[13]がいた。

ビセンテ・ウイドブロ財団に、この食事会の時のものと思われる一枚の写真が保管されている。写真家ハロルド・ステイン[14]が撮影したそれのなかでは、ウイドブロは五人の美女たち——くだんのリア・デ・プッティ。1926 年のミス・アメリカ、ノルマ・スモールウッド。1926 年と 1927 年のミス・フランス、ロベルト・キュ。当時の著名なダンサー、トムリス。「ニューヨークのヴィーナス」の異名を取ったジャクリーヌ・ローガン[15]——に囲まれて座っている。

白い立派なソファ。少し椅子の左に寄っているのだろうか、右のひじ掛けはフレームの外だが、詩人はその真ん中を占めていて、左隣のリア・デ・プッティの手を取って視線を交わしている。彼女が親しげに、しかし慎ましやかに微笑んでいるのに対して表情が若干固くも見える。女優が寄せかけるそろえた足から身を引いているようでもあるが、かえって横顔に笑みを浮かべたスモールウッドに密着してしまっている。頭の上まであるソファーの背もたれの後に立つ三人の女たちは、向かって左側からローガン、キュ、トムリス。女優の二人はカメラに目線を送っていて撮影に慣れた様子がうかがえるが、トムリスは下を向いてしまっている。いずれにしても後列の三人はウイドブロを見ていない。女性たち全員が、

---

12) Lya De Putti（1897-1931）ハンガリー出身の女優。サイレント時代の映画で運命の女（ファム・ファタール）を主に演じた。作品に『サタンの嘆き』（1926）、『深夜の薔薇』（28）など。
13) Acario Cotapos（1889-1969）チリの作曲家。ウイドブロと同じ 1916 年にチリを出国、37 年に帰国するまでの二十余年をアメリカ合衆国、フランス、スペインで過ごした。ピカソ、ストラヴィンスキー、ファリャ、オネゲル、メシアン、コープランドら、多数の芸術家たちと交流。この年、ヴァレーズとともに国際作曲家組合を創設している。
14) Harold Stein（1902-66）アメリカ合衆国の写真家。映画やラジオ・スターを主な被写体にした。
15) Norma Smallwood（1909-66）、Roberte Cusey（生没年不詳）、Tomris（生没年不詳）、Jacqueline Logan（1901-1983）。リア・デ・プッティ以外の人物の同定は、ウイドブロ博物館の年表 http://www.museovicentehuidobro.cl/en/linea-de-tiempo/（2016 年 8 月 31 日確認）とそれぞれの女優たちの写真による。

頭にはそれぞれ違ったスタイルの帽子を載せており、おしゃれに余念がない。様々な著名人との交流があったウイドブロの肖像でも、おそらくもっとも華やかな一枚となっている。

　詩人がリア・デ・プッティの手を取っている写真は、クローズアップされて、「リアの手を勝ち取る」の見出しとともに、これも7月30日付けの「モーニング・テレグラフ」紙に載っている。「リア・デ・プッティが向けるまばゆいばかりの称賛のまなざしに比べれば、優良映画連盟のシナリオ・コンクールで得た一万ドルもささやかなものだ、と王家の侯爵[16]は思っているに違いない」とのキャプションが下についている[17]。

　ニューヨークにおける映画人たちとの交流は、優良映画連盟の受賞式をめぐるものばかりではなかった。アメリカ合衆国の映画関係者を紹介したのはもっぱら、アメリカ合衆国に帰化したばかりのエドガー・ヴァレーズ[18]であった。このパリ出身の作曲家は1921年に「捧げもの」[19]（オフランド）――ニューヨークとボストンのC・C・バーチャード社から出版されたその楽譜を、この機会にチリからの客人に贈っている――で、ウイドブロの詩編「天上の歌」[20]にソプラノとオーケストラのための曲を付けており、二人は旧知の仲であった。そのような経緯からヴァレーズは、チャールズ・チャップリン[21]やグロリア・スワンソンといった名優たちに

---

16) ウイドブロのこと。家系に因んで、このように呼んでいる。
17) 'Poesía' 30-31-32（1988-1989）p.251.
18) Edgar Varèse（1883-1965）フランス出身のアメリカ合衆国の作曲家。アレーホ・カルペンティエル、ミゲル・アストゥリアス、ホセ・フアン・タブラダ、カルロス・チャベスといったラテンアメリカ出身の作家・詩人・作曲家たちと、あるいはキューバの血を引くフランス人作家アナイス・ニンとも交流があった。
19) Offrandes は7分ほどのオーケストラ作品で、もう一編、メキシコの詩人フアン・タブラダの詩編「南十字星」La Croix du Sud が取り上げられている。
20) 'Chanson de là-haut' は、ロベール・ドローネーの絵を表紙にあしらい、1918年にマドリードで出版された詩集『エッフェル塔』Tour Eiffel（1918）Madrid, Imprenta Pueyo の第36行から第50行を抜粋したもの。
21) ウイドブロは好きな映画スターとして、チャップリンの他に、マルクス兄弟やハリー・ラングドンの名前を挙げており、彼らについて記事も書いている。'Harry Langdon' en 'Feuilles Volantes' 1（París, 1 juin 1928）, p.14 ; 'El hombre y el ángel Chaplin' en 'Crítica'（Buenos Aires, 13 de agosto 1936）recogido en Huidobro, V., Montes, Hugo (ed.), *Obras Completas I*,（1976）Santiago de Chile, Andres Bello, p.900.

詩人を紹介する労を取った。1934年に発表される近未来小説『来るべきもの（近い未来に起こった物語）』[22]でウイドブロは、主人公がアフリカに築いたユートピアに喜劇王を移住させ、そこに建設されたハリウッドにも比肩する映画都市にチャプリニアの名前を冠している。また彼の所有する全盛期のスワンソンのブロマイドには、女優の直筆で「ビセンテ・ウイドブロに。いつかスペインに行けますように。心をこめて。グロリアより……」[23]と書かれている。

なおウイドブロのブロマイドのコレクションには、グレタ・ガルボが写るものも見つかる。7月23日というと、先の受賞の記事が掲載された日だが、その日にウイドブロはスウェーデン出身の女優と食事をしている。この時、ガルボがニューヨークに移り住んでまだ二年ほどに過ぎなかったが、前年に公開された『肉体の悪魔』が彼女の演技への評価を確かなものにしていた。詩人の備忘録に残されたメモには、同じ月の8日と18日にもガルボに会ったという記録が残っている。とにかく受賞によって、ウイドブロは多忙をきわめたに違いない。7月28日には、ジャクリーヌ・ローガン[24]——グリフィスを上回る予算を与えられてセシル・デミルが監督したこの年の話題作『キング・オブ・キングス』に出演していた——とも会見している。

さて、ダグラス・フェアバンクス[25]との再会の場を設けたのもヴァレーズであった。ウイドブロは、監督やプロデューサーとしても活躍していたこの高名な俳優の知遇を過去に得ていた。というのも、1926年、フェアバンクスが妻のメアリー・ピックフォード[26]を連れてヨーロッパへ旅行した際に、映画の題材として、スペインのレコンキスタ時代の英雄、ロドリゴ・ディアス・デ・ビバル[27]を

---

22) Huidobro, V., *La próxima*（*Historia que pasó en poco tiempo más*）（1934）Santiago de Chile, Walton.
23) César Antonio Molina, *En honor de Hermes*（2006）Madrid, Huerga y Fierro. p.480.
24) Jacqueline Logan（1901-83）アメリカ合衆国の女優。
25) Douglas Fairbanks（1883-1939）アメリカ合衆国の俳優。ピックフォード、チャップリン、グリフィスらと映画製作会社ユナイテッド・アーティスツを創設した。息子ダグラス・フェアバンクス・ジュニアも著名な俳優。
26) Mary Pickford（1982-1979）カナダ出身の女優。
27) Rodrigo Díaz de Vivar（1043頃-1099）カスティリャ王国の貴族。イスラム教徒たち↗

取材してほしいという依頼を受けていたのである[28]。この時の話題もそれに関連していたはずだ。結局、フェアバンクスの企画は実現しないまま終わり、同主題の映画化は、サミュエル・ブロンストン[29]による1961年の大作、アンソニー・マン監督、チャールトン・ヘストン、ソフィア・ローレン主演の『エル・シド』を待つことになる。

一方、ウイドブロ自身、ロドリゴの物語に熱中し、ホセ・ソリーリャの『シドの伝説』[30]をはじめとして様々な資料の収集に努めた。その成果は、1929年に小説『わがシド・カンペアドル（武勲）』[31]として結実する。この作品を構想するに当たってフェアバンクスの依頼が寄与するところが大きかったことは、著者自らが認めており、謝意を表するためにその名前を記す、と巻頭に載せた「ダグラス・フェアバンクスへの手紙」で述べている[32]。

ただし、ウイドブロがロドリゴに執心したわけはそれだけではない。実はニューヨークでしばらく暮らすことになった理由の一つでもあるのだが、18歳年下の少女、ヒメーナ・アムナテギとの禁断の恋愛が背景にあった。

先にそのいきさつに触れておくと、ウイドブロは1912年にマヌエラ・ポルタレス・ベリョと結婚し、四人の子供をもうけていたが、1926年、チリ大学の学長や国務大臣を歴任したドミンゴ・アムナテギの娘、ヒメーナと知り合う。ウイドブロが33歳であったのに対して、彼女は15歳。しかも、兄弟の姻族であった。周囲は当然のこと、この交際に猛烈な反対をし、勘当騒ぎにまでなった。アムナテギ家は、娘の忌まわしい誘惑者に死の脅しをかけた。身の危険を察したウ

↘ からエル・シド・カンペアドル（勇敢なる主君）の異名を取った。現存するスペイン最古の叙事詩『エル・シード』（1207頃）をはじめ、ピエール・コルネイユの『ル・シッド』（1637）など、いくつかの文学作品の題材になっている。

28) ウイドブロはこれをパリのオテル・ド・クリヨンでのことだとしている。'Carta a Mr. Douglas Fairbanks' en Huidobro, V., *Mio Cid Campeador (Hazaña)*, (1929) Madrid, Compañía Iberoamericana de Publicaciones, p.7.
29) Samuel Bronston（1908-1994）アメリカ合衆国の映画製作者。他に『北京の五十五日』（1953）や『ローマ帝国の滅亡』（64）のような大作を手がけた。
30) Zorrilla, José, *La leyenda del Cid* (1882) Barcelona, Montaner i Simon.
31) Huidodbro, V. (1929).
32) ibid., p.7.

イドブロは汽船でヨーロッパに逃れる。9月には、長く暮らしたパリの住まいも引き払った。そして翌1927年に家族と別れた後、新天地をニューヨークに求めたのである[33]。ヒメーナとは、1928年の帰国後に誘拐同然に家から連れ出して、自動車でアンデス越えをした後、ブエノス・アイレスから船でパリへ旅立っている。

　話をロドリゴへの情熱に戻すと、このカスティリャの貴族が王の暗殺に加担した疑いで郷里ブルゴスを追われた時、残していった妻の名前がヒメーナで、それは映画『エル・シド』ではローレンが演じたシメンに当たるが、ウイドブロが心を奪われた少女の名前と同じであった。そこから中世の武将に深い因縁をおぼえたウイドブロは、この方面の権威である碩学、メネンデス・ピダル[34]に手紙を書き、自身の家系がブルゴスの貴族につながること、それがアルフォンソ十世の遠縁であることを、さらにこの賢王がロドリゴの末裔であったことを認めてもらった[35]。

　最初にスペイン語で発表された『わがシド・カンペアドル（武勲）』は、『戦士の肖像(パラディン)』[36]の題名で英語版が、1931年にイギリスで、翌年にはアメリカ合衆国で出版された。改題の理由は、シド・カンペアドルというロドリゴの通り名が、英語圏では、スペインでそうであるようには誰もが知るものでなかったせいだろう。それまでに若書きの短編こそ発表していたものの、これはウイドブロにとって初の小説であった。現代の読者の感覚に訴えかけるために、時間と空間を自由に切り重ねた構成など、前衛的な手法が取り入れられており、中世の武人の

---

33) 前年、渡欧に際して寄港したハバナでのインタヴューで、パリにしばらく滞在した後、ニューヨークとハリウッドに行くつもりだ、と語っている。Cecilia García-Huidobro McA., *Vicente Huidobro a la intemperie* (2000) Santiago de Chile, Sudamericana, p.73.
34) Ramón Menéndez Pidal (1869-1968) スペインの文学史家、言語学者、歴史家。『わがシドの歌——文献、文法、語彙』(1910) や『エル・シドのスペイン』(29) などの著作がある。
35) de Costa, René, *Huidobro: Los oficios de un poeta* (1984), Ciudad de México, Tierra Firme, pp.162-163.
36) Huidobro, V (autor). Warre B. Wells (trad.) *Portrait of a Paladin* (1931) London, Eyre and Spottiswoode ; (1932) New York, Horace Liverwright.

伝記をただ単に同時代の言語で語りなおしただけの作品にとどまっていない。著者は序において、ロマンセのような過去の詩形をもってでもなければ、詩人たちが書く「小説家の小説」としてでもなく、真正な「詩人の小説」として、真実のロドリゴを描くべく物語を再創造したと自負をもって語っている。

　さてヴァレーズはウイドブロの献身的な友人で、フェアバンクスとの対面の機会を設けただけでなく、往時の名優ジョン・バリモア[37]に手紙を書いて、ウイドブロの『ジル・ド・レ』を下敷きにした映画を撮影し、その主役を務めるように勧めている[38]。原稿は、1925年から1926年にかけて執筆されてたものだった。ジル・ド・レは、十五世紀に実在したフランスの貴族だが、その残虐な性癖から、シャルル・ペローが「青髭」に仕立てている。この「青髭」に対するウイドブロの関心は、どこから生まれたのか。十九世紀の末には、J・K・ユイスマンスが『彼方』(1891)で、少年殺しというジル・ド・レの忌むべき所業に中世の暗黒面を見出していた。またバルトークの『青ひげ公の城』(1911)やポール・デュカスの『アリアーヌと青髭』(1907)といったオペラの公演について見聞する機会が、パリにいたウイドブロにはあったかもしれない。それとも、ジャンヌ・ダルクについての伝説のなかから、その盟友としてのジル・ド・レにたどり着いたのだろうか。その場合には、ジュール・ミシュレの『ジャンヌ・ダルク』(1841)、あるいはアナトール・フランスの『ジャンヌ・ダルクの生涯』(1908)やバーナード・ショーの『聖女ジャンヌ・ダルク』(1923)などが詩人に霊感をもたらした可能性が考えられる。

　ヴァレーズの熱意にもかかわらず、この『ジル・ド・レ』も映画化にはいたらなかったが、1932年になって戯曲として日の目を見た[39]。さらに全編ではない

---

37) John Barrymore (1882-1942) アメリカ合衆国の俳優。舞台ではハムレット役が高評を得た。映画の出演作に『ドン・ファン』(1926)や『グランド・ホテル』(32)がある。
38) 3月13日付けのその手紙のなかでヴァレーズは、ウイドブロが「パリから着いたばかりで、二、三週間を当地で過ごす予定だ」だとしている。'Poesía' 30-31-32 (1988-1989) p.316.
39) ウイドブロにとって最初の戯曲ではなかった。1913年5月にサンティアゴのバレ ↗

がその一部が、翌年の 4 月 10 日にパリのウーヴル劇場で上演された。パリで出た初版[40]には、ピカソによる著者の肖像の他、シュルレアリスムの画家、ジョゼフ・シマ[41]の挿画があしらわれている。実験的性格を帯びた作品で、アンリ・ベアールが『ダダ・シュルレアリスム演劇史』[42]で同作を取り上げている[43]。青髭の猟奇的行為への恐怖よりも前に、その心理の描写にウイドブロの関心があり、それはまさに処刑台の上での主人公の贖罪の場面に顕著に現れている。

ニューヨークでの再会と言えば、第一次世界大戦中に救護車両の運転手を務め、その後、パリで放蕩生活を送ったマルカム・カウリー[44]とも邂逅を果たしている。ウイドブロはこの時期のあるインタヴュー[45]で、彼と、e・e・カミングズ、チャールズ・ノーマンの三人をアメリカ合衆国で知った、もっとも新しく、もっとも力量のある詩人だとしている。インタヴューは 9 月 30 日に行われており、1927 年 10 月の「シグサグ」誌に掲載されたが、そのなかに、サンティアゴ・デ・チレに「ニューヨークから到着したばかり」というくだりがある。密かに一時帰国したのだろうか。

摩天楼がそびえる都市の印象を問われて、ウイドブロは、そこに暮らす「途方もない想像力を秘めた」同国人の作曲家アカリオ・コタポスと、ブラック・ボトム、キンカジュー、ナンブルといったダンス[46]を挙げている。次いでインタヴュアーは「映画の偉大な中心」での生活がどのようなものか尋ねているが、答え

↘ ース・シアターで、ガブリ・リバスとの共作『愛が去りゆくとき』 *Cuando el amor se vaya* が上演されている。
40) Huidobro, V., *Gilles de Raiz*（1932）Paris, Totem.
41) Joseph Sima（1891-1971）チェコ出身のシュルレアリスムの画家。
42) Béhar, Henri, *Étude sur le théâtre dada et surréaliste*（1967）París Gallimar, pp.275-280.
43) Langowski, Gerald J., *El surrealismo en la ficción hispanoamericana*,（1982）Madrid, Gredos, p.25.
44) Malcolm Cowley,（1898-1989）アメリカ合衆国の批評家、詩人、編集者。『失われた世代』のひとりであり、『亡命者帰る』（1934、51 改訂）で同世代の文学者たちの二〇年代の活躍を記録した。
45) 'Vicente Huidobro' en 'Zig-zag'（Santiago de Chile, Nº1184, 29 octubre 1927）en Cecilia García-Huidobro McA.（2000）, pp.78-81.
46) それぞれ、the black bottom、el kiu[n]kajou、el Nambul と呼んでいる。

は、皆が想像するほど、映画に関わる人々が常日頃から愉快な時間を過ごしているわけではなく、仕事に追われているというもので、われわれの関心を引くようなことは出てこない。さらに質問はニューヨークの離婚の状況に及ぶが、これはウイドブロの私的な結婚生活の危機を念頭に置いてなされたものだろう。

　いつ『カリオストロ』の映画の撮影に入るのかという最後の質問にウイドブロは、二、三ヶ月のうちには、と答えている。そして、自身の意見が取り入れられないにしても、撮影現場には居合わせたいと希望を述べている。一見、謙虚な姿勢に思えるが、小説は作家のものであり、映画は監督のものだから、それは当然のことだと割り切っておきながら、最後になって、同時にその両方になれることを忘れてはならない、と付け加えている。そうなれば、相談を受ける十分な資格が自分にはあるだろうと。この時点でウイドブロが、ニューヨークに戻り、映画の製作に積極的に関わる意欲にあふれていたことがうかがえる。

　ウイドブロの快挙をチリに伝える報道は、「シグサグ」の記事以前、受賞の時点でもなされていた。セバスティアン・ダクスという署名のある記事がそれで[47]、「昨日のニュースの網の釣果は、アメリカ合衆国で優良映画同盟の賞を獲得したわが国の詩人、ビセンテ・ウイドブロの名前であった」と始まる。次いで「預言者郷里に容れられず」[48]ということわざを引いて、チリでは多くの才能ある芸術家が埋没してしまっていると嘆き、ウイドブロがチリ社会で常にスケープゴートにされてきたことを指摘する。しかし、スペインでは、1921年の彼のマドリード訪問が、かの地で強い影響力を持つ作家カンシノス＝アッセンスによってその年のもっとも重要な出来事とされたこと[49]、さらに、当時すでに頭角を現し

---

47) Morelli, G., 'Introducción' en Huidobro, V., *Cagliostro* (2011), p.19. 切り抜きであるため、新聞紙名と発行日が確認できない。記事の末尾に、下に切り残された次の記事の見出しか、A.J.C.F. という略号が見つかる。チリでは1921年に設立された Asociacion de la Juventud Católica Femenina（カトリック女子連合会）のことか。
48) 新約聖書ルカ福音書4章24節にある言葉。たとえば、ウイドブロ自身が、自分の作品がフランス語詩のアンソロジーに収載されただけで、非国民のレッテルを貼られてしまうと嘆いている。Rojas Giménez, Alberto, *Chilenos en París* (1930) Santiago de Chile, la Novela Nueva, p.13.
49) ウイドブロはそれ以前にもマドリードを訪れていたが、1921年4月にはこの街で ↗

ていた、後の「二七年代の世代」の詩人の一人、ヘラルド・ディエーゴがウイドブロに心酔していることを挙げて、その才能を擁護している。そして、肝心の映画賞の受賞については、次のように述べている。

　　昨日のニュースは、知性の世界選手権における勝利を示している。ウイドブロはその才能をもって、アメリカの巨万の富から一万ドルを掠め取った。おそらく、キンティン・ロメーロ[50]と彼だけが、巨人からドルを稼げるチリ人である。誰もいないよりもましだ。エル・テニエンテとチュキカマタ[51]のささやかな代償である。(一文不明)。熟達の詩人に勝利を与えた作品は『カリオストロ』と題されている。おそらくは、そのプロテウス的人物――人間が生んだもっとも突飛な人々のひとり――の冒険譚である。『赤道』[52]の著者の芸術的気質を理解していれば、われわれは、それが洗練された、劇作法を極限まで集成したものとなるのを信じられる。もう5年ほど前になるだろうか、モンマルトルの小劇場で演じられた『サッカー』と題されたロシア・バレエで見せたように[53]。そして、もっとも愉快なことだが、いつの日にかわが国のいくつもの劇場で、受賞した映画『カリオストロ』が、われわれの忘恩の悲しむべき証拠が見られるだろう、そしてこの映画は、わが国の鉱山が

　'Creación'(「創造」)誌を創刊し、12月に文芸協会で'Estética moderna'(「現代美学」)と題した講演を行った。
50) Quintín Romero Rojas (1896-1972) サンティアゴ・デ・チレ出身のボクサー。南米のヘヴィー級のタイトルを獲得したが、アメリカ合衆国では全盛期にタイトルマッチの機会を与えられなかった。
51) エル・テニエンテ El Teniente もチュキカマタ Chuquicamata のいずれも、チリにある世界有数の銅山。後者は原文で Chuqiacmata と誤ってつづられている。
52) *Ecuatorial* (1918) ウイドブロの詩集。第一次世界大戦がもたらした黙示録的なイメージをキュビスムの手法を用いて表現した長詩。
53) 記事では、上演されたかのように記されているが、誤り。当時、マドリードにいたウイドブロは、セルゲイ・ディアギレフのロシア・バレエ団のために台本を執筆するはずだったが、途中で妹メルセデス Mercedes と詩人ディエーゴ・ドゥプレ・ウルティア Diego Dublé Urrutia の結婚式に出席するためにチリに帰国してしまう。そのため作品は未完に終わった。ストラヴィンスキーが音楽を、ロベール・ドローネーが舞台装置を担当するはずだった。

産出する銅で作られた鍋や針金のごときものになるのだろう。つまりそれは、正当な対価が支払われることなく原料のままここから出て行くが、製品となってれわれわれのもとに戻ってくる時には正当な対価を支払わなくてはならないということだ。

　ジュネーヴにおけるアラウ[54]の、そしてアメリカ合衆国におけるウイドブロの勝利は、われわれを喜ばせると同時に憂鬱にする。

　このダクスの記事は、『カリオストロ』のニューヨークでの受賞を祝福するというよりも、チリにおいてウイドブロの支持者と敵対者のあいだの激しい舌戦に投じられた一石といった色彩が濃い。作品そのものへの関心はさして強く感じられず、代わって鮮明になるのは、ウイドブロが母国で置かれていた微妙な立場である。映画がまだ撮影されておらず、受賞したシナリオに関して何も手がかりがないことを考慮すれば、それは仕方のないことだろうか。

　いずれにせよ、ここまでに取り上げてきた新聞の掲載記事や1927年のニューヨークにおける行動は、ウイドブロが実際にアメリカの映画産業に近いところに身を置いたこと、映画『カリオストロ』が実現の可能性を与えられたことを客観的に示している。しかし、一万ドルという高額の賞金を与えられたそのシナリオは、結局、一本のフィルムとして完成しなかった。アメリカ合衆国で撮影された『カリオストロ』がチリの映画館で封切られる、というダクスの期待は裏切られる。

　映画の企画が頓挫するのは珍しいことではない。しかし、『カリオストロ』の場合には、制作側ではどうにもならない事情があった。最初のトーキー作品となるアル・ジョルスン主演の『ジャズ・シンガー』が、同じ年の10月に公開されたのである。映画史に刻まれたこの出来事の詳細は、ここに繰り返すまでもない

---

54) Claudio Arrau León（1903-1991）チリ出身のピアニスト。多彩な受賞歴を誇るが、記事が書かれた1927年にはジュネーヴで開催された国際ピアノ・コンクールで優勝している。

だろう。さらに映画のサイレントからトーキーへの移行は、ウォルト・ディズニーの『蒸気船ウィリー』（1928）における、フィルムに音声を直接載せるサウンドトラックの導入によって決定的となる。

　1928年から1930年にかけて音声のない映画は徐々に、しかし逆らえない強い流れで、過去の娯楽として駆逐されていく。ことにアメリカの映画産業——ニューヨークからハリウッドへと拠点を移していく——においてその動きは顕著であった。そうした時代の奔流にもてあそばれるようにして、少なからぬ企画が『カリオストロ』と同様、お蔵入りしたり、大幅な見直しを求められたりしたに違いない。その事情やその後の成り行きは様々であっただろう。企画としてそのまま倒れてしまうものもあれば、あるいはトーキー用に脚色されてよみがえった幸運な作品もあったのかもしれない。

　ウイドブロの『カリオストロ』の場合にはどうか。映画化の頓挫したシナリオは、後年、小説としてよみがえる。1931年には英語で執筆された『魔術師の鏡』が、そして、1934年にはスペイン語による『カリオストロ』が出版されるのである[55]。しかし、この二つの版の小説を取り上げる前に、映画シナリオとしての『カリオストロ』について今しばらく話を続けたい。というのも、ニューヨークで受賞したシナリオはいきなり優良映画連盟に送られたものではなく、その前史を持つからだ。まず、1921年から1922年にかけて、いくつかの「先鋭的な」雑誌[56]でデクパージュ（コンテ）が断片的に発表されていたことが、小説の英語版とスペイン語版の両方の序章で明らかにされている。ただし、ウイドブロは複数あるとするその掲載誌の誌名を記していない。だが少なくとも、この時期のシナリオの存在は確認されており、フランス語によるタイプ原稿が、さらには、その

---

[55] 英語版は、Huidobro, V.（autor）, Warre B. Wells（trad.）*Mirror of a Mage*.（1931）New York, Boston, Houghton Mifflin、および Huidobro, V.（autor）, Warre B. Wells（trad.）*Mirror of a Mage*（1931）London, Eyre and Spottiswoode。スペイン語版は Huidobro, V., *Cagliostro*（*Novela-film*）（1934）Zig-Zag, Santiago de Chile。

[56] "This book was first published fragmentarily in "advanced" reviews in 1921 and 1922." と記すだけで、デクパージュを掲載した誌名を挙げていない。Huidobro, Vicente, *Mirror of a Mage*（1931）Boston ; New York, Houghton Mifflin, p.20.

シナリオを発展させた、これもフランス語で執筆された「映画的小説」[57]が残されており、チリのビセンテ・ウイドブロ財団がそれらを保管している。

では、シナリオが存在したとして、その撮影は実際に行われたのだろうか。ウイドブロは、そのシナリオに基づいて映画が過去に製作されていたと述べている。それは1921年から翌年にかけてのことで、つまり、デクパージュが一連の雑誌に掲載されたとされる時期に並行している。

この「秘密裏に行われていた」映画の製作は、1923年4月4日に「出版情報」で「ウイドブロ氏が、人々を驚かすであろう映画を密かに準備している」と、4月28日の「パリ・ジャーナル」では「観客の習慣を革新するであろうキュビスムの映画を撮影している」と報じられている[58]。また「詩人たちと映画」と題する「新時代」紙の記事[59]は、彼が映画『カリオストロ』のシナリオを完成させたと、そのなかでは映画的行為が「光学的かつ動的な」リズムでもって視覚化されると伝えている。これらの報道は、自己顕示欲の強いウイドブロの性格を考えた時、あるいは意図的に情報を流したものかもしれないが[60]、映画の製作が具体的に進んでいたことを十分に示している。

さらにフアン・ラレーアが1924年6月7日にウイドブロに送った書簡は、それを補強する。ラレーアはスペインの詩人で、一時期、ディエーゴとともにウイドブロの詩学クレアシオニスムに傾倒した。この書簡でも、ウイドブロに厚い信

---

57) novela-fílmica。『魔術師の鏡』の序文では、映画の文学への影響について論じて、その技法を応用していることをうたっているが、この語に相当する表現は用いていない。『カリオストロ』では、novela-film と、映画が形容詞ではなく小説と対等な関係にあることを示すかたちに表記を変更している。

58) 'Argus de la presse' および 'Paris-Journal'。Costa, René de, *Huidobro: Los oficios de un poeta* (1984) Ciudad de México, Fondo de Cultura Económica. p.173 ; Morelli, G., 'Introducción' en Huidobro, V. (2011) p.12.

59) 'Les poètes et le cinéma' en 'L'Ere Nouvelle', París, 6 de mayo de 1923. Costa, R. de (1984), p.173.

60) パリの日刊紙 'L'Intransigeant' の批評家に3月27日付で、アナトール・フランスやブラスコ・イバニェスといった著名な作家たちからも高評を得ているとして、製作中の映画を記事にしてもらえるように手紙を送っている。Morelli, G., 'Introducción' en Huidobro, V., *Cagliostro* (2011), p.12.

頼を寄せていることを明かし、彼を頼ってパリに一年でも二年でも行ってみたいと訴えている。オリンピックのサッカーのこと、おそらく『わがシド・カンペアドル』に関連するものだが、フランシスコ・ガルシア・デ・ウイドブロ[61]に連なる系図調査についてのことなどを書き連ねた後、ラレーアは「パテ社[62]のスタジオで、あなたが映画を監督していると聞いた」と記している[63]。この証言には作品の製作会社が明示されており、さらにそれが映画創業期に設立されて同産業における一大帝国を築いたパテ社であることは、『カリオストロ』の映画が撮影されたという主張に信憑性を与えている。

　それでは、撮影の話自体が虚言でなければ、ほぼ完成していたはずの映画が公開されなかった理由は、いったい何だったのだろうか。ミメ・ミズ[64]は、1923年に制作されたと思しい映画『カリオストロ』の監督を務めたとされる人物だが、「ウイドブロ氏の映画『カリオストロ』のデクパージュが、ミズ氏の意見に反して書かれたものであることを宣する」という覚書がウイドブロの残した文書のなかに見つかっている[65]。1923年6月14日の日付のある文書の末尾には、二人の芸術家が署名している。この書類は映画の撮影が進行していたことを裏付け

---

61) Francisco García de Huidobro（1697-1773）スペインの金融家。1743年、フェリーペ五世の勅命を受けてチリ造幣局を創設した。その功績により、初代のマルケス・デ・カサ・レアル（「王家の侯爵」の意）の爵位を授かった。注16で触れたように、ビセンテ自身がこの称号で呼ばれることがある。
62) Pathé-Cinema は、Compagnie Générale des Etablissements Pathé Frères Phonographes & Cinématographes の映画製作部門。シャルル Charles、エミール Émile、テオフィル Théophile、ジャック Jacque の四兄弟が1896年に設立した Société Pathé Frères が発展したもの。映画製作の他、配給、映画館運営、撮影機材やフィルムの製作販売なども手がけ、同社の活動はヨーロッパだけではなく大西洋の対岸にまで及んだが、第一次世界大戦の影響を受けて、イギリスやアメリカ合衆国の支部は多くが現地資本に譲渡された。
63) Huidobro, V., Morelli, Gabriele（ed.）. *Epistolario : Correspondencia con Gerardo Diego, Juan Larrea y Guillermo de Torre : 1918-1947*（2008）Madirid, Residencia de Estudiantes. p.176.
64) Mime Mizu（1888-1953）ルーマニア出身。詳細は不明だが、ドキュメンタリー映画 *Balul "Rampei"*（1922）を撮影したという記録がある。
65) Costa, R. de（1984）, p.173. 'Poesía' 30-31-32（1988-1989）, p.215 に、この文書の写真が載る。

ると同時に、原作者と監督の関係の破綻を意味している。それは、パリで撮影された『カリオストロ』が完成に近づきながらも公開されなかった理由をしっかりと説明するようにも思われる。

　このミメ・ミズとの映画がお蔵入りになったあとのことか、別の機会にウイドブロ本人は、異なる名前を映画の演出家として挙げている。アルベルト・ロハス・ヒメネス[66]は、1930年に唯一の著書となる『パリのチリ人たち』[67]を出したが、その冒頭に、1924年にまとめられたウイドブロとの対話が載る。まずはヨーロッパ各地で行われる講演や、イギリスの帝国主義を糾弾する『フィニス・ブリタニア』[68]が理由と思われるが、詩人が被害者となった最近の誘拐事件が話題になる。その後、ウイドブロが、映画の撮影で多忙であると近況を語り出す。チリでは誰も知らないだろうし、パリでも最新のニュースだと念押しした上で、才能豊かな俳優、イワン・モジューヒン[69]を主役に据え、その映画を自身が監督するつもりだと明かしている。その際、ウイドブロは、自分が最高の映画監督に、最高の役者になる素養があるという自負を示し、ナポレオンになりたいという願望を打ち明けさえする。ロハス・ヒメネスは、この時のウイドブロの様子を「ここで詩人は立ち上がり、額の髪をかき上げながら、一方の腕を胸に当てて、もう一方の腕を背中に回す。まなざしは遠くの夢想のなかの地平線を見つめていた」と描写している。最後にウイドブロは「わたしの映画は『カリオストロ』と題されるだろう。さらに、わたしが発行する「創造(クレアシオン)」誌に定期的に掲載される手はずだ」と予告している。この後、話はウイドブロのチリへの帰国や、あるいはこれが本来もっとも関心を寄せるべきテーマであろうが、詩の創造に転じていき、

---

66) Alberto Rojas Jiménez（1900-34）チリの詩人、コラムニスト。
67) 前掲の Rojas Giménez, A.（1930）。Morelli, G., 'Introducción' en Huidobro, V., *Cagliostro*（2011）の導入部にも、この会話の一部が引用されている。
68) Huidobro, V., *Finis Britannia*[e]（1923）Paris, Editions Fiat Lux.
69) Ivan Mosjouwkine（1889-1939）ロシア出身の俳優。1917年の二月革命後、フランスに移住。パリで『秘密の家』（1922）や『キイン』（1922）などの作品で名声を築いた後、さらにアメリカ合衆国に移って活躍した。同じ映像が前後のカットによってまったく違った印象を与えることを明らかにした、クレショフの「モジューヒン効果」によっても知られる。

『カリオストロ』に戻ることはない[70]。

ロハス・ヒメネスに語った『カリオストロ』の映画が、ミズとともに撮影していたものなのか、あるいはその共同作業が破綻した後にあらためて撮りなおそうとしていた新たな企画なのか不明だが、ともかくウイドブロの自身が、映画を何としても実現したいと望んでいたことが分かる。

1934年に出た小説『カリオストロ』のスペイン語版の初版、および1942年に初版同様、サンティアゴ・デ・チレのシグサグ社から出た版[71]に付された注記は、未完の映画の撮影のいきさつに触れてこう述べている。「1922年、『他人の過ち』(ラ・フォート・デゾートル)を撮り終えたばかりの演出家(メトゥル・アン・セーヌ)、ジャック・オリヴェ[72]とともに、著者はフランスの映画製作会社の依頼を受けてこの小説のデクパージュに取りかかった。作業が四分の三以上も進んだ段階で会社が破産した。翌1923年、著者はモジューヒンから原稿を求められた。この人物は、その映画化に強い関心を示したが、しかし……まさにその時期にフランスを去らなくてはならなくなった。ドイツ、次いでアメリカ合衆国がパリよりもよい条件の契約を提示したのである」[73]

まず目を引くのは、ここにミメ・ミズの名前が出てこないことである。代わりに、演出をしたとされるオリヴェは、記録に残る唯一の監督作品『他者の過ち』を撮り終えたばかりであったことにされているが、この映画は1923年に公開されているので、ウイドブロがいくつかの雑誌に発表したという1921年から1922年にかけてのコンテの作成時期や、この注記で明らかにされている1922年という年号は整合性を欠くようにも思える。あるいはオリヴェの映画は1922年の、ことによっては早い時期にクランクアップしており、翌年までその公開を待ったということなのだろうか。カリオストロを演じることになっていたモジューヒン

---

70) Rojas Giménez, A.（1930）, p.12.
71) Huidobro, V., *Cagliostro*（1942）Santiago de Chile, Zig-Zag.
72) Jacques Oliver *La faute des autres*（1923）は唯一の監督作品。関わった別の三作品では、撮影監督してクレジットされている。
73) Morelli, G., 'Introducción' en Huidobro, V., *Cagliostro*（2011）, p.28.

は、当時、人気の絶頂を誇っていた俳優であり、フランスの国外で契約することになったのはつじつまの合わない話ではない。ただし、ロハス・ヒメネスに語ったように、もしウイドブロ自身が役者を務めるとしたら、おそらくそれは、自らを生まれ変わりとみなしたカリオストコその人の役以外ありえないであろうから、モジューヒンを起用するキャスティングと矛盾する[74]。それとも、ロシア人の俳優には、カリオストロの敵役の魔術師を演じさせるつもりだったのだろうか。

　またこの注記は、映画撮影の中断の原因を製作会社の倒産に帰している。それは一見合理的だが、ラレーアが証言する通り、パテ社が製作の主体であったとすれば、この頃、アメリカ合衆国では映画製作部門を売却していたものの、会社自体は安泰であったはずであり、時期が重なる、ミズとの意見の相違による破局を糊塗しようとしたように思われてならない。いずれにしても真相は不明で、ミズとの決裂の場合のように、映画製作にまつわる直接的な証拠がさらに出てこないことには、憶測を重ねるしかないだろう。

　それにひきかえ、小説『カリオストロ』の出版の経緯に関しては、もう少し具体的な事実が知られている。先に述べたように、この小説には英語の版とスペイン語の版とが存在するが、厳密には著者の生前、四つの版が出ている。既述の通り、英語の版は『魔術師の鏡』と題されており、これはロンドンではエア・アンド・スポティスウッド社から、ニューヨークとボストンではホートン・ミフリン社から出版された。基本的に両者に異同はない。いずれもウォーレ・B・ウェルズ[75]の名前が翻訳者として記されている。

---

[74] 本稿では詳細に触れないが、英語版の序文として用意された未発表の原稿に、ウイドブロは、ある降霊術の会において前世で自身がカリオストロであったと告げられたこと、カリオストロから授かった指輪をニューヨークで盗まれたこと、小説の執筆のあいだずっと、夜ごとカリオストロが憑依して草稿に意見したことなどを記している。Morelli, G., 'Introducción' en Huidobro, V., *Cagliostro*（2011）, pp.23-26.

[75] Warre B. Wells（1892?－没年不詳）1919 年から 1920 年にかけてアイルランド自治同盟の非公式な機関紙 'Irish Statesman' の編集に関わり、イェーツやショーの寄稿を受けた。著作にアイルランドの政治家、ジョン・レドモンドの評伝がある。1932 年には *The Spanish Omnibus* を、やはりエア・アンド・スポティスウッドから出した。↗

イギリスにおいてもアメリカ合衆国においても『魔術師の鏡』の出版を引き受けたのは大手出版社であり、この小説のセールスが期待されていたことがうかがえる。実際に反響は小さくなかった。アメリカ合衆国では、1931年11月1日付の「ニューヨーク・ヘラルド・トリビューン・ブックス」紙にアンヘル・フロレスによる「高速度のカリオストロ」[76]が載ったを皮切りに、同年11月28日「ボストン・イブニング・トランスクリプト」、翌29日に再度「ニューヨーク・ヘラルド・トリビューン・ブックス」、1932年3月13日「ニューヨーク・タイムズ」、同月16日「ボストン・トランスクリプト」（「ボストン・イブニング・トランスクリプト」）が、一方、イギリスでは、1931年4月9日「ロンドン・タイムズ」、1932年4月7日「タイムズ・リテラリー・サプルメント」が『魔術師の鏡』の書評を載せている[77]。「ロンドン・タイムズ」掲載の書評の日付がもっとも早いのは、ロンドンでの出版が先であったことを示唆する。

　他方、スペイン語版の『カリオストロ』は『魔術師の鏡』に遅れて、1934年にチリの重要な出版社、シグサグ社から刊行された。こちらも5,000部もの宣伝用の小冊子を刷るなど、広告に努めた甲斐があって、「今日」紙の記事[78]をはじめ、多くの反響を得たようだが、その出版は必ずしもウイドブロの望むように進まなかったと思われる。そのいきさつを、ウイドブロとヘラルド・ディエーゴのあいだで交わされたいくつかの書簡が説明している[79]。

↘　『戦士の肖像』の訳者でもある。

76) Flores, Ángel, 'A High-Speed Cagliostro', 'New York Herald Tribune Books' (29, November, 1931).筆者のフロレス（1900-1990）は、プエルトリコ出身の批評家、アンソロジト。英語文学とスペイン語文学を研究の対象としたが、ことにラテンアメリカ文学を世に広く紹介した貢献は大きい。「魔術的リアリズム」の語を文学に初めて援用したことでも知られる。

77) Morelli, G., 'Introducción' en Huidobro, V., *Cagliostro* (2011), p 22、Costa, Réne de, 'Del cine a la novela : *Cagliostro*, "novela-film" en Huidobro, V., *Cagliostro* (1993) Madrid, Anaya, p.11、および Hey, Nicholas, 'Bibliografía de y sobre Vicente Huidobro' en 'Revista Iberoamericana', nº 41 : 91, 1975, pp.293-353.

78) 'Cagliostro, por Vicente Huidobro' en 'Hoy', III, 143 (17 agosto 1934), pp.17-18. Hey, N. (1975), p.330.

79) Huidobro, V., Morelli, G. (ed.) (2008), pp.211-212.

まず1932年3月10日（もしくは13日）にディエーゴに宛てた手紙でウイドブロは、マドリードのシグノ社が『カリオストロ』の原稿を買い取ったので、序文を寄せてくれるようにと依頼している。その際、原稿を保管している編集者のフェルナンド・デ・ラ・プレーサ[80]からそれを受け取るようにと指示している。ところが、4月14日の手紙では、序文を書かなくてもよいと態度を変えて、シグノ社がくだんの小説をすぐにも出版する運びとなるだろうから、原稿をそのまま手元に置いて同社に渡すようにデ・プレーサに伝えてくれと頼んでいる。このやり取りから、この時点では、シグノ社からの『カリオストロ』の刊行が順調に進んでいるようにうかがえるが、結局、その話は立ち消えてしまう。

そして、すでに述べたように、1934年にシグサグ社から『カリオストロ』が出版される。この年、やはりチリの出版社であるウォルトンから『パパ、あるいは、アリシア・ミルの日記』[81]、そして『来るべきもの（近い未来に起きた物語）』[82]が出ている。同年7月、ウイドブロはサンティアゴからマドリードのディエーゴにこれら3冊の書籍を送ろうとして手紙をしたためているが、そのなかで『カリオストロ』については「海賊版のようなものだとみなしており、ゆえに悩みの種になっている」とこぼしている[83]。

次いでウイドブロは友人にその経緯を説明する。前に引いた手紙にあるように、『カリオストロ』の原稿はマドリードのシグノ社に売却されていたが、チリにも、小説の出版先を見つけるために別に用意された二通の写しがあった。そのうちの一通は友人の手に委ねられた。問題となるのはもう一通の写しで、1927年に「ラ・ナシオン」紙の編集部に預けられたものである。著者としては同紙に

---

80) Fernando de la Presa（生没年不詳）ウイドブロはこの人物に、フランスで出していた *Manifestes*（1925）Paris, Éditions de la Revue Mondiale のスペイン語版の出版の仲介も期待していたようだが、実現しなかった。
81) Huidobro, Vicente, *Papá o el diario de Alicia Mir*（1934）Santiago de Chile, Walton. 同年に第二版が出ている。
82) 前出の Huidobro, V., *La próxima*（*Historia que pasó en poco tiempo más*）（1934）。同年のうちに二回版を重ねている。
83) Huidobro, V., Morelli, G.（ed.）（2008）, p.219.

連載されることを望んでいたが、大衆受けしないという理由で提案は退けられる。その原稿が、ウイドブロの意に反してシグサグ社の手に渡ってしまったのである。詩人は弁護士に相談するが、当時のチリでは著作権が尊重されず、何も打つ手がないという回答を得たのみであった。彼にとって「滑稽なこと、馬鹿げたこと」だったが、それを甘受するしかなかった。

　ウイドブロはさらに続ける。書籍の発売に先立って、サンティアゴ・デ・チレでの『カリオストロ』の「広告(レクラム)」は盛んになされた。しかし、為替管理が行われているおかげで、チリにスペインの本が入ってこないのと同じように、『カリオストロ』はチリだけで売られることになる。従って、他の国で出るはずの別の版に悪い影響を及ぼすことはないはずだ。そうはいっても、シグノ社が『カリオストロ』を早急に刊行し、他のアメリカ諸国にはそれが届くようになればよいのだが、と。

　3年近く出版を棚上げにしているシグノ社[84]には、不満と不信を抱いてはいたものの、それでもウイドブロは、同社が『カリオストロ』を出版してくれるという期待を捨てずにいたようである。ディエーゴには、チリの版を一冊送るので——本が汚されることがあれば、新しいものを贈るからと気遣いながら——シグノ社に届けてほしいと頼んでいる。つまり、チリで自分の同意なしに出た版の中身のほうが、デ・ラ・プレーサを通じてマドリードの出版社にすでに渡している原稿よりも好ましいと考えたのである。またシグサグ社の版に対して、チリでは通常そうしているように、もっと厚手の紙にしたい、判型を大きくしたいと製本についての希望を伝えている。

　なお、シグサグ社版の『カリオストロ』の巻末には——ウイドブロの言によれば、チリの出版の慣行に従って——著者もしくは作品に関する複数の論考が収められているが、なかにディエーゴが書いた一編が混ざっていた[85]。1932 年 3 月

---

[84] 『カリオストロ』初版の注記は、原稿がもっと早い時期、1923 年にマドリードのある出版社に預けられて、三年のあいだ放置されていたとしている。Morelli, G., 'Introducción' en Huidobro, V., Cagliostro (2011), p.28.
[85] ibid.

10日の手紙で執筆を依頼したものと思われるが、それもウイドブロには不満であったらしく、誰が版元に渡したのだろうかと先の書簡で犯人探しをしている。やり玉にあげたのは、当時、二十歳前の若者だったエドゥアルド・アンギータ[86]で、彼がシグサグ社にその原稿を渡したのではないかと臆断している。アンギータはこの年、処女詩集『終わりへの移行』を出すが、まだ駆け出しの詩人で、様々な新聞や雑誌、あるいは出版社のために働いていた。シグサグ社にも出入りしており、それがウイドブロの疑いの一応の根拠となったのだろう。またアンギータは、ウイドブロの他にパブロ・ネルーダやパブロ・デ・ロカらの詩編を収載し、チリの詩史に重要な位置を占めることになる『新しいチリの詩のアンソロジー』[87]をボロディア・テイテルボイム[88]と共同で編んでいるが、その版元もシグサグ社であった。

このようにウイドブロはディエーゴに容疑が薄い犯人——この若者がいったいどのようにしてスペインから送られた草稿を入手しえたというのか——を差し出しているのだが、モレッリはそれについて、スペインの友人に断りなくチリの版に原稿を使用してしまったのを取り繕おうとしたのであり、自分の意図しないところで『カリオストロ』が出版されたというのが作り話である可能性を示唆している[89]。そのように考えると一見筋が通らないでもない。

しかしながら、これもモレッリが同じ場所で指摘しているのだが、1922年5月、パリで開かれた絵画詩の展覧会に際して、ウイドブロは、そのパンフレットにディエーゴとラレーアの書簡からの抜粋を断りなく載せておきながら、モーリ

---

86) Eduardo Anguita (1914-1992) チリの詩人。「一九三八年の世代」の一人。クレアシオニスムや「マンドラゴラ」グループのシュルレアリスムに接近した。当時の新しい傾向を捉えた重要な選詩集、*Antología de poesía chilena nueva*（1915）の編者である。年長のウイドブロとは友人で、選詩集 Huidobro, V., Anguita, Eduardo (prólogo), *Antología*（1945）Santiago de Chile, Zig-Zag を編んでいる。
87) Anguita, E. (ed.), Volodia Teitelboim (ed.), *Antología de poesía chilena nueva*（1935）Santiago de Chile, Zig-Zag.
88) Volodia Teitelboim (1916-2008) チリの作家。「一九三八年の世代」の一人。ネルーダと深い親交を結び、後に評伝 Teitelboim, V., *Neruda*（1984）Madrid, Michay を発表した。
89) Morelli, G., 'Introducción' en Huidobro, V., *Cagliostro*（2011）, p.31.

ス・ライナルのような高名な批評家たちとともに彼らの名前がないのはしのびがたく、ぜひそれを出さなくてはならないと感じたのだと、詫びるのではなく、義務と考えたのだと弁解している[90]。そうしたエピソードはこれ一つではなく、それがシグサグ社の『カリオストロ』が海賊版だというような話の捏造をウイドブロがいとわない根拠となるとしているのだが、スペインでであれ、チリでであれ、『カリオストロ』を出版しようという時、そのために依頼していた原稿を載せたということであれば、アンギータまでを巻き添えにして、あえて作り話をする必要もないように思える。ディエーゴやラレーアは概ねウイドブロの性格を把握しているだろうし、彼らの師弟的な関係を考えれば、一言あやまれば済むことではないだろうか。

むしろシグサグ社から本が出て問題となるのは、3年間も音沙汰がないとはいえ、すでに原稿を売却していたシグノ社、そして著者と出版社のあいだに立っていたディエーゴへの配慮の欠如であろう。そうすると確かに、自分の預かり知らぬところで海賊版が出たのだとすればウイドブロにとって好都合である。しかも、望み通り、ディエーゴの原稿も印刷されての上だ。

もしそうであるとすれば、ウイドブロの行為を正当化するのは、『カリオストロ』の出版の3年間の遅延だろう。さらに言えば、1923年の映画の破綻であり、1927年の映画化の頓挫である。ウイドブロは悠久の時をさまよう魔術師のごとく、成就の瞬間をじっと待ち続けてきたのである。『魔術師の鏡』が成功を収めていたとはいえ、翻訳のそれは、スペイン語やフランス語で自身執筆した作品とは、異なったものに感じられたとしても不思議はない。むしろスペイン語での出版をいっそう強く期待するようになったのかもしれない。これ以上出版が先に延びるのは耐えがたいことだった。

状況証拠はまだある。シグサグ社からは、それまでもハンス・アルプとの共著『三篇の模範小説集』[91]や政治的小説『サテュロス、あるいは言葉の力』[92]を出し

---

90) Huidobro, V., Morelli, G. (ed.) (2008), p.112.
91) Huiobro, V. (autor, trad.), Arp, Hans (autor), *Tres novelas ejemplares* (1935)

ており、社名と同名の雑誌にも寄稿するなど、関係はむしろ良好であったはずである。結局、スペインのシグノ社が『カリオストロ』を出版することはなく、1942年にシグサグ社が第二版を出した。これも初版が海賊版であったとすれば、8年ほどのあいだに和解した可能性があるとはいえ、不自然さが感じられる。また、ウイドブロが1934年に発表した小説のうち[93]、『来るべきもの（近い未来に起こった物語）』と『パパ、あるいは、アリシア・ミルの日記』がウォルトン社から出ているのに対し、『カリオストロ』がシグサグ社からとなっているのは、海賊版という話を意識して出版社を変えたためだと考えるのはうがちすぎであろうか[94]。

ちなみにディエーゴの原稿を勝手に持ち出したとされるアンギータは、若さゆえの過ちだとして許されたのか、それとも嫌疑が晴れたのか、その後もウイドブロと良好な関係を保ち続ける[95]。

ここまで寄り道を重ねながらも確かめてきたように、ウイドブロが完成を夢見た映画『カリオストロ』は、「小説／映画」として体現されることとなった。当初の企図通りサイレント映画として上映されていたとしたら、はたしてそれは『メトロポリス』や『イントレランス』のように伝説になっていただろうか。『カリガリ博士』や『吸血鬼ノスフェラトゥ』のように時代の芸術に衝撃を与えただろうか。『黄金狂時代』や『戦艦ポチョムキン』のように今日なお心を動かすだろうか。それとも、忘却を運命づけられた記録がひとつ、フィルモグラフィーに、加わるだけだったろうか。いずれにしても、幻となった映画を紆余曲折の果てに、小説として現在も享受できるのは幸運なことである。

  Santiago de Chile, Zig-Zag.
92) Huiobro, V., *Sátiro o el poder de las palabras*（1939）, Santiago de chile, Zig-Zag.
93) やはり同じ年の『月にて』Huidobro, V., *En la luna*（1934）Santiago de Chile, Ercilla は戯曲。
94) 『月にて』の版元はエルシリャ社だが、この本は7月の時点でまだ刊行されていない。
95) たとえば、'Vital/Ombrigo'（1934）や 'Vital'（1935）といった雑誌を共同で編集している。

参考文献

村山匡一郎編『映画史を学ぶクリティカル・ワーズ（新装増補版）』（2013）東京、フィルムアート社。

G・サドゥール『世界映画史Ⅰ』（1984）東京、みすず書房。

H・ベアール『ダダ・シュルレアリスム演劇史』（1972）東京、竹内書店。

イアン・マカルマン『最後の錬金術師　カリオストロ伯爵』（2004）東京、草思社。

Hurtado, María Elena, *Acario: el músico mágico*（2009）Santiago de Chile, Ril.

Larrea, Juan, 'Vicente Huidobro en Vanguardia' en 'Revista Iberoamericana' 106-107（1979）, pp.213-273.

Salle XIV: Vicente Huidobro y las artes plásticas（2001）Madrid: Museo Nacional Centro de Arte Reina Sofía.

Ciné Ressources http://www.cineressources.net/recherche_t.php（2017年2月19日確認）

宗教から実存へ

"From Religion to Existence"

川神　傅弘

Morihiro KAWAKAMI

Abstract:

Paul Valéry believed that Christianity introduced the concept of the inner life ('interiority') to people in the West. The present article first examines the differences among various kinds of existential thought, as well as the history of the ideas dominant in each era, from the perspective of a conflict between the 'religious' mind, which enabled expressions of anthropocentric interiority, and the individual, existential mind. Secondly, the article clarifies the problems of faith by revelation versus faith by reason, and fanaticism versus tolerance, by chronologically comparing expressions of anthropocentric interiority which devolved from pietism to deistic existentialism or atheism.

Keywords:

atheism, deism, pietism, reason, religious fanaticism, tolerance

はじめに

　ジャン=ポール・サルトル、アルベール・カミュそしてニコライ・ベルジャーエフらは、一般に実存主義の思想家と謳われている。しかし思想傾向の相違や社会・政治活動に対する情熱の温度差を考慮すれば、彼らにそのような一色の冠を

被せることにいささか不具合を感じる向きは少なくないであろう。ただ、少なくとも基本的に彼らには人間存在のあり方の追究という共通の姿勢があった。ルネサンス以降の西欧でその傾向が徐々に芽生えるのであるが、19世紀になると人間の基本的生活は客観的真理を拠り所とする本質論的な人間観のみでは、掬い取ることのできない人間心性の領域の増大に伴い、人間的実存の主体的内面性を重視する人々が現れ、20世紀になるとその傾向は顕著になった。実存主義の呼称で括られる思想家に共通する性格・特質はせいぜいそのレベル、主体的内面性の重視ということになるであろう。

　人びとの生活のなかで、内面性の吐露がそれ以前になかったわけでは勿論ない。が、それが主体的内面ということになると、別の話になるのである。いわんやそれを体系的な思想・哲学として表現することには越えがたい壁があった。西欧中世社会では建前として、個人主体という考えそのものがなかった、というより否定されていたからである。個人はあくまでも神の前の、神の僕としての存在であり主体ではなかったから、人々は宗教の教義という客観的真理あるいはそれに由来する道徳・慣習を順守しながら生きていた。しかしながら、キリスト教の教会権力が頂点に達したときすでに腐敗は始まっていた。かくしてキリスト教思想の分裂と、キリスト教からの主体の分離がはじまる。ここに大っぴらに個人的実存の主体的内面を重視する時代が到来した。

　ところで、ポール・ヴァレリーはその著『精神の危機』において「内面生活を西欧の人間に教えたのはキリスト教である」と語る。彼は続けて「キリスト教は人間の精神にこの上なく微妙な、この上なく重要かつ豊饒な問題を提起した」としてその例をいくつも挙げているが、なかでも「知識のよってきたる源泉・確実性とか、理性と信仰の区別とか、理性と信仰の間に起こる対立とか、信仰と行為・奉仕の間の矛盾とか、自由・隷属・恩寵」などの項目はそのまま主体的内面・内省の問題に繋がるものと思われる。

　拙稿では人間存在の主体的内面表現の究極的露呈化を可能にした要素の一つである宗教的心性と個人的心性の相克を取り上げて、西欧近代が宗教の軛を逃れる

ことで徐々に獲得してきた実存表現の段階的歴史をたどることにするが、前述したようにサルトル、カミュ、ベルジャーエフらそれぞれの主体的内面性の分析と描写については、実存主義という同じレッテルを付し難い思想内容を見せているので、それぞれの思想家の相違の指標を宗教からの解放が果たした役割に止め、その観点から便宜的に「敬虔 piétiste 的なもの」から「理神論 déisme 的実存主義」、そして「無神論 athéisme 的実存主義」のはざまに蠢く人間主体の内面性の表現を時間の流れに沿って比較しつつ、狂信 folie・fanatisme と寛容 tolérance の側面から彼らの業績の歴史的意味の考察を試みる。

1. 神の実在と不在

サルトルは「神が存在してもそうでなくても、そのこと自体は問題にならない」と語り神の存在の問題を棚上げしていた時代があったが、1946 年『実存主義はヒューマニズムである *l'Éxitencialisme est un humanisme*』において無神論の立場を明確にした。

「私の代表する無神論的実存主義はいっそう論旨が一貫している。たとえ神が存在しなくても、実存が本質に先立つところの存在、なんらかの概念によって定義されうる以前に実存している存在が少なくとも一つある。その存在は人間、ハイデッガーのいう人間的現実である、と無神論的実存主義は宣言するのである」[1]とその立場を明言したが、このような無神論の考えは 20 世紀になって初めて現れたものでは勿論ない。

古代ギリシャの「プラトンはどんなに無神論に徹した人でも、たいていの場合、危険が迫れば神の力を認めるようになると言った・・・無神論者は、判断の推理によって、地獄だの来世の救いだのをつくりごとだと主張する。けれども、老衰や病気のために死に近づいて、死を経験する機会を目の前にすると、死に対

---

1) ジャン - ポール・サルトル、『実存主義とは何か』、伊吹武彦訳、人文書院、1955 年、p.16.

する恐怖から・・・まったく新しい信仰を抱くようになる」[2]。

　以上はモンテーニュのエセーからの引用であるが、無神論の考えはいつ時代にもあったし、常に無神論者は存在しただろう。モンテーニュの時代つまり宗教戦争の時代はユマニストの活躍した時代であったので、殊更に宗教、信仰、神の実在・不在の問題が識者の関心を集めた。

　こうした機運のきっかけはイタリアで始まったルネッサンス・文芸復興の運動である。ルネッサンスの精神的本質は人間性の尊重、神中心の中世思想に対して人間中心の考え方を強く押し出したところに意義がある。ルネッサンス精神の特徴を概略述べておく。

　特徴（1）現実主義。自然にあるがままの人間を肯定する。ラブレーが小便の話をしたり、お産の話をしたりするのは、それが人間として当然の営みであるという考え方からであるし、ロンサールが官能の美を歌うのも、それが自然によって人間に与えられたものであるからに他ならない。女性のヌードの絵はイタリアで始まったボッティチェリーの『ヴィーナスの誕生』『春』からであるが、それは神話や聖書を題材にすることで許された。人間を原罪によって堕落したものとみて、特にその肉体を蔑視する中世の考え方と基本的に対立するものである。

　（2）合理主義。科学主義的な傾向が顕著になる。聖書そのものをギリシャ語、ヘブライ語の原典と比較検討し、合理的に解釈しようとする傾向が現れる。たとえば〈神と子と聖霊〉の三位一体説を否定する説が現れ、これが新教の生まれるきっかけになった。

　（3）自由検討の精神。合理主義的・実証主義的な探求を推し進め、文芸復興の推進者には一切の権威を否定し、自由で何ものにもとらわれない立場から研究論議する姿勢がある。天上的、地上的権力の圧迫に抵抗する精神ゆえに弾圧を受けることも辞さない気概を持ち続けた。

　（4）才能の多面性。人間性高揚の見地から、人間のあらゆる可能性を育て発揮させようとした。

　（5）古代崇拝。古代の文化は16世紀の失っていた唯一の非キリスト教文化で

あったのみならず民主主義的文化、都市文化であったので、中世のキリスト教的・封建的・農村共同体的文化に対する強力な武器となった。

2. 16世紀　モンテーニュの時代

　以上のように、ルネッサンスまで西洋の人々の心性を一方的に支配していたのは宗教であった。1517年10月ドイツの聖書学者ルターがヴィッテンベルク城教会の門に〈95箇条の提題〉を貼り付けた。後に「貼り紙事件」と称される彼の行為は、歴史的に大いなる渦を巻き起こすことになったが、貼り紙そのものは単に神学・教義上の論争をいざなう手段として普通に行われていたことであった。それは贖宥状（免罪符）販売の是非を問い、聖餐論の明確化を要求するものであったが、あくまで聖職者に向けられたもので、一般人を巻き込んで政治・社会運動に発展させる意図に基づくものでなかった事実は、提題が庶民に親しみのないラテン語で書かれていたことからも明らかである。

　フランスでもジャン・カルヴァンが現れ、法皇権を頂点とするローマ教会の階層性と教義を根本的に批判した。形式的には、教会や教皇は不要で〈聖書のみ sola fidé〉によって救われるという共通の原理に立って展開された改革の嵐はやがて各種のプロテスタント教会を生みだす広範な宗教の改革運動となり、16世紀半ばスイスのジュネーヴを中心に新教は南仏、西仏などフランス全土に広く浸透し、彼ら新教徒はユグノーと呼ばれた。そしてついに旧教徒との間で1562年戦争が起こる。その内乱は1598年アンリ4世の公布したナントの勅令まで30数年間にわたる宗教戦争となった。

　従来人々の日常的生活習慣を支配していた客観的真理の基盤は、キリスト教の信仰箇条に象徴される宗教的な戒律であり、それは一方では順守さえしていれば安堵を保証するものであったが、他方では一種の軛を意味していた。教義・戒律は少なからず人を陥れる罠として利用されることもあった。ジャンヌ・ダルクを火あぶりの刑に付した宗教裁判などもその一例である。

　しかし、中世において民衆が戒律を唯々諾々と受け入れ順守していたどうかは

別問題である。彼らはすでに世俗的現実生活のなかで宗教者の語る美辞麗句的な教義や厳格な戒律を真摯に受け止めていた訳ではないようだ。城主を中心とした町 bourg が形成され、市民（町人）階級の世界が成立し、市民の発言が力を持つようになったからである。彼らは、宗教者が求める理想的な道徳をすべて実践することは不可能であると認識していたふしがある。たとえば、フランス中世の民衆説話やお伽草子において、僧（聖職者）は常によその女房を寝取る者として描かれている。あるいは、この時代女性は他の理想的な文学では崇められ尊敬される存在（その原型は聖母マリア）であったが、庶民文学では亭主を裏切って浮気する存在として描かれている事実がそれを物語っている。そして宗教戦争が起きた。予め認識しておかねばならないのは、それがイエスを神と崇める者同士の争いであり、無神論者との争いではなかったということである。

　したがって、イエスを神と崇める者同士の長い戦闘は神そのものへの不信を性急に招いたわけではないが、少なくとも宗教と宗教者の権威の失墜を招き、延いては宗教の世俗化につながる社会の倫理的・思想的雰囲気 éthos を醸成することにはなったであろう。元来、領主対農民の社会関係が中心で、キリスト教思想がその精神内容であったのが中世社会であった。その中世社会が農民上層部の上昇と都市の発展、つまり市民階級の興隆という新事実に対応できなくなったとき、ルネッサンスという文化運動が起きたのであるが、それは実質的にはユマニスムという古典語・古典文学研究であった。かくしてキリスト教以前の古代ギリシャ文明・古代ローマ文明に範を仰ぐユマニストが登場し、彼らは従来の宗教観と教会の在り方に数多疑問を投げかける発言を繰り返した。基本的には啓示信仰に発する啓示神学の在り方を批判し、自然的理性の光によって神の存在を認識すべしとする自然神学の優位を説く学説で、こうした学識者の意見は無視しがたいものになっていた。ルターは「信仰のみ」の立場を崩すことなく、自然神学は理性の越権であるとして、あくまで信仰と理性の分離を叫び、信仰を理性によって

2）モンテーニュ、『エセー（上）』、原二郎訳、筑摩世界文学大系 13、昭和 55 年、p.316.

説明することは不可能であるとする態度をとり続けた。

　16世紀の偉大な思想家であったモンテーニュの『エセー』第二巻第十二章「レーモン・スボンの弁護」は当時の知識人の心中で信仰と理性がせめぎあう姿を見事に映し出している。モンテーニュは、

　「学問はきわめて有益で偉大な能力であり、これを軽蔑するものは自分の愚かさを十分に証明するものであるが、私にある人々のようにあれほど極端には学問の価値を認めない」[3]と予め断わったうえで自然神学に関して次のような事例を取り上げている。レーモン・スボンの章は自然神学の危険性に関するモンテーニュの懐疑的な考察である。

　そもそもレーモン・スボンという人に、信仰を理性に基づいて証明しようとしたスペイン生まれの神学者・哲学者で、彼は『自然神学、あるいは被造物の書』を著し、無神論者に対してキリスト教の信仰箇条を人間的かつ理性的に説明することを試みた人物である。

　あるとき、ピエール・ピュネルという高名な学者がモンテーニュの館を訪れ、彼の父親に『レーモン・ド・スボン師の自然神学、あるいは被造物の書』と題する書物を贈呈したのであるが、その際モンテーニュはピュネルの語る、その書に関する個人的見解にいたく感動した様子を記している。

　「当時はルターの所説が勢いを得てあちらこちらで、われわれの昔からの信仰をゆるがしはじめた時代であった。これについてピュネルはきわめて正しい意見を持っていて、理論的に推論して、この初期の病気がたちまちのうちにいまわしい無神論にまで悪化することを立派に見抜いていた。大衆は物事をそれ自体で判断する能力を持たず、偶然や外観から、それまで信じていた説を軽蔑したり批判したりするようになり、自己の信仰のすべてが怪しく見えて、権威も根拠もないように見えてくるのである」[4]。

　上記記述の就中〈初期の病気〉なる言辞からは、哲学的神学ともいえる自然神

3）ibid., p.310.
4）ibid., p.311.

学は当時すでに信仰の危機を招きかねない訪問者と見なされていたことが窺える。また当該の著書についてはこう語る。

「この著書の目的は大胆で勇敢である・・・キリスト教のあらゆる信仰箇条を、無神論者の反対に抗して確立し、証明しようと企てているからである。（・・・）彼の著作に対する第一の非難は「キリスト教徒が人間の理性によって信仰を支えようとするのは間違いである。信仰は信心と恩寵の特別な霊感だけによって心に宿るからだ」[5]」ということである。

こうして見ると、宗教の在り方や神の存在を理性によって理解し合理的に説明すること自体に無神論の萌芽を認める人びとが既にいたということになる。

モンテーニュの文体の特徴の一つは冷徹な自己観察にある。彼の人間観察の極致ともいえる言に Schadenfreude という言葉（ドイツ語）がある。フランス語では la volupté maligne à voir souffrir autrui となるその意味は「他人が苦しむのを見ることで生まれる邪な喜び」というものだが、それは冷徹な自己観察から生まれた哀惜と苦衷の情動を表したものである。この深い自己観察から生まれたのが、彼の文体の二つ目の特徴である相対主義の思考である。宗教戦争の時代モンテーニュが関心を注ぎ、最も心を痛めていたのは<u>狂信</u> fanatisme についてであった。彼は同胞が敵味方に分かれて殺しあう原因を狂信と見ていた。また、狂信が<u>不寛容</u>を招くと考えた。『エセー』において彼は、物事をある一つの立場から固定的、断定的に捕捉するのでなく、それをあらゆる角度から眺めて「その本性ではなく、その動き」を描くことに心を砕いた。いわば相対的な見方をとることを心掛けたのである。それは徹底した相対的思考であった。人々が視野の狭さに由来する無理解のために相争う動乱の時代にあって、先入観にとらわれない相対主義の立場を取り続けることは、ある意味で危険な行動でもあった。宗教的不寛容の時代がそうさせたのであろうが、彼は外面的にはキリスト教の伝統を重んじ、習慣を順守して旧教の権威に従ったが、同時に権威に対する批判精神を持ち続け

---

5) ibid., p.31.

た。われわれはもっと寛容になれる筈だという信念を彼は変えることはなかった。彼は寛容 tolérance と中庸の人であった。

3. 17〜18世紀　デカルト〜パスカル〜ヴォルテールの時代
デカルト

　1637年デカルトは『方法序説 Discours de la Méthode』を著す。その冒頭で「良識は、この世で一番公平に分け与えられているものである」[6]と述べている。ここでデカルトの言う良識 bon sens は、物事を正しく判断できる能力、すなわち理性をも意味している。彼は「理性をよく導き、諸学において真理を見出す」ために、明証・分析・総合・枚挙などの方法について「婦女子などにもよく理解できる」生活の言葉（フランス語）で語った。学術書はラテン語で書かれるのが通例であった時代、それは新機軸の試みであった。

　彼は明晰と判明と思えることだけを真理の基準とする方法を採用し、一切を方法的に疑ったのち、疑いえぬ真理を発見する。疑う自己の存在＝思惟する自分が在ることの意味、それが〈考える自己・われ思う cogito〉であった（疑いえぬ真理の第一原理）。

　「〈わたしは考える、ゆえに存在する〉というこの命題において、わたしが真理を語っていると保証するものは、考えるためには存在しなければならないことを、わたしがきわめて明晰にわかっているという以外にはまったく何もないことを認めたのでした」[7]。

　こうして彼は〈思惟する精神〉と〈延長ある物体〉とを相互に独立した実体とする二元論の哲学体系を樹立する。つまり Cogito ergo sum「われ思う、ゆえにわれあり」という真理の第一原理から精神と物体という二つの実体（存在するために何ものも必要としないもの）が措定されたが、それらはあくまでも有限実体であるとした。デカルトはさらに、

6）デカルト、『方法序説』、谷川多佳子訳、岩波文庫、1997年、p.8.
7）ibid., p.48.

「続いてわたしは、わたしが疑っていること、したがってわたしの存在はまったく完全ではないこと——疑うより認識することのほうが、完全性が大であるとわたしは明晰に見ていたから——に反省を加え、自分よりも完全である何かを考えることをわたしはどこから学んだのかを探求しようと思った。(・・・) 何らかの不完全性を示すものは神の内には一つもなく、そうでないものはすべて神の内にあるとわたしは確信していたからである。(・・・) たとえば三角形を想定して、その三つの角の和は二直角に等しくなければならないことはよくわかるが、しかしだからといって、この世界にこうした三角形が存在することを保証するものは、この証明の中には何も認められなかったのである。これにひきかえ、完全な存在者についての観念の検討に立ち戻ると、存在が観念のなかに含まれていることをわたしは見出した。それは、三角形の観念のなかに三つの角の和は二直角に等しいということが含まれ、また球の観念のなかにそのすべての部分は中心から等距離にあるということが含まれているのと同じように、あるいはそれ以上に明らかなのであり、したがって、あの完全な存在者である神があること、存在することは、少なくとも、幾何学のどの証明にも劣らず確実であるのをわたしは見出した」[8]のように思索し、精神と物体の二つの実体のほかに神という第三の実体の存在を証明し、これを無限実体とした。

かくして彼は『省察』第三章「神について。神は存在するということ」[9]という項目で神の存在証明を試みる。その概略は次のようなものである。言うまでもなく彼の方法的懐疑は基本的に、絶対的に確実なものを求めてすべての感覚知を否定することから始まる。感覚は人を欺くからである。たとえば $2+3=5$ の等式は真であろうか。全能の神あるいは邪悪な霊がわれわれを欺いているのかもしれない。よって数学の命題も絶対的な確実性はもたない。しかしそれを思惟する自己の存在だけは疑いえない。疑うものとしてわれわれは不完全であるが、不完全であることを知っていること自体が逆に、自己の中に〈最完全者〉の観念が宿る

---

8) ibid., pp.48-52.
9) デカルト、『省察』、野田又夫他訳、筑摩世界文学大系19、昭和54年、p.55.

ことを示すものである。こうした〈最完全者〉の観念は不完全なわれらが作為できるものではないし、感覚が外から伝える観念でもない。結局、現実に存在する神がわれわれの精神に刻み付けた観念（生得観念 idea innata）なのである。そのことをデカルトは次のように説明し、結論づける。

「私が存在し、そしてもっとも完全な実有すなわち神の観念が私のうちにあるということ、ただこのことから、神もまた存在するということがきわめて明証的に論証せられると、どうしても結論しなければならない」[10]。

あるいは、下記のような比喩によって表現する。

「神が私を創造するにあたって、この観念を私のうちに植えつけたということは何ら怪しむにあたらない。それはちょうど芸術家が彼の作品に自己のしるしを刻印するようなものである」[11]。

また、最後はこのように締めくくっている。

「このことをさらに立ち入って検討し、同時にまたここから引き出されることのできる他のもろもろの真理の中へ訪ね入る前に、私はここでしばらく〔まったく完全な〕そのものの観想にふけり、その〔驚嘆すべき〕もろもろの属性を心静かに考量し、そしてその無辺なる光明の〔比類ない〕美を、これにいわば幻惑せられた私の精神の眼の堪えうる限り、凝視し、賛嘆し、崇敬するのがふさわしいと思う。なぜなら、ただこの荘厳なる神の観想のうちにのみ別世界の生活の至高の浄福があることをわれわれが信仰によって信じているように、むろんはるかに不完全なものではあってもその同じ想いによって、およそこの世の生活においてわれわれが享受しうる最大のよろこびを享受しうることをわれわれは今においても経験するからである」[12]。

デカルトはこのように、仮令不完全であれ別世界の浄福の存在を信じ、荘厳なる神の観想に身を委ねることの意義を伝えることによって、神の実在の証明に成

---

10) ibid., p.56.
11) ibid., pp.64-65.
12) ibid., p.65.

功したが、それはいわば徹頭徹尾合理論の方法に則るものであった。

パスカル

ところで、デカルトからおよそ四半世紀後に生まれたパスカルの宗教観はどうであったろうか。デカルト同様、彼も数学者・科学者として斯界において赫々たる成果を挙げたが、突如華々しい世俗生活から半ば身を引き信仰生活に入った。病気の悪化にともない、医者に勧められて気晴らしに社交界に出入りした時期もあったが、父親の奇禍が縁となりパスカルはジャンセニスム jansénisme に帰依し、ポール゠ロワイアル修道院に出入りするようになる。この教派はカトリックの小教派であり、アウグスティヌスの晩年の<u>恩寵 grâce efficace</u> と<u>無償の救霊予定 prédestination gratuite</u> の考えを強調する禁欲的な他力主義を旨とし、王室と教会に反抗する政治的党派の性格を持ついささか異端的な宗派であり、その教義は新教派カルヴァンの唱える決定論に近似するものであった。

他力の意味するところは、旧約聖書創世記に発する<u>原罪</u>を背負って生まれてくる人間は自由に善を選ぶ能力を働かせることができなくなっており、神の恩寵によってしか救われないということであるが、更に恩寵が与えられなければ人間の意志は必然的にこの世の欲にとらえられ、罪の状態から脱することはできない。しかも恩寵は神の選択によるので、すべての人に等しく与えられるものではない。したがって、人が救われるか地獄に落ちるかは人が生まれる前にすでに決まっているとする教義であり、それが他力・「決定論」と称される所以である。

対してローマ教会の正統的見解は、原罪のもとにあっても人間の意志は自ら善を選ぶ能力を全く失ったものではないとした。こうした自力主義の急先鋒にイエズス会派があった。因みに、青少年期のデカルトは八年間ラ・フレーシュ校でスコラ哲学と人文学を学んだが、その教育機関の属していたのがイエズス会 jésuite である。後に、イエズス会とジャンセニストの間で激しい教義論争が始まり、パスカルはジャンセニスト擁護の論客として矢面に立ち、18 通の書簡体の論文『田舎人への手紙 *Les Propvinciales*』を刊行することになる。

ところでデカルトの場合とは対蹠的に、パスカルのキリスト教への入信は論理の紆余曲折を経たものではなかった。それは突然啓示信仰のように彼に舞い降りてきたものである。1654 年 11 月心の中に突如神の声を聞き、科学と理性は自分の心の無限の広さを満たしえないことを知り、決定的な回心を果たし、以降一層信仰を固めてゆく。

今日その名を不朽のものとしているのは、彼が無神論者をキリスト教信仰に導くべく書いた『パンセ Pensées』である。その著書でパスカルは合理主義、宗教的無関心、懐疑主義思想、無神論など、当時の反キリスト教思想に対してキリスト教を弁護したが、読者を説得しようとした訳ではない。なぜなら信仰を決定づけるのは神の恩寵のみであるからだ。さらに彼の徹底した禁欲主義は人間の〈空しさ〉を執拗に暴く。人間は気を紛らわすことでなんらか誤魔化しをしており、快楽や野心によって得る幸福感は偽りの幸福で、それらはすべて空虚である。パスカルは〈気晴らし〉に divertissement というフランス語を充てているが、それは娯楽という意味でもある。彼にとってはある意味で学問さえも気晴らしに過ぎない。

「学問のむなしさ。外的な事物についての学問は、苦しい時に、道徳についての私の無知を慰めてはくれないだろう。ところが徳性についての学問は、外的な学問についての私の無知をいつも慰めてくれるだろう」（断章 67、以下パスカルの言については断章番号を付す）[13]のような思索がそれを表している。

要するに、神を選ばない限り永遠の幸福を手に入れることは出来ない。その神なき人間の悲惨については『パンセ』の第二章〈神なき人間の惨めさ〉で次のように示される。たとえば、

「人間の状態は定めなさ、嫌気、不安」（127）[14]

「クレオパトラの鼻、それがもう少し低かったら全地表は変わったものになっ

---

[13] パスカル、『パンセ』、前田陽一訳、中央公論新社、2009 年、p.39.
[14] ibid., p.88.

ていただろう」(162)[15]

「むなしさ、恋愛の原因と結果。クレオパトラ」(163)[16]

同様に第二章では、

「そもそも自然における人間というものは、いったい何なのだろう。無限に対しては虚無であり、虚無に対してはすべてであり、無とすべてとの中間である」(72)[17]と語り、中間的存在者としての人間の定めなさに言及する。

「二つの無限。中間。あまり早く読んでも、あまりゆっくり読んでも、何もわからない」(69)[18]

「あまり多くの、またはあまり少ない酒」「彼に酒をやらないでみたまえ。彼は真理を見出せなくなる。あまり多くても同様」(71)[19]また、

「われわれは、あらゆる方面において限られているので、両極端の中間にあるというこの状態は、われわれのすべての能力において見出される。われわれの感覚は、極端なものは何も認めない。あまり大きい音は、われわれをつんぼにする。あまり強い光は、目をくらます。あまり遠くても、あまり近くても、見ることをさまたげる。話があまり長くても、あまり短くても、それを不明瞭にする。(・・・)あまりに多くの快楽は、不快にする。あまりに多くの協和音は、音楽では、気にさわる。あまりの恩恵は、われわれをいらだたせる。〈恩恵は返却可能と見られるあいだは好ましいが、度をはるかに超えれば感謝に代わって憎悪にて報いられる〉。(・・・)あまりの若さも、あまりの老年も、精神を妨げる。多すぎる教育も、少なすぎる教育もまた同様である。すなわち、極端な事物は、われわれにとっては、あたかもそれが存在していないのと同じであり、われわれもそれらに対しては存在していない。これがわれわれの真の状態である。そのために、われわれは確実に知ることも、全然無知であることもできないのである。わ

---

15) ibid., p.111.
16) ibid., p.111.
17) ibid., p.44.
18) ibid., p.40.
19) ibid., p.41.

れわれは広漠たる中間に漕ぎ出でているのであって、常に定めなく漂い、一方の端から他方の端へと押しやられている」(72)[20]。

　かくして彼は科学を知ることによって科学の領域の狭小であることに思い至る。科学だけでは人間は、存在の実体も原理も原因も認識しえない。つまり科学は相対的なものであることを悟り、絶対的なもの、無限に確実なものを求めて半ば科学を捨てたと考えられる。二つの無限のはざまに揺れ動く人間の理性のはかなさに対する絶望感が信仰の中に、理性以上に高度な認識を求めさせたのである。それは言わば、パスカルが到達した人間理性の限界性とも言うべきものであり、彼にとって〈論理の整合性は必ずしも万能でない〉事実を示すものでもあった。

　また『エセー』の断章（メモ書き）に見られるモンテーニュやデカルトに関する記述はパスカルの信仰に対する想いをより鮮明にしてくれるはずである。

　「モンテーニュの欠陥は大きい。みだらな言葉。軽信、無知。自殺や死についての彼の気持ち。彼は救いについての無関心をふきこむ、恐れもなく悔いもなく。彼の著書は人を敬虔にさせるために書かれたのではないから、この義務はなかった。(・・・)人生のある場合における彼の、少し手放しで、享楽的な気持ちは許すことができる。しかし、彼の死に対する全く異教的な気持ちは許すことができない。なぜなら、すくなくとも死ぬことだけはキリスト教的にしようと願わないのだったら、敬虔の心をすっかり断念しなければならないからである。ところが彼はその著書全体を通じて、だらしなくふんわりと死ぬことばかり考えている」(63)[21]のように、その評は信仰に関する限り、必ずしもかんばしいものではないが、それは主にモンテーニュの品行についてのことに限られているのである。それを離れると、

　「モンテーニュにあるいいものは、なかなか手に入れにくいものである。彼にある悪いもの、といっても、品行の点を別にしての話であるが、それは、彼がど

---

20) ibid., p.38.
21) ibid., p.39.

うでもいいことをくどくど言いすぎるし、また自分のことを話しすぎるということを彼に注意してやりさえすれば、すぐにでも改められたことだろう」(65)[22]や、「人は自分自身を知らなければならない」(66)[23]という断章などは明らかにモンテーニュの自己観察の態度を評価したものである。結局、

「モンテーニュのなかで私が読み取るすべてのものは、彼の中ではなく、私自身のなかで見出しているのである」(64)[24]のように彼の思索の価値を認め、人間観察に対する尊敬の念さえ感じられる。

他方、信仰や宗教観に関しては、デカルトに対する筆鋒は鋭い。
「学問をあまり深く究める人々に反対して書くこと。デカルト」(76)[25]

「私はデカルトを許せない。彼はその全哲学の中で、できることなら神なしですませたいものだと、きっと思っただろう。しかし、彼は、世界を動き出させるために、神に一つ爪弾きをさせないわけにいかなかった。それからさきは、もう神に用がないのだ」(77)[26]。

「デカルト。大づかみにこう言うべきである。〔これは形状と運動からなっている〕と。なぜなら、それは本当だからである。だが、それがどういう形や運動であるかを言い、機械を構成してみせるのは、滑稽である。なぜなら、そういうことは、無益であり、不確実であり、苦しいからである。そして、たといそれが本当であったにしても、われわれは、あらゆる哲学が一時間の労にも値するとは思わない」(79)[27]。

以上のようなデカルト評は一層パスカルの心性の在りようを鮮明に伝えている。

---

22) ibid., p.39.
23) ibid., p.38.
24) ibid., p.56.
25) ibid., p.56.
26) ibid., p.56.
27) ibid., pp.56-57.

ヴォルテール

　18世紀はヴォルテールの世紀といわれる。いわゆる啓蒙主義の時代であるが、フランスでは「光明の世紀 siècle des lumières」と言い、光は理性を意味する言葉であった。その他に悟性、認識、精神の明晰などを指すこともあり、また精神が獲得する知識を意味することもあった。〈光明の人＝哲学者〉は科学の探求者であり、彼らには宗教の束縛を脱して、一切を理性の立場から批判しようとする精神態度が窺える。その批判精神は時として直接行動に結びつくこともあり、その意味でヴォルテールは文学者の政治・社会参加の草分け的な存在である。

　批判精神は言い換えれば自由検討の精神であり、18世紀の思想・文学を特徴づける一つの指標である。いわば理性が活動の自由を得て、あらゆる分野に懐疑と批判の目を向ける時代が到来したのである。理性を普遍的審判者とする点では17世紀と符号を一にするが、伝統的権威を否定し、政治問題、社会問題を主目標とした点において若干異なる。

　デカルト以降、人々はますます人間の本質を理性と見てひたすら合理性の追求に奔走したが、実はこのような合理主義思想の潮流を生んだ主要因の一つに"宗教的不寛容"に対する反発があった。17世紀デカルトが理性尊重を標榜して以来、理性と合理主義の普遍的性格は徐々に社会に浸透していった。

　1762年「カラス事件 l'affaire Calas」が起きる。ツールーズの織物商人ジャン・カラスが無実の訴えをよそに処刑された。カルヴァン派のカラスは長男がカトリックに改宗するのを阻止しようとして、息子を絞殺したとする冤罪を着せられたのである。不審を抱いたヴォルテールは調査をすすめカラスの冤罪を雪ぐために立ち上がり、彼の名誉回復の実現に成功した。他にもラ・バール事件などで狂信や偏見のために死刑判決を受けた人たちの名誉回復に奔走した。『寛容論 Traité sur la tolérance』はこうした実践行動の産物である。ダランベールの書簡でヴォルテールは"卑劣なるものを粉砕せよ！Écrasez l'infâme."という有名な言辞を残すことになるのであるが、その"卑劣なるもの"とは聖職者と聖職者の行為すなわち"合理的でないもの"を指し示していた。つまり理性的観点から見

て「客観的真理」とは認められないものを意味していた。また〈卑劣なるもの〉は教義に示唆され、教会によって行われる<u>不寛容</u> intolérance をも意味した。なかでも彼が弾劾したのは宗教的偏見による狂信 fanatisme についてであった。迷信・狂信は不寛容の源であり〈賢明なる母の愚かな娘〉である。対して寛容は〈理性の娘〉である。理性の時代の精神「啓蒙哲学」によって狂信を乗り越え、退けて、平和な社会を取り戻さなければならないことを彼は様々な文書で訴えた。

狂言に対して寛容の精神の重要性を説くヴォルテールは、その著『哲学辞典 *Lettres philosophiques*』で人間性と人類愛に満ちた想いを吐露しているので、いくつか紹介しておきたい。

〔狂信〕「狂信と迷信の関係は逆上と興奮、憤激と立腹のそれと同じである。法悦に浸り、幻影をいだき、夢を現実と思い込み、自己の空想を予告と信じる人は熱狂者である。自己の狂気を殺戮によって押し進める人は狂信者である。(・・・) 法律もこうした激高の発作にはきわめて無力である」[28]。

〔寛容〕「寛容とはなんであるか。それは人類愛の領分である。われわれはすべて弱さと過ちからつくりあげられている。われわれの愚行をたがいに宥しあおう。これが自然の第一の掟である」[29]。

「自分の兄弟である人間を自分と同意見でないという理由で迫害する者は明らかにすべて〈怪物〉である」[30]。

「あらゆる宗教のうちでキリスト教がおそらくもっとも寛容を鼓吹すべきであろうに、今日までのキリスト教徒はあらゆる人間のうちでもっとも不寛容であった」[31]。

「イエスが生涯ユダヤ教を守ったからには、われわれもみなユダヤ教をまもるべきであろうか。もし宗教に関して首尾一貫した推論が許されるならば、われわ

---

[28] ヴォルテール、高橋安光訳、『哲学辞典』、法政大学出版局、1988年、pp.193-194.
[29] ibid., p.386.
[30] ibid., p.388.
[31] ibid., p.389.

宗教から実存へ

れがすべてユダヤ人となるべきことは明白である。なぜならば、われらが救世主イエス・キリストはユダヤ人に生まれ、ユダヤ人として生き、ユダヤ人として死に、ユダヤ教を果たし、全うする、と明言しているからである。しかしわれわれがたがいに許し合うべきことのほうがいっそう明らかである。なぜならば、われわれはみな脆弱で無定見であり、不安と誤謬に陥りやすいからである。沼の中で風に倒された葦が逆の方向に倒れている隣の葦に言うであろうか、「怪しからん奴だ、俺みたいに這え、さもなきゃ、おまえを引き抜いて焼くように訴えるぞ」と」[32]。

ヴォルテールの根底にあった素朴で単純な人間的情熱と良識は、イギリス亡命によってより明確な思想形成を可能にした。その特徴は宗教批判の激しさと政治批判の穏和主義であり、彼が当時の世相全般について合理的説明を果たした事実は18世紀合理主義の典型と称して差し支えないであろう。

4. 19〜20世紀　ベルジャーエフ〜サルトル〜カミュ

ベルジャーエフ

彼の神的実在や信仰に対する考え方は若干パスカルのそれに似ている。ベルジャーエフは何より信仰と理性の関係を整理しようとした人であった。それは「真理は論証によって導き出せるか」という問いに表れている。

「真理とは導き出されるものでも論証されるものでもなく、出会われ看取されるものだとしたら、どうだろう」[33]として神的な実在（真理）の理性による捕捉は疑わしいと語る。また、

「啓示とはそも何か。現代人はこの言葉を聞くぎょっとする。この言葉は、合理主義的実証主義に感染したすべての人々にとって、無縁であり敵対的である。（・・・）信仰心を容認し、これへの心理的要求を感ずるこの上なく繊細な人々

---

32) ibid., p.392.
33) ニコライ・ベルジャーエフ、青山太郎訳、ベルジャーエフ著作集Ⅱ『新たな宗教意識と社会性』、行路社、1994年、p.7.

も、啓示を認めることには決して同意しない」[34]と、啓示に関する人々の無思慮を指摘した上で、

「現代世界は神秘体験を軽視している。神秘体験は、われわれの世界がそれによって生きている現実的理解からはほど遠く、また、われわれの時代がかくも心砕いている社会機構の整備を、神秘体験と結びつけることはむずかしい。この世の支配的意識が神秘体験の内に見るものは、精神異常か、個人的奇行かであり、この領域に踏み込んだものを、人は救い難いものと見做して、真面目には相手にしなくなる。(・・・) 現代の「意識的な」人々が神秘体験に対してとる態度とはこうしたものであり、彼らにとって神秘体験の問題は存在しない。(・・・) 宗教の真理が粗野な迷信と、神秘的体験がオカルト的・降神術的いかさまと混同されている。人々は、合理性の陽光が神秘思想の月光に最終的に打ち勝ったと信じた。しかし、合理主義の病を病む人々には、陽光は見えない」[35]と言う。

ベルジャーエフは啓示信仰、神秘体験などによって、人間存在の在り方そのものの神秘性を示しているように思われる。しかし、それ以上に彼の注意を惹きつけていたのは、その理性と合理主義から派生した〈歴史哲学〉の問題であり、それは世界のどの民族もが体験した、啓蒙時代のもたらした功罪についての省察である。

「啓蒙時代は聖なるものと、有機的な伝統と歴史的な伝承を破壊したのであった。およそ一切の人間文化と地上の民族の命を流出させる根源であるあの生の神的秘儀から抜け出して、自己を向上させる時代である。この啓蒙時代において、あの直接的な生の秘儀の外に、あるいは上に、人間理性の僭越がはじまる」[36]と、人間理性の跳梁跋扈する危うさを指摘している。また、

「啓蒙主義は《歴史的なもの》を否定する」[37]と述べ、《歴史的なもの》と啓蒙

---

34) ibid., p.30.
35) ibid., p.30.
36) ibid., p.13.
37) ニコライ・ベルジャーエフ、『歴史の意味』、氷上英廣訳、白水社、1998年、pp.14-15.

宗教から実存へ

時代に始まった〈歴史主義〉には大きなへだたりがある、とベジャーエフは見る。そのわけは、一方には《歴史的なもの》、他方には認識する自分という分離した対立が生じてしまうからなのだ。つまり啓蒙時代にはじまる分裂と反省が問題なのである。それは、

「啓蒙時代にはじまった歴史哲学には宿命的に深淵が欠け、歴史の神秘への突入がなされない」[38]からである。ベルジャーエフの示唆する《歴史的なもの》とは、

「存在と生の秘儀、およそ一切の人間文化と地上の民族の命を流出させる根源であるあの生の神的秘儀」[39]のことであって、彼にとって啓蒙的歴史主義は、深淵が欠け神秘性が失われた歴史観なのである。自己を理性的に、言い換えれば客観的に捉えるがゆえにその歴史観は有機性に欠けるということである。

18世紀ヴォルテールは狂信に由来する不寛容を寛容に導くために理性の効用を説いた。しかしベルジャーエフの考えでは、やがて人間理性の僭越がはじまり、合理主義の病がはびこって神聖な伝統の破壊工作がはじまり、聖書そのものの破壊に至るであろう。それは宗教改革の時代に始まった問題であるが、この問題がマルクスの唯物論的歴史観を招いた事実について次のような言及を見せている。

「マルクスの経済的唯物論は歴史哲学の領域における最も興味ある動向のひとつであるが、その大きな貢献は、あの歴史の聖物と伝統の裸形化の過程を最後の結論にまでつきつめたところにある」[40]。

ここでベルジャーエフの言いたかったことは、啓蒙主義的方法の理性主義と理論偏重の有害性であろう。さらに啓蒙主義の危険性について語っている。

「一切の歴史的聖物と歴史的伝統をとことんまで、情け容赦なく、論理的に破壊し殺戮すること、マルクス主義の歴史観以上のものを私は知らない」[41]と。か

---

38) ibid., p.14.
39) ibid., p.14.
40) ibid., p.14.
41) ibid., p.18.

くして18世紀に始まった啓蒙理論が人間存在の在り方を無機的な経済理論に変えてしまった事実を彼は嘆くのである。

「歴史的過程における唯一の本来的な実在として、ただ唯物的経済的生産の過程だけがあることになり、これが生み出す経済的諸形態が、唯一の存在論的、真に第一義的、実在的なそれとして出現するに至る。その他一切のものは、単なる第二義的なもの、単なる反映、単なる上部構造にすぎない。宗教、精神、文化、芸術、人生そのものが単なる反映であって、本来の実在性を欠いている」[42]。

このように内的秘儀を素裸にするによって、歴史的唯物論は歴史の魂である内的秘儀を生産の条件と人類の生産力に還元し、必然的に人間の尊厳性も失われることになった。

ところで、啓蒙主義時代にはじまった批判的破壊工作は完成したが、その批判の勢いはとどまるところを知らず、マルクスの経済学的唯物理論は「啓蒙主義」を超えた歴史的進化論を打ち立てるに至る。ここにおいてマルクス主義における「啓蒙理性」の自負と僭越は極限に達したのである。

理性、「それは人類の宇宙的歴史的運命を超出し、その全精神生活と人間的イデオロギーのすべてを超出した理性――啓蒙的、すなわち光に満たされ、光を放つ理性――の所持者であるとみずから信じている。経済過程の反映にほかならない一切の迷妄と幻想を暴露して見せたと信じている。このマルクス主義に見られるものは、啓蒙理性の要求を、古代イスラエルに見られたようなメシア（救世主）的要求に結び付けようとする努力である。なぜなら、これは、光――他のイデオロギーと並ぶものではなく、唯一の、最後的な光であって、歴史の進行の秘儀をあらわにするところの光――を持っている唯一の認識だと主張するものだからである」[43]。

こうしてマルクス主義の主張する啓蒙理性は、メシア的要求を満たす唯一最後の光となった。そして、その要求に向かって歴史は進行するということになる。

---

42) ibid., p.18.
43) ibid., p.19.

結果的に歴史には方向性 sens があり、その方向に向かって<u>歴史は進歩すること</u>になった。

　時期的にも〈ダーウィンの進化論〉という追い風を受けて、進化論的歴史尊重主義は圧倒的なものになる。しかしながら、進化論と人間社会の進歩の概念はまったく違うと主張する思想家ニコライ・ベルジャーエフは進化論と社会の進歩の違いをより詳しく説明する。

　「進歩の観念は...進化の観念と混同されてはならない。進歩の観念は歴史的過程の目標を設定し、この目標の光に照らして歴史的過程の意味をわれわれが発見することを要請する。(…) 進歩の観念は、歴史の中に存在していないような、いかなる時代、過去・現在・未来のいかなる時期にも結び付けられず、むしろ時代を超えているような目標を要請する」[44]。

　このようにベルジャーエフは、進化の観念と進歩の観念の混同を戒め、進歩の観念に潜む危険性を指摘する。

　「進歩の観念、(…) この観念の古い根源は宗教的・メシア的なる根源である。それはメシア的解決の観念、<u>歴史の運命</u>の理念、<u>地上的解決の観念</u>という古いユダヤ主義的観念である」[45]「それは神の国の到来の観念、いつの日か実現すべき完全の国、真理と正義の国の到来という観念である。このメシア的至福千年説の観念が進歩の理論において世俗化されている。(…) <u>19 世紀の人々は進歩の宗教に帰依したのであり</u>、それが (…) <u>キリスト教の代用品</u>となったと言っても言い過ぎではない」[46]。

　とも語っている。結果として進歩の観念はソヴィエトにおいて、キリスト教の「千年王国説」と結びつき、平等主義的・共産主義的幻想である「プロレタリア革命思想」となり、ロシアのスターリン体制下、強制収容所における 2000 万人とも 3000 万人とも言われる大量の犠牲者を生み出すことになる。

---

44) ibid., p.21.
45) ibid., p.228.
46) ibid., p.229.

絶滅収容所とも称される強制収容所は思想犯・政治犯を収監する施設であり、その存在は全体主義体制を象徴する恐怖政治である。この体制は体制維持のためにイデオロギーに依存し、人民の行動を方向づけるために恐怖政治を利用し、個人の利益追及を禁止するが、無制限な権力支配にその特徴がある。この時点においてなお、果たして狂信と寛容の問題からわれわれは縁を切ることができていない事実には詠嘆を禁じえない。

　ところで、至福千年説とも訳される千年王国説であるが、このキリスト教の宗教思想ないし幻想的信仰については、それが生まれた時代や思想の内容が複雑かつ多岐にわたっていて、様々な解釈や分析がなされており、明確な見解が確定しているといったものではない。しかし信仰の根底にあったのは、〈ヨハネの黙示録〉を拠り所にする貧民たちの間に生じたメシア（救世主）待望論であったことは間違いない。8世紀から16世紀にかけて中世ヨーロッパの各地で起きた宗教的異議申し立ての、無政府主義的な運動の総称であるようだ。

　ノーマン・コーンの『千年王国の追求』によると、キリスト教は〈終わりの時〉〈終わりの日〉あるいは〈この世の終わりの姿〉に関する教理と言う意味で、常に一種の〈終末論〉を内包してきた。キリスト教的千年王国主義はキリスト教的終末論の変形に過ぎなかった。

　そのセクトや運動が描く救世観の特徴は、共同体的であること、彼岸でなくこの地上で実現されるという意味で現世的であること、単なる現状改善でなく完璧を期すという意味において絶対的であること、ほどなく忽然と現れると言う意味で緊迫的であること、超自然的力によって完成されるという意味で奇跡的であることなどであるが、この幻想的信仰である現世的宗教を奉じる千年王国主義的セクトの人々の境遇は過酷なほど不安定であり、彼らは狂暴で、無秩序で、時には文字通り革命的であった[47]。

　「千年王国主義高揚の世界と社会不安の世界とは、当時ぴったり重なり合って

47）ノーマン・コーン、『千年王国の追及』、江川徹訳、紀伊国屋書店、p.5.

宗教から実存へ

いたのではなく部分的に重なっていた。(・・・) 生活の物質的条件を改善したいという貧民通有の願望が、最後の黙示録的大虐殺を通して無垢へと再生した世界の幻想と混じりあっていった。悪人たちは・・・皆殺しにされ、その後で<u>聖徒たちすなわち当の貧民たち</u>が、彼らの王国、苦しみも罪もない国土を築くことになるというものであった。このような幻想に駆り立てられて、あまたの貧民たちが果敢な行動に走ったが、それは (・・・) 一揆とはまったく異質なものであった。(・・・) そしてまたそれはある点において、今世紀のいくつかの大きな革命運動の真の先駆であったことを示唆するものである」[48]。

またノーマン・コーンは千年王国に関連してヨーロッパの平等主義的・共産主義的起源に関しても語っている。

「ヨーロッパの革命的終末論を形成するに至った他のさまざまな幻想と同様に、平等主義的、共産主義的幻想の起源も、古代世界にまで遡ることが出来る。中世ヨーロッパが、万人が身分・財産において平等であり、なにびとも他人から抑圧や搾取を受けることのない状態、普遍的信頼と同胞愛、そして時には財産と配偶者さえ完全に共有することを特色とする状態、つまり〈自然状態〉なる観念を継承したのは、ギリシャ・ローマ人からであった。ギリシャおよびラテンの両文学の中では〈自然状態〉は遠い昔に失われた黄金時代に地上に存在したものとして描かれている。オヴィディウスの『転身物語』にあるその神話表現は、後世の文学の中で反復して表現され、中世時代の共産主義思想に著しい影響を及ぼすことになった」[49]。

このように、当時のロシアのプロレタリア革命が目指した《均質的かつ普遍的な国家》や平等主義の観念の基盤は、幻想的信仰や文学が養い育てた、ある意味では神話とも言えるものなのである。が、その観念の原動力となったのはヘーゲルの『歴史哲学』であった。たとえば歴史崇拝について『全体主義の起源』(1951年) の著者ハンナ・アーレントがマルクスとヨーロッパ思想の項で記述し

---

48) ibid., p.6.
49) ibid., p.191.

た要約を示すと、「ヘーゲルの哲学は全体として歴史哲学であり、彼はあらゆる哲学思想を他のすべての思想とともに歴史の中に解消した。ヘーゲルが理論さえも歴史化し、さらにダーウインが発展の観念によって自然さえも歴史化して以降は、歴史概念に対する攻撃に耐え得るものはなにも残されていないように見えた」[50]。

　歴史は段階的に発展するというヘーゲルの歴史哲学において、進歩の観念は極めて重要な意義を持つ。しかし、この進歩という考え方は比較的新しいもので、18世紀ヨーロッパで生まれ19世紀全般を通じて次第に一般的な常識として定着した。

　ここで、前章で紹介したベルジャーエフの著書『歴史の意味』に窺える進歩観を再度詳述してみよう。進歩の観念は歴史的過程の目標を設定し、歴史的過程の意味をわれわれが発見することを要請するが、それは歴史の中に存在していないような、過去、現在、未来の如何なる時期にも結び付けられない、時代を超えた目標である。進歩の観念は宗教的・メシア的な古い根源を持つメシア的解決の観念、歴史の運命の理念、来るべきメシアの観念など、地上的解決を期する古いユダヤ主義的観念であり、いわばこのメシア的・千年王国説が<u>宗教的な性格を失い</u>、<u>現世的で反宗教的なもの</u>となり、進歩の理論において世俗化されたものである。そして「進歩の理論」は多くの人々にとって、一個の〈宗教〉を意味した。すなわち、<u>19世紀のひとびとは進歩の宗教に帰依したのであり</u>、もはや信じ難くなったキリスト教の代用品になったのである。そしてベルジャーエフは次のように続ける。

　「進歩の理論は、<u>過去と現在を犠牲にして未来を神化する</u>のであり、科学的見地からも哲学的ないし道徳的見地からもこれを正当化することはできない。<u>進歩の理論は一個の宗教的帰依</u>、<u>一個の信仰</u>を示す。なぜなら、われわれは進歩についての科学的・実証的な理論を基礎づけることができず、また、科学的・実証的

---

50) ハンナ・アーレント、『カール・マルクスと西欧　政治思想の伝統』、佐藤和夫訳、大月書店、2002年、p.12.

な仕方ではせいぜい進化論までしかできないのであって、進歩の理論はしたがってたんに信仰の対象、信頼の対象たりうるのみだからである。進歩の理論は「見えざるものについての告知」であり、来たらんとするものについての告知であり、「その信仰を抱くものへの福音」である。(・・・) 進歩の理論は (・・・) 人間世界の歴史の諸課題が未来において解決されるであろうということ、人類の歴史において、人類の運命において、高次の完全な状態が到達されるような瞬間が到来するであろうということを前提としている。(・・・) 人類の歴史の運命を満たすあらゆる矛盾が解消され、あらゆる問題が解決されることを前提としている。これはコントとヘーゲルとスペンサーとマルクスの信仰であった。この仮定は正しいのだろうか」[51]。

このようにベルジャーエフは、進化については科学的に実証できるとしても、<u>進歩の理論は科学的に証明しがたい一種の信仰対象</u>と見ていることが分かる。また、この信仰とも言える「進歩の理論」を推し進めた思想家の内に、前に挙げたヘーゲルとマルクスが含まれている。そして進歩主義の危うさは、<u>目的のために人間を犠牲</u>にすることであると指摘する。

「進歩はあらゆる人間的世代、あらゆる人間的人格を、終局の目標に対する一個の手段、一個の道具に代えてしまう。(・・・) 進歩の宗教は、いっさいの人間的世代、いっさいの人間的時期を無価値、無目的、無意味なものとして、ただ未来の手段であり道具であるものとしてみる。ここに<u>進歩の理論の宗教的道徳的な根本的矛盾</u>が存在し、それがこの理論をわれわれに受け入れがたく、承認しがたいものとする。進歩の宗教は死の宗教であり、(・・・) 未来の完成は過去の世代の一切の苦難を贖うことはできない。(・・・) あらゆる<u>人間的運命を犠牲に供せしめる進歩の宗教</u>は、過去と現在に対しては血も涙もない態度をとる」[52]。

ベルジャーエフは後のスターリンの全体主義的抑圧体制を見越していたかのように、1922年の段階ですでに進歩思想の危険性を見抜いている。進歩にたいす

---

51) ibid., p.230.
52) ibid., p.232.

る絶対的信頼にもとづく信仰的歴史観、それは言ってみれば楽観的進歩史観とも言えるものだ。が、ベルジャーエフは既に1922年の時点でその傾向を洞察していた。

「それは未来に関しての無限の楽観論と、過去に関しての無限の悲観論とを結びつける」[53)]のように語っていることからも明白である。また彼は、『共産主義とキリスト』教のなかで「歴史的進歩などというものはない。現在は決して過去の上に築かれた改良品ではない。過去にはもっと多くの美があった」[54)]とも語っている。

ベルジャーエフはまた、ロシア人の宗教観と革命、共産主義とキリスト教の関係について次のような見解を示している。1926年から1933年にかけて書かれた『共産主義とキリスト教』の内容の中から拙稿に関係するものを要約してみよう。

〈19世紀ロシアのインテリゲンチャ・・・この階層はロシア国の成功を自分自身の成功〉であるとは感じなかった。現実の生に基盤ないし根を持たないということが、19世紀のロシアの魂の特徴であった。そのことから、思想の大いなる自律と大胆さが生まれてきた。スラブ主義者であれ西欧主義者であれ、知識人はすべて、自分たちの時代をロシア民族の使命が果たされない時代として拒否した。同時代の生に対するこのような否定的態度は一つの革命的な要素である。スラブ主義者は過去に、すなわちピョートル大帝以前のロシアに目を向け、一方西欧主義者は西欧に目を向けた。しかし、昔のロシアも西ヨーロッパも共に夢であり、現実ではなかった〉[55)]。

このように、時代の現状を否定する態度が革命に結びつく経緯は充分納得のゆくメカニズムである。

---

53) ibid., p.232.
54) ニコライ・ベルジャーエフ、『共産主義とキリスト教』、峠尚武訳、行路社、1991年、p.38.
55) ibid., pp.58-59.

宗教から実存へ

サルトル

　第二次世界大戦の終戦前後にすでに兆候はあったが、とりわけ戦後になってソ連国内の凄まじい抑圧体制の存在に関して陸続ともたらされる報告は徐々にフランス知識人たちの牢固とした認識の隙間に浸み込んでゆくことになる。就中、革命的暴力の象徴とも言うべき強制収容所の存在が隠しようもなく露呈するにいたって、知識人らはロシア国内の<u>抑圧体制</u>と<u>マルクス主義理論</u>とのはざまに整合性を見出だすことが、可能であるか否かを模索し、コミュニズムに対する信頼を継続することに逡巡せざるを得ない仕儀に立ち至り、一部フランス知識人のコミュニズムを支える信念が揺らぎはじめる。

　全体主義の非道な体制はファシズムの社会にのみ限定されるものと信じていた彼らにとって、人民の理想を追求するコミュニズムの祖国が、実際には一党独裁の支配体制であり、密告の奨励、追放、強制収容所送り、拷問、暴力、虐殺などの手段を駆使する過酷で抑圧的な体制であって、その内実が恐怖政治 terreur であるとはとうてい信じられなかったのである。しかし、もたらされるさまざまな情報は、全体主義がファシズム、コミュニズム、左右いずれの側にも発生しうる現象である可能性を否定しがたいものにしてゆく。ナチス Nationalsozialist ドイツが代表するファシズムとは対蹠的位置にあって、180度異なる"理想の体制"とみなされてきた共産主義国家の実情報告によって共産主義とファシズムを同一視する人々が現れてくる。このような情況の中で徐々に反共産主義 anti-communisme に傾く者が生まれることになるのだが、時宜を得て、ハンガリー生まれの作家アーサー・ケストラーによる『真昼の暗黒』が出版され、反共的動向に拍車をかけることになる。"モスクワ裁判"に取材したこの小説作品は1945年にフランス語訳されている（フランス語訳では『ゼロと無限』）。

　1947年このような反共産主義者的気運が醸成されつつあった情況に大きく揺さぶりをかける一書が刊行される。メルロ=ポンティによる『ヒューマニズムと恐怖政治 Humanisme et Terreur』である。あらかじめ『ヨガ行者とプロレタリア le Yogi et le Prolétaire』のタイトルでサルトル主幹の『現代』誌上に掲載された

この論稿は、先のアーサー・ケストラーの『真昼の暗黒』に対する批判的考察を試みたもので、右傾化しつつある世論に歯止めをかけるための論考であった。彼の主張を鮮明に特徴づける言説を紹介する。

「歴史は本質的に闘争である。主人と奴隷の闘争であり、階級の闘争である。人間の条件の必然性によってそのようになるのである。それはまた、人間の精神と肉体、つまり無限と有限が分かちがたいものであるという根源的パラドクスによるものである。具体的な人間存在のシステムとして、各人は他者を客体として扱うことによってしか自分を肯定することが出来ない」[56]

「革命は、歴史哲学に基づくものであってさえ強制された革命であり、暴力である」[57]

「歴史上の恐怖政治は革命において最高度に達する。また歴史とは恐怖政治である」[58]

こうした文言が示唆するように、彼は未来のヒューマニズムのための、暴力を伴う革命の必要性を説く。この著書でメルロ゠ポンティは《進歩的暴力》violence progressive の理論を展開し、革命のための暴力を容認する発言をする。骨子となる内容はほぼ次のようになる。

〈非暴力のリベラルな原則は政治的弁別の基準としてはまったく役に立たない。なぜなら、万一この観点においてコミュニズムがファシズムと同一視されるとしても、それはリベラリズムについても同じことが言えるからである〉。さらに、

「革命は、ブルジョワ社会が失業や戦争を許容し、運命の名においてカムフラージュしてきた暴力に責任をもち、指揮を執る。しかしすべての革命を束にしても、さまざまな帝国が流した血を超えるわけではない。暴力しかないのである。革命の暴力は、ヒューマニズムの未来を有するがゆえにより好ましいものである

---

56) Merleau-Ponty, *Humanisme et Terreur*, Gallimard, 1947, Le Yogi et le Prolétaire, p.110.（拙訳）
57) ibid., p.99.
58) ibid., p.98.

はずだ」[59] 次に彼はプロレタリアートは《普遍的階級》であるとして、その暴力とファシズムの暴力の違いに言及する。

「万一プロレタリアートが革命社会の基礎となる力であるとすれば、またプロレタリアートが、マルクスに倣ってわれわれが述べたあの《普遍的階級》であるとすれば、その時この階級の利益は歴史に人間的価値をもたらす。プロレタリアートの力は人間性の力であるからだ。逆にファシストの暴力は普遍的階級の暴力ではない。それは《人種》の暴力もしくは後進的な国家の暴力である」[60]。

また多方面から批判の対象となった革命の目的と手段の齟齬について次のような弁明を試みる。スターリンの〈恐怖政治〉に対する論拠としてリベラリストたちは〈ヒューマニズム〉を引き合いに出す。彼らは、人間は単に手段としてのみならず、目的として扱われなければならないとするカントに準拠している。しかしスターリンの問題に関するこのような取り組み方は〈理想主義〉である。現在人間が目的として扱われているようなところはどこにもない。そしてメルロ=ポンティはこう述べる。

「実際には、目的とか手段とかいうものはない。あえて言うなら目的しか、手段しかない。言い換えれば、革命のプロセスというのはその一瞬一瞬が《究極的》なユートピアの瞬間と同じくらい不可欠で、価値あるものなのである。弁証法的唯物論は手段と目的を切り離さない。目的は必然的に歴史の生成から演繹される。手段は有機的に目的に従属する。差し迫った目的はその後の目的の手段となる」[61] と語り、論旨は次のように展開する。

世界中どこにも"主人と奴隷""死刑執行人と犠牲者"は存在する。したがって、《リベラリズム》が《スターリン主義》よりも価値があるとは言えない。カント的な態度表明の裏には、人間による人間の搾取や植民地、帝国主義がある。それらは避けがたいものとして受け入れなければならない。政治は常にそういう

---

59) ibid., pp.115-116.
60) ibid., p.113.
61) ibid., p.138.

ものであった。ヒューマニズムは精々のところ、現実との接触を持たぬ哲学者のもたらした心地よい夢でしかなかった。非暴力？万一それをまともに取り上げるというなら、われわれはヨガ行者にならなければなるまい。そのようなことができるだろうか。人間は本質的に〈社会に組み込まれ位置づけられた存在〉un être engagé, situé である。人間は自分が自分を作ると同時に他人が作るものである。われわれはこの歴史から逃れることはできない。

メルロ゠ポンティはこのように語り、〈未来のヒューマニズム〉実現のために、現今の〈恐怖政治〉はやむを得ないと考える。現在の共産主義の暴力はおそらく、新たな歴史の創造に伴う小児疾患（はしか）であり、いつの日かヒューマニズムに到達するために辿らなければならない迂回 détour である。ゆえに、

「歴史哲学のなかでヘーゲルが説明していることだが、個人が不正な行為に苦しむことは充分にありうるが、そのことは個人が歴史の奉仕者であり、歴史の道具でしかないのだから、普遍的な歴史と歴史の進展・進歩には関係ない」[62]ということになる。

さて、サルトルの歴史観は先述したメルロ゠ポンティの〈歴史の動向に由来する進歩史観〉にほぼ重なるものである。サルトルとメルロ゠ポンティは共にアレクサンドル・コジェーヴが1933-39年にかけて「精神学現象学」の講義を行った際の聴講者で、いわば弟子であった。その講義はマルクスとキルケゴールを意識したヘーゲルの読み直しであり、後に『ヘーゲル読解入門』として出版されたが、それは"超マルクス主義的ヘーゲル解釈"であった。

ヘーゲルの歴史認識は、個人は歴史の奴隷・道具であって、個人的実存の内面的境涯とは無縁な理論体系である。キルケゴールが「ヘーゲルの高慢な汎神論的体系のなかには、罪の意識も不安も、絶望も冒険も出てこない。生きている現実的存在＝実存は忘れられている」と批判した所以である。歴史の動因をあらゆるもののなかに内在する〈矛盾〉に見るヘーゲルの弁証法においては、例えばA

---

62) ibid., p.139.

という現象は自然にBになるのではなく、Aが否定されてBが生まれる構図になっており、A・B間の対立があらゆる現象の変化や運動の原動力である（「一般に世界を動かしているのは矛盾である」『エンツィクロペディア』（119節））のだが、現象の変化・運動の過程はその矛盾を内包したまま全体として総合されてゆく。それがいわゆる弁証法の総体性であり完結性なのである。

　ヘーゲルの弁証法法は、現象の変化・運動の原動力は現象そのものの中に内包（蓄積）された矛盾であり、ゆえに必然的にAが否定されてBになるという否定性の哲学で、こうした進歩史観を敷衍すると革命による暴力や虐殺、または強制収容所の存在でさえ歴史の発展過程の一コマであり、〈絶対者〉が自己の本質を実現する過程でしかないことになる。ヘーゲルは、絶対的な理性が世界を支配しており、世界史の発展を支配するものは世界精神（神）であり、世界史は神の摂理によって目的論的に決定されていると考えた。したがってナポレオンのような英雄も、目標実現のためにある段階で利用された操り人形（道具）にすぎない。闘争と矛盾の継続と見える世界の歴史も、合理的につまり必然的に進展してきたということになる。このようにして"手放しの"という表現は言い過ぎであろうが、いささか楽天的な〈進歩史観〉が識者の間に蔓延したことは想像にかたくない。

　このようにして歴史には方向性がある、つまり「歴史の動向・傾向」があって、それは常に未来に向かって前進・進歩するという考え方はサルトルの信念となっていた。それは、サルトルの「自己の脱自性」の認識にも表れている。国家、地方、体制、時代、政体等の違いがある以上、個々の人間が置かれた状況はそれぞれ異なるものであるから、われわれは万人共通の生き方を求めることはできない。脱自とは各人が時代の子であり状況の子であるかぎり、一人一人が自由と責任の主体である事実に覚醒し、その都度自らの方向性を選択し、新たな生き方を模索しつつ創りだすことである。つまり今ある自分の殻を打ち破る困難を自らに課し、自己を超え出ることを「脱自」は意味している。また、それは自らが埋没している日常性の枠を超え出る行為であるが、人間は誰しも時代（時期）の

子であり、状況（場面）の子であるがゆえに、各状況における超出（自己超越）transcendance のあり方は時代と状況によって異なるものとならざるを得ない。以上のような「自己の脱自性」「自己超越」の考えなども彼の進歩史観と無縁ではない。

　1951年こうした情況を背景にして登場するのがアルベール・カミュの『反抗的人間 l'Homme révolté』である。

　「激情的な犯罪と論理による犯罪がある」[63)] という鮮烈な書き出しで始まるこの評論の内容は、端的に言って「論理による悪の系譜学」généalogie du mal であるが、たちまちサルトルをはじめとする進歩的左翼の攻撃に晒された。この本の内容を一言でいえば「歴史の発展のために人の血が流され、《進歩的暴力》の名のもとに暴力が容認される」ことに疑問を提示するものであった。カミュは発作的犯罪とは別の、用意周到な「論理的整合性」の衣裳をまとう犯罪、すなわち"論理の悪"の存在することを訴え、過激と中庸を比較する思考の重要性を強調するのである。言い換えれば、それは狂信に対して寛容を求めることにほかならない。

　その著作のなかで、「"死刑執行人"と"奴隷"は世界中どこにもいる」とするメルローポンティの主張に呼応してカミュは、『犠牲者も否、死刑執行人も否』Ni victime ni boureau を著し、〈目的は手段を正当化する〉la fin justifie les moyens という社会主義者の主張に待ったをかける。つまり理想の未来を実現するという目的は、いかなる残虐非道も許容しうるのかと。カミュは〈人の命を救うことこそが重要である l'essentiel est le sauvetage des vies〉として、「できるだけ流血と苦痛を避けなければならない」[64)] という自説を提示するが、その考えは宗教戦争時代のモンテーニュの想いに似ている。この『反抗的人間』が発端となってカミュとサルトルの論争に発展することになるのであるが、その中心的な問題の一つが"進歩的と称される暴力"を特別に優遇することは許されるか否か、と

---

63) Albert Camus, l'Homme révolté, Gallimard, 119ᵉ édition, p.13.
64) Albert Camus, Ni victime ni boureau , O.C.t.II. p.336.

いうことにある。カミュは一貫して人命尊重の立場をとり続ける。

　『反抗的人間』全体の基調精神は"大切なのは人命の救助" l'essetiel（était）le sauvetage de vie である。同書の書き出しが「激情による犯罪と論理による犯罪がある」ではじまること自体がそのことを明瞭に表している。作中延々とライトモティーフのように殺人の不当性を訴える表現が頻出する。論理的犯罪 crime logique とは理論づけられた犯罪 crime qui se raisonne のことで、あらかじめ計画された犯罪 crime prémédité である。カミュは、「われわれは予謀の時代、完全犯罪の時代に生きており」[65]、それを可能にするものは、「あらゆることに役立ち、殺人者を裁判官にさえしてしまう哲学である」[66]と語る。このように『反抗的人間』のテーマは哲学体系や思想の教義が暴力を正当化し、かつ暴力を招来する危うさを問題にするものであった。

　カミュは、プロレタリアートによる《均質的かつ普遍的国家》の実現、彼らにとって〈絶対的なもの〉への到達は不可能と考えていた。元々キリスト教を嫌うカミュは、マルクス主義的なメシア思想を拒んだのである。『反抗的人間』で述べているように、彼の目には、歴史に関するマルクスの理論はユートピアもしくは欺瞞と映っていた。

　こうしてカミュとサルトルの間に論争が始まった。論争のきっかけは1952年5月サルトル主幹の『現代』誌79号に掲載されたフランシス・ジャンソンの『反抗的人間評——A．カミュ　あるいは反抗心』である。カミュが1951年に著した『反抗的人間』に対する知識人界の反響は絶大であった。ジャンソンは自著の冒頭で、ある意味で左右両翼からカミュの著書に高い評価が寄せられた事実を皮肉交じりに紹介する。

　「本書は一挙に思想界の各方面の賛同を得ている。「非常に重要な書」「大作」「近年の大収穫、世紀の半ばにあらわれた偉大なる書」「西欧思想の転換点」「〈人間にならいて〉ともいいうる、気高く、人間的な作品」「かくも価値ある書は、

---

65) op. cit., p.413.
66) ibid., p.413.

戦後フランスに現れたことがない」——こうした賛辞は、いくぶんの差はあれ、すべての批評家のうちに見られた。『モンド』紙のエミール・アンリオ氏から、同じ『モンド』紙のジャン・ラクロア氏まで、またクロード・ブルデ氏（『オプセルヴァトゥール』紙）から、『生ける神』誌のマルセル・モレ氏を経て、アンリ・プティ氏（『解放されたパリ人』紙）にいたるまですべてしかりである。右翼の方へと、万古不易のフランスの高嶺を襲った、この熱狂的旋風が決定的だと思わぬにしても、カミュの立場に立ったら、僕ならどうにも不安でかなわないことだろう。（・・・）彼の著書が、多種多様の精神の持ち主を・・・有頂天にさせたのは、ふしぎな力によるものか・・・みんなが欣喜雀躍して迎えた「福音」とはなんだろうか」[67]。

　以上のような書き出しではじまる『A. カミュ　あるいは反抗心』はカミュを批判する書であり、これに応えてカミュは同誌 8 月号に「『現代』誌主筆への手紙」を書く。また同号にはサルトルも、カミュの反抗の理論を激しく弾劾する『アルベール・カミュに答える』*Réponse à Albert Camus* を発表した。カミュにたいしては、当然のことながらコミュニストやシュールレアリストの側から反対の声が上がっていたが、右翼や中立左派を含む多くがカミュに賛辞を贈ったことへの対抗心も手伝って、サルトルの筆鋒は凄まじいものであった。

　論争の重要なポイントの一つに、ソ連の強制収容所の存在をめぐる両者の見解の相違がある。カミュの言い分は、サルトルやジャンソンがソ連の強制収容所について多くを語らない事実を指摘するものであった。この問題についてサルトルは次のように応じる。

　「あなたが、私の本のいかなる批評もロシアの強制収容所をなおざりにしては成立しないと書いたとき、あなたは彼の論文がそのことに触れなかったことで彼を責めている。それについては恐らくあなたが正しい」[68]とカミュの言い分を認

---

67) フランシス・ジャンソン、『革命か反抗か―カミュ=サルトル論争』、佐藤朔訳、新潮文庫、平成 22 年、pp.9-10.
68) Jean-Paul Sartre, *Réponse à Alebert Camus,* in Situations IV, Gallimard, 1993, pp.103-104.

めたうえで、「あなたは、ジャンソンが自分の権利であるかのごとく、あなたの本のなかのソヴィエトの強制収容所のことについて触れなかったという否定しえない事実を利用して、社会参加を主張する雑誌の編集長の私がこの問題に取り組まないだろうと示唆しているが、それに公正にたいする重大な過ちであり、偽りである」[69]と語り、次のように弁明する。

「ルッセの声明の数日後われわれは、強制収容所に関する数本の論文を掲載する論説を発表している。日付を調べれば、その号はルッセの介入以前に作成されたことがわかる」[70]。

しかしサルトルは弁明のすぐあとで、自らの偽らざる本音を吐露している。

「そうだカミュ、わたしもあなたと同じように強制収容所は許しがたいものだと思う。ただし、いわゆるブルジョワ新聞がそれを毎日書き立てるやりかたも同様に許しがたい」[71]。

サルトルもソ連の強制収容所の存在を非難するが、論点の比重はむしろ後半部の〈ブルジョワ新聞に対する非難〉にかかっている。現に存在する犠牲には目をつぶらざるを得ないとする態度と言えよう。いわば、サルトルにとって〈絶対的なもの〉l'absolu は〈未来〉futur であり、カミュのそれは〈ここ・今〉hic et nunc であった。したがってサルトルはカミュと逆に〈ここ・今〉を相対化するのである。カミュにとっては現在こそ絶対的なものであり、ここ・今の喜びを味わうことが重要なのである。一方サルトル的意識は、今この瞬間を味わうというより、現在を超える意識である。彼に憑依する意識は輝ける〈未来〉であるが、それはある意味で永久に捕捉しえない、未だないものを志向する恒常的不満の源泉ともいえるものである。

そしてサルトルの意識が志向する未来の内容は、プロレタリアートによる〈均質的で普遍的な社会〉の実現した姿であろう。強制を伴いながらも、その理想に

---

[69] ibid., p.103.
[70] ibid., p.104.
[71] ibid., p.125.

向かって革命は進行するはずであり、また進行しなければならない。それがサルトル側の歴史認識であった。要するに、サルトルは現状否定の未来志向派であり、彼の実存哲学の基底にはヘーゲルの弁証法につながる「否定性」Négativité がある。進歩主義と否定性の哲学である。

カミュ

　一方カミュは〈現実への忠実〉と〈大地への同意〉を表明してはばからない。現状を否定し未来を志向するサルトルとは対蹠的である。『シジフの神話』『裏と表』『結婚』の一部を既に少部数公刊していたが、カミュの作家としての出発点はやはり『異邦人』であるとしたい。構想から5年後の1942年に刊行された当作品は絶大な評価と反響を呼んだ。因みにこの作品が構想された1937年カミュは共産党を脱党している。

　ところで、極力接続詞を避け、細切れのフレーズを並べ、もっぱら複合過去形を用いたこの作品が、それでも"みずみずしい文体"と称される理由はどこにあるのだろう。要因の一つは主人公が自然を享受する姿に求められる。享受の対象は主人公ムルソーが恋人マリーと戯れる「海」であり、夕方勤務から解放されたムルソーが岸壁を歩く帰途に感じる「さわやかな空気と新鮮な息吹」であり、「目いっぱいに空がひろがり、それは青くまた黄金色であった」[72]のような「空」、また小説『異邦人』の主役とも言える「太陽」でもある。かくして初期の書きものが示しているように、カミュには〈自然への同意〉consentement à la «physis» が明瞭に見て取れる。それは1939年刊行の自伝的随筆『結婚』において、フィレンツェのピッチ美術館裏手にある16世紀のイタリア式庭園ボボリの高台から見下ろしながら観想するカミュが感じた「大地への同意」«consentement à la terre» でもある。カミュはいくつかの著書で倦むことなく繰り返す。

　「世界は美しい、世界の外に救いはない」[73]と。大地への同意は人間を幸福に導

---

72) Albert Camus, *Étranger*, folio, p.34.
73) Albert Camus, *Noces*, O．C.t.II, p.87.

くためのキーワードとして存在する。つまりカミュは自然 nature を、大地 terre を、また世界 monde を愛する人であり physis（ものごとの自然の形）を肯定する姿勢が彼の根底にある。ここまで見てきたようにサルトルとカミュの対比は反自然 antiphysis と自然 physis の相反する姿勢に顕著に現れている。この姿勢の違いがさらに「行動 action」に対する「観想 contemplation」、「自己投企 projet」に対する「郷愁 nostalgie」、「自己超越 transcendance」に対して「大地に根を張ること enracinement」、「義務存在 devoir-être」に対する「存在 être」・・・という形で平行線をたどるのである。

『異邦人』の主人公について言えば、確かに母の棺を前にしてタバコをくゆらせ、葬儀の翌日マリーと海で戯れるムルソーの行為は社会の慣習にそぐわない。いわば社会的なお芝居 théâtre social の配慮に欠けるため、外見上利那的に見えるのであるが、それはまさに「ここと今」hic et nunc に生きる無頼な青年そのものである。また、社長がムルソーにパリ行きを打診する場面がある。

「『君は若い。気に入ってもらえる生活になるはずだ』僕は、そうですね、でも結局どちらでもいいのです、と言った」[74]。

主人公の言葉は、彼が野心家でないこと、出世や進歩・発展とは縁遠いタイプであることを示している。つまり彼は未来志向のない、生成の観念とも無縁な、"ここ・今"を享受する人間と言える。エリック・ヴェルネールが《カミュ的享楽》frui camusien と呼ぶものがこれである。ヴェルネールの解釈はこうである。

「不条理の壁は乗り越えがたいという意識が人をして悲劇的であるが、それゆえ精神的高揚をもたらすここ・今に追い込む。逆に言えば、カミュ的享楽は不条理の苦い体験である」[75]。

つまりある意味で不条理が「ここ・今」に人を誘うとヴェルネールは解釈している。確かに一方でそのような理解も可能であろうが、それだけでは利那主義の境域を超えるものではない。『異邦人』のムルソーは、通夜の式場でタバコを吸

---

74) *Étranger*, op.cit. p.68.
75) Eric Werner, *de la Violence au Totalitarisme*, Calmann-Lévy, 1972, p.73.

い翌日はマリーと遊ぶ、事務所のトイレの濡れたタオルに我慢できない、後方から来て追い抜いてゆくトラックを突然友人と一緒に追いかけて飛び乗る、世辞を含めた世間的な儀礼に対応できないなどの不器用な行為に見られるように、自己の欲求に素直で正直、言い換えれば五感の要求や本能の誘惑のままに行動する、いわば幼児性を宿した青年のごとくに描かれている。

ところでムルソーは確かにカミュの分身であり、一面でカミュにそのような傾向があるとしてもそれがそのままカミュ自身というわけではない。先ほど述べた不条理の苦い体験としてのカミュ的享楽は実は、絶望の裏返しの顔なのである。

「その喜びはカミュにあっては、世界の外に救いはないという確信のなかに源泉を見出す、絶望の裏返しでしかない」[76]。

カミュは今ある世界を享受する人間であり、宗教的来世を希求することもなければ、サルトル的生成 devenir に興味を示すこともない。世界を肯定するその姿勢は現実を超える transcender le réel ことを拒むものである。カミュは暴力による革命よりも、不完全であってもこの世界との調和 s'accorder au monde を選ぶが、実はそれは中庸というカミュの「反抗」の思想そのものなのだ。『反抗的人間』の第五章〔正午の思想〕において彼は、「反抗自体は、相対的正義しか願わず・・・世界は相対の世界である」「絶対視された歴史では、暴力は正当化される」「現代の熱狂的信徒は、中庸を軽蔑する」と語り、暴力を伴う革命よりも反抗を選ぶことを勧める。その意味で、つまり狂信を避け寛容を説く点で、彼はモンテーニュの衣鉢を継いでいると言える。

おわりに

1955年レイモン・アロンが『知識人の阿片 *l'Opium des Intelletuels*』を発表した。アロンはカミュ、サルトルらと共に1930年代アレクサンドル・コジェーヴの『精神現象学』の講義を受けた一人であったが、その後は反－反共主義（共産

---

76) ibid., p.73.

主義）に対抗する論客になっていた。その著書の巻頭に、英語版には掲載のないカール・マルクスとシモーヌ・ヴェイユの警鐘的な銘句二つが併記されているので、紹介しておきたい。

〈宗教は不幸に打ちひしがれた人間の嘆き、精神なき時代の精神であるのと同様、愛なき世界の魂である。それは人民の阿片である〉カール・マルクス[77]

〈マルクス主義はその語彙の最も背徳的な意味で完全に宗教である。それはとりわけ宗教生活として、またマルクスの正鵠を得た言葉に従うなら絶えず人民の阿片として使用されてきた事実を共有している〉シモーヌ・ヴェイユ[77]

　宗教は阿片であろうか。マルクスは宗教を人民の阿片と規定して否定した。シモーヌ・ヴェイユはマルクス主義こそが宗教であり、したがって阿片であると切り返したことになる。上記二つの文言は著者アロンの意図を明確に示唆する指標である。結局、古いユダヤ主義的観念であるメシア的解決の観念がマルクスによって進歩の観念となり、歴史の運命の理念となり、地上的解決の観念となったのである。それは神の国・完全な国の到来、真理と正義の国の到来の観念で、メシア的千年王国説が進歩の理論によって世俗化されたものであった。ベルジャーエフの言うように、19世紀の人々は進歩の宗教に帰依したのであり、それがキリスト教の代用品になったのである。
　アロンはその本の第9章に〈宗教を探し求める知識人〉Intellectuels en quête d'une Religion というタイトルを付して、当時の知識人の心的傾向について次のような批判的推察を試みている。

---

[77] Raymond Aron, *L'Opium des Intellectuels,* 2004.

「われわれが見てきたようにマルクス主義の予言は、ユダヤ・キリスト教の予言の典型的図式と一致する。予言はすべて現状を非難し、かくあらねばならぬもののイメージを描き、輝ける未来と忌まわしい現在を隔てる壁を乗り越えるための個人やグループを選ぶ。政治革命なしに社会の進歩を可能にする階級無き社会は、理想国家を待望する人々が夢見たキリスト教の千年王国に匹敵するものである。プロレタリアートの不幸はその使命を証立てるものであり、共産党は《教会》である。この教会に対して、福音に耳を傾けようとしない異教徒＝ブルジョワや、長年月自らその到来を予告してきた革命を認めようとしないユダヤ人＝社会主義者が反対している」[78]。

　また「マルクス主義者らの言う革命が実現しなかったのは観念そのものが神話的 mytique であったからである」と語り、次のように結論づける。「すべての過去の革命と同様、プロレタリアートを引き合いに出す革命も、エリートから他のエリートへの暴力的交代を示すものである」[79]と。革命思想は組織・機構の維持を優先するあまり、恐怖政治的全体主義 caractère terroriste-totalitaire の性格を帯びるのかもしれない。

　こうした革命思想が神話的であるという考えはカミュも『反抗的人間』のなかで述べている。時代の中にキリスト教の理想を導入することは可能であろうか。カミュは疑問を提示する。彼にとってもそれは神話でしかない。しかも危険な神話である。二世紀にわたり人類は世界のあちこちで革命的希望に根拠を与えようとしてきたが、試みはすべて失敗によって清算された。「革命家たちは不可能なことに挑戦していた」とカミュは言う。ニーチェ同様カミュがキリスト教的・ヘーゲル主義の否定性を拒否するのはそのためである。世界（この世）をなおざりにした彼方の幸福の可能性はまことに疑わしいものであるからだ。

　ハンナ・アーレントも『カール・マルクスと西欧政治思想の伝統』第一章で、19世紀の二つの主要な問題は労働の問題と歴史の問題であったとして、こう語

---

78) ibid., p.53.
79) ibid., p.53.

っている。

　「ユートピア社会主義の主要な欠点は、マルクス自身が考えたように非科学的であるという点にあるのではなく、労働者階級を無権利な貧しい集団とみなし、彼らの解放のための闘いだとみなした点にあった。キリスト教的な隣人愛という昔からの信念が社会的正義の激しい情念へと発展した」[80]。

　こうしてプロレタリアート革命がはじまり、社会正義の名のもとに不寛容が始まった。宗教改革の時代モンテーニュが心を痛めた狂信と不寛容の問題は20世紀を越えた今なお続いている。全体主義思想による恐怖政治、強制収容所と暴力の支配する社会の現前である。18世紀ヴォルテールは狂信と、宗教人による不寛容をデカルト以来の理性と合理論によって乗り越えようとした。宗教改革の時代、当初反教会的ということで、手を携えて改革に取り組んだユマニストとカルヴァンが袂を分かつ原因になったのは、宗教教義の教条主義にあった。ユマニストの合理主義的で実証主義的な自由検討の精神と、「・・・すべし」の宗教的教条は元より相容れないものであったからだ。

　しかし、その合理主義（理性）は無神論的唯物史観となった。歴史には動向があり、一つの方向に向かって進歩する歴史主義という名の進歩史観が生まれた。人々はキリスト教の代用品である進歩の宗教に帰依し、歴史の運命の理念と地上的解決の観念を奉じ、目的のために人間を犠牲にすることを躊躇わなくなったのである。

　善悪二元論の考えはわれわれにつきまとって離れないもの、仏教で言うところの業のようなものである。サルトルが言っていることだが、一般にわれわれは良いと思うことしかしないが、ひとたび、ある考えに執りつかれると、あとは一瀉千里その方向に向かって奔るのみ。異なる思想の持主には不寛容になりがちだ。あとは、紀元前古代ローマのプラウトスの言葉 homo homini lupus「人間は人間にとって狼である」の出番となる。

---

80) ハンナ・アーレント、『カール・マルクスと西欧政治思想の伝統』、佐藤和夫訳、大月書店、2002年、p.11.